P9-DEH-334

ST. MARTIN'S
MINOTAUR
MYSTERIES

Other titles from St. Martin's **Minotaur** Mysteries

MURDER WITH PEACOCKS by Donna Andrews
A COLD DAY IN PARADISE by Steve Hamilton
CROSSROAD BLUES by Ace Atkins
ROMAN BLOOD by Steven Saylor
TELL NO TALES by Eleanor Taylor Bland
FAREWELL PERFORMANCE by Donna Huston Murray
DEATH AL DENTE by Peter King
JITTER JOINT by Howard Swindle
LARGER THAN DEATH by Lynne Murray
A GIFT OF SANCTUARY by Candace Robb
THE SILLY SEASON by Susan Holtzer
SEARCH THE DARK by Charles Todd
EMERALD FLASH by Charles Knief
DEAR MISS DEMEANOR by Joan Hess
AGATHA RAISIN AND THE WITCH OF WYCKHADDEN by M. C. Beaton
THE BEST-KEPT SECRET by Les Roberts
THE IRISH COTTAGE MURDER by Dicey Deere
BIG EASY BACKROAD by Martin Hegwood
ROOTS OF MURDER by Janis Harrison
THE COMPANY OF CATS by Marian Babson

St. Martin's Paperbacks is also proud to present these mystery classics by Ngaio Marsh

ARTISTS IN CRIME
BLACK AS HE'S PAINTED
CLUTCH OF CONSTABLES
LIGHT THICKENS

A SMALL TOWN WITH A BIG SECRET . . .

"His blood still runs through my veins and I want to know who killed him. Don't you?" I asked.

"Not really."

"It doesn't bother you at all that, number one, you've been lied to your whole life? You obviously believed the hunting story," I said. My father only shrugged his shoulders and lit up another cigarette. "Number two, you knew this man and it doesn't bother you that somebody just killed him? Killed him violently and left him on the front porch for his wife, your grandmother, to find?"

"You don't know what you could be stirring up."

"Your grandmother lied to you, your parents lied to you," I said. "I don't know about you, but I would want to know just what the big secret was that they had to lie about it."

"This thoughtful cozy explores an intriguing paradox: close families and small towns can hide big secrets." —*Booklist*

"A pleasant return to a charming series." —*Library Journal*

St. Martin's Paperbacks Titles
by Rett MacPherson

A Comedy of Heirs
A Veiled Antiquity
Family Skeletons

A Comedy of Heirs

Rett MacPherson

St. Martin's Paperbacks

A COMEDY OF HEIRS

Library of Congress Catalog Card Number: 99-22065

ISBN: 0-312-97133-8

Printed in the United States of America

St. Martin's Press hardcover edition / August 1999
St. Martin's Paperbacks edition / August 2000

10 9 8 7 6 5 4 3 2 1

This book is dedicated to
my husband, Joe Lange.
For reasons beyond words.

Acknowledgments

The author wishes to acknowledge the people who helped bring this book to publication.

First of all, my editor, Kelley Ragland: I am most grateful for the fact that she always makes the final version of my manuscripts better than the first.

My writers group, the Alternate Historians: Tom Drennan, N. L. Drew, Gus Elliott, Laurell K. Hamilton, Debbie Millitello, Marella Sands, Mark (MC) Sumner, and Sharon Shinn. Thank you not just for professional advice but for all of the personal friendships, each one unique, that have developed among us.

Thank you to my husband, for all the times that I said, "Honey, can you . . . ?" and he, without hesitating, said, "Certainly." Deadlines are a sure test of a marriage.

And the following people who really did a lot for me in 1998: The couple whose organizational skills have saved me more than once, Suzi and Matt Seeker. Jackie, Nickole, and Andrea, for their beautiful singing voices. Bekah and Ellie for smiling at me when I needed it. Joe Weir and Matt Steins, for their hard work on my Web page.

And last but not least, to all those twentysomething cousins of mine. Although the characters in this book are all creations from my imagination, the property on which the murder takes place is based on my grandparents' old farm. And even though the characters are not based on anybody real, thank you to my family for providing me with anecdotes and inspiration. You made my childhood rich.

One

December in New Kassel is the greatest. I walked along Jefferson Street on my way to the Gaheimer House. The handmade dresses that I give the tours in were on hangers, draped over my shoulders. All seven of them. I tried desperately to keep them from dragging on the ground, but when you're short that's an impossible task. My wrist ached from the strain on it and I tried not to slip on the icy sidewalk.

It hadn't snowed yet. Used to be when I was a kid we got our first snow before Thanksgiving. Now, I can't remember the last time it snowed before December. It rained last night, though, and little patches of ice had frozen to the low spots on the sidewalk.

All the homes and shops were decorated for Christmas as if there might never be a Christmas again. Some of it was really tacky plastic stuff, but some, like the Gaheimer House, were decorated as authentically as possible with live greenery, candles and antiques. I passed by the lace shop with its red lights strung through the low front window and the big green sign that said CHRISTMAS SALE.

The next building was the Gaheimer House, my point of destination and the place where I am employed. I stopped on the step and looked up at the sky. It was gray-white and heavy as if it were just waiting to dump ten feet of snow on Missouri. I took a deep, cleansing breath. Yup, there was snow in those clouds, I could smell it. People laugh at me when I tell them I can smell snow. I can smell rain, too. I smiled and entered the Gaheimer House with that peculiar contentment that I get when I am reminded how much I love winter and how happy I am with my life.

"Absolutely no!" I heard Sylvia scream.

"You're not God!" I heard a woman yell back.

"God or not, you're not wearing a conventional brassiere with historic costumes!"

I went through the ballroom as quickly as possible to get to my office where all the trouble seemed to be coming from. Wilma Pershing stood in the hallway, in a blue dress with tiny little Santa Claus's printed on it, wringing her hands. She was a nicely plump old woman in her nineties. Her nearly white hair hung down loose, rather than in the braids she usually wore. Her green eyes were wide and worried. "Oh dear," she said. She covered her mouth and pointed into my office.

I turned the corner and stopped in my office doorway. Sylvia Pershing, Wilma's sister, stood behind my desk in a forest green pantsuit, shaking her finger at Helen Wickland who stood on the other side of the desk. Sylvia's hair was in its usual double braids wrapped around her head with not so much as one loose hair.

"Victory, thank goodness," Sylvia said when she saw me. Only Sylvia and my mother call me Victory. Everybody else calls me Torie. "Tell Helen she cannot wear a conventional brassiere with the historic costumes. It is abominable."

"Uh," I said, standing in the doorway. "Helen, you cannot wear a conventional brassiere with the historic costumes." The words sort of fell out of my mouth, without any great emotion.

"Thank you," Sylvia said. She seemed happy that I had sided with her until she got a good look at me. "Get those costumes up! You're dragging the floor with them. I bet you dragged them on the ground outside, didn't you? Do you know how long it takes to make those? Do you know how much money they cost?"

"Which of those questions did you want me to answer first?" I asked.

Sylvia's face turned a purplish color. "Hang them out there on the coat rack," she said. "No better yet, just give them to me. I'll take them," she demanded and took the dresses from my hand.

I shook my wrist, trying to get the blood to flow back into it. Sylvia marched out into the hall and Wilma still stood at my doorway, still wringing her hands.

"Good morning, Wilma," I said. "Your hair looks very pretty."

She reached up and touched a strand of her hair and blushed. "Why, thank you," she said, and left.

Helen stared at me from across my desk. Helen was forty-nine and fought turning fifty with every ounce of energy she had. Her frosted hair was cut short, and the frosting was so heavy that you couldn't tell which was gray and which was frosting. I think she did that on purpose. She owned the Lick-a-pot Candy Shoppe down on the corner of Hermann and Jefferson; it was her pride and joy.

"I can't thank you enough, Helen," I began. I took my brown bomber jacket off and hung it on the coat rack by the door in my office. I was wearing beat-up jeans and my husband's big olive green sweater that hung almost to my knees. It seemed as though I never wore my own clothes if I didn't have to.

Helen just stared at me. I sat down. Helen glared at me from above. "Please, sit down," I said. Helen had graciously agreed to take over giving my tours here at the Gaheimer House for the upcoming week because I was going on vacation. Being a tour guide for an old house in a historic river town is really a lot of fun. I also compile all of the genealogical data and land records and that sort of thing for the historical society. Sylvia is the president of the historical society and Wilma is the vice-president.

Helen sat down, although it seemed as if it were against her will. "I'm going to kill her," she stated. "I'm going to kill her and then I'm going to go to jail."

"She's really not that bad," I said. "You were referring to Sylvia, I presume."

"Who on God's green earth do you think I was talking about?"

"Oh," I said. I smiled a big wide, fake smile. "Just pretend she's Wilma."

Helen did not find me amusing. "Why do you have to take a week's vacation in December?" she asked. "Why do you have to take a vacation at all? Ever?"

"My dad's family gets together every December. Every year, somebody sets aside their house and their town for a whole week and all week long aunts, uncles, cousins and whoever come to visit. There are activities and stuff, like caroling, and of course the big dinner. Everybody tries to make it to the big dinner."

Helen rolled her eyes.

"It's my turn to host it," I said. "Actually, it's my dad's but you don't want him hosting something like this, or all they'd get is coffee, cigarettes, and pork rinds. So, I'm hosting it for him."

"You sure you can't work and host this thing?" Helen asked, obviously still miffed at Sylvia. "She's gonna be on my case all week."

"If I want to keep my sanity, I need to be free from work to host this thing," I said. "Some of my family have really loose screws."

"I'm going to kill her and then God's going to be mad at me," Helen said. "And I think He was just starting to forgive me over the Woodstock thing."

I laughed and tried to hide it as quickly as possible.

"Well, you're about ten pounds heavier and three inches shorter than me," Helen stated, changing the subject.

"Gee thanks, Helen," I said.

"I'm just saying that I think the costumes will fit, but I may have to let the hems down," Helen said.

"Don't you even think about touching those costumes!" Sylvia yelled from the hallway as she was passing by. "Except to put them on!"

Helen and I looked at each other. Talk about Big Brother. We had Big Sylvia and that seemed to be far worse. "How does she do that?" Helen asked.

"I don't know," I said.

Sylvia came to the door of my office. "You got a package over there on the computer table," Sylvia said. "There's no return address."

"Oh, thank you," I said and got up to go get it.

"And need I remind you of what your family did to this town back in 1991, at the last Christmas reunion you hosted?" Sylvia asked.

"I was young then," I said, trying to come up with whatever excuse I could to plead my innocence to Sylvia. I sat back down at my desk with the manila envelope that was addressed to me clutched in my hands.

Wilma walked by the office, smiling and carrying a white poinsettia. Sylvia saw her and raised an eyebrow. "What are you doing with your hair down?" she asked and headed in the direction that Wilma had gone. "A woman of your age should never have her hair down." Her voice trailed off as she went farther down the hall, berating her sister over her loose hair. I wondered if there was ever a day in their lives that Sylvia hadn't berated Wilma over something.

"Really, Helen, I can't thank you enough," I said. "I really really appreciate this. You will never know."

Helen just stared at me.

"I'd offer you my firstborn, but I already promised her to Sylvia for putting the soda machine in. I hate to make you settle for second, but I only have one other child—"

"I'll take her," Helen said and laughed. The laughter told me that she would do the tours for me and she would forgive me for it.

"Just smile and say, 'Yes Sylvia,' " I said. "That's what I do."

Helen stood and walked over to get her coat. "What kind of bra do I get to go with those costumes?"

"Ask Sylvia," I said. "It's one of those weird things that push you up and all that."

Helen rolled her eyes yet again as she put her coat on. "What if you don't have anything to push up?" she asked and looked down at her rather flat chest.

"Uh, well, . . ."

"Never mind," she said. "So, your whole family is coming?"

"On my dad's side."

"The *whole* family?"

"Not necessarily on the same day, we have it for a whole week, but yeah, there's like seventy of them or so," I said. "And they just keep coming and coming."

"Like a swarm of killer bees," Sylvia said as she walked by the office, once again in perfect timing. I couldn't imagine what it would have been like to be raised by this secret agent.

Helen stared at me, frozen, as she was putting her scarf on. I looked around the room, trying to seem innocent. "She really isn't all that bad."

Two

Mom," I said. "Where did I put the cake pan of Santa's face?" I was standing on top of my kitchen counter trying desperately to see into the deepest recesses of the top shelf of my kitchen cabinets.

My mother, who was working on her handmade pen and ink Christmas cards never looked up from the snowman that she was sketching. "Downstairs in the seasonal stuff."

"Are you sure? It's bakeware. Would I put bakeware in the seasonal stuff?" I asked. The deep fryer that we never use came tumbling out of the cabinet and I caught it with my right hand, my left hand keeping my balance by gripping the cabinet door.

She looked up over the rim of her granny glasses, pen poised above the paper. "Well, obviously you would put a Santa bakeware with the seasonal stuff, because you did. That's where it's at." She went back to drawing the Christmas card. She was quite the gifted artist and I am very happy the polio that claimed the use of her legs and confined her to a wheelchair did not damage her arms.

I stood there for a moment and then decided that she was probably right. I stuffed the fryer back into the cabinet and then slammed the door shut before it had a chance to jump back out at me. I jumped down off the countertop. It would be just my luck that one of my two daughters would come in while I was up there and I'd have to explain how come I was allowed up there and they were not.

"Well, I'll go downstairs and see if I can find it," I said.

"Okay," Mom said.

Flipping on the basement light, I cautiously descended the steps. I don't like basements, not even mine. And ours isn't one of those nice finished basements with a family room and a bar. Ours is just the plain old concrete floor with metal suspension posts. The girls' bikes were leaning up against the west wall. Rachel's, which had yellow smily-face stickers all over it, was parked perfectly. Mary's, which was decorated only with dings and scratches, was parked just however it happened to land. My husband Rudy's workshop was in the very back. My brand-new washer-dryer was down here along with an extra refrigerator and a deep freeze. We like food.

We also had a big storage area that I actually spent one whole month buying rubber tubs for and organizing all of our junk. If it's not used enough to be upstairs in the real part of the house, it's junk. I wasn't too upset about having to haul out the seasonal tubs, because we had to put the Christmas tree up within the next few days, and I'd need the lights and ornaments anyway.

I walked over to the storage area and pulled and shoved on tubs until I found the three or four labeled Seasonal.

Then I saw something move. I screamed, my hand flying instinctively to my throat. Well, now I knew where Mary's missing rubber snake was, I tossed the rubber snake over my shoulder and grumbled.

I opened up seasonal tub number one. Red tablecloth, red tablecloth with Christmas geese, matching napkins, ta dah; cake pan in the shape of Santa's head. I put the lid back on the tub and noticed that it felt a lot colder down here in the basement than it did when I first came down.

I looked around the room. The basement door stood wide open.

It wasn't wide open when I came down here. It was shut. All the way. Now it wasn't.

"Rudy?" I yelled. I couldn't imagine a single reason why he would leave the Rams game that was on television to come down here in the basement. No answer.

I never know what to do at times like this. I wanted to just walk over and close the door, but then I could be shutting Marilyn Manson in the house with me. I cleared my throat and walked on over to the door, anyway. I shut it, turned around and screamed again.

Uncle Jedidiah Keith stood at the bottom of my basement steps, smiling with a mouth full of . . . well, of nothing. He didn't have any teeth. He held a filthy and ancient pipe between his gums. The whites of his eyes were as yellow as his tobacco-stained beard, and his pants were pulled up nearly to his armpits.

"Hey, Torie," he said. "Come give Uncle Jed a hug." He held his arms out wide and winked. His armpits had a permanent stain on them. This red and blue plaid shirt had to be twenty years old. "I wore my Christmas socks for you."

He didn't have to raise his pants legs for me to see them. He was expecting the next great flood and I could see bright red and green socks blazing above dingy brown work shoes.

"Uncle Jed, you scared the bejesus out of me."

"What you want to go gettin' all scared for?" he asked. "Ain't like it's Halloween or nothin'. You gettin' your holidays all mixed up, missy."

"Can't you knock?" I asked, trying to let my heart get back to some kind of regular rhythm. "Or use the upstairs door?"

He looked at me peculiarly as if I'd just suggested something really far out. "Don't never use the front door. That's for company," he said. "And I did knock, nobody answered."

"Probably because we didn't hear you upstairs," I said.

"Well, I went on up to say hello to your mother and then remembered that I forgot to shut your door," he said.

"Oh," I answered. I finally walked over and gave him a hug, but I held my breath the whole time. Sometimes he forgot what soap was for. I remember one time when I was a kid I asked him why he never took a bath and he told me that water was for drinking, not sitting in. I didn't argue with him at the time, because it seemed rather logical to a seven-year-old.

"Ya miss me?" he asked.

"Of course," I said. I started back up the steps and he followed close behind. His wife had died about ten years ago, so he usually came to these things alone. His five children were all grown with families of their own, and would attend at their own leisure.

We reached the kitchen and I flipped off the basement light and shut the door.

"Look what the cat dragged in," I said to my mother.

"Yes, I know," she answered.

"Well," Uncle Jed said, and let out a long sigh. He patted himself on the stomach and smacked his gums together, his pipe bobbing up and down as he did so. "Where's the whiskey?"

"We don't have any," I said. "We're not big drinkers, Uncle Jed."

"I ain't talkin' about drinkin'," he said. "I'm a-meanin' for medicinal purposes. Lordy, missy, every house gotta have medicine."

"And just what do you need medicine for?" I asked. "I've got Nyquil, that's about as close to whiskey as you're gonna get. It's twenty-five percent alcohol."

He scratched his head and looked around the kitchen. He was probably trying to figure out just how much Nyquil he'd have to drink to get drunk. "Well. I got this pain a-goin' in my foot. And bad eyes. Got real bad eyes—"

"Whiskey isn't going to cure bad eyes," my mother said.

"Oh, you just go on and stay outta this, Jalena," Uncle Jedidiah said. "Well, you know, Torie. Hmmm, when's your dad gonna get here?"

He knew my dad would come armed with some sort of alcohol.

I wasn't ignorant of the ways my uncle thought in. Uncle Jed was the oldest of the group of seven kids. He'd just turned seventy-eight. And let me just say for the record that having an uncle that is seventy-eight is freaking me out completely. If he's seventy-eight then I must be in my thirties. It's like, you say you're thirty-whatever, but you don't really think you are in your thirties. Having an uncle this old has to mean I'm actually, no way out of it, in my thirties. Jeez. I hate family reunions. All the pregnant cousins always freak me out, too. There's always at least five pregnant women at every reunion. That's been the number for the last ten years.

"Dad should be here tomorrow," I said.

"So, what? I'm early?" he asked.

"Yup, you are the first one to arrive," I said.

"Well, that oughta mean that I get a free bottle of whiskey," he said and smiled.

"Give it up, Uncle Jed," I said. "You want anything stronger than Nyquil you're going to have to go down to the Corner Bar," I said.

"You mean I gotta pay for it?" he asked totally offended.

"Yeah," I said.

"What's the name of the corner bar?" he asked all slump-shouldered.

"The Corner Bar," I said. "That's the name of it."

"Hmm," he said.

"What's this?" Mom asked, pointing to the manila envelope that I had thrown on the table when I came in.

"I'm not sure, I haven't had a chance to look at it, but I think it's some information on Rudy's family tree," I said.

"There's no return address," my mother said.

"I know, but the postmark is St. Louis. The only thing in St. Louis that I've sent off for is Rudy's stuff. I'll look at it later.

"Well, Uncle Jed," I went on, "I think I'm going to head in to town and go to Fräulein Krista's Speisehaus. I can drop you off at the Corner Bar, or you can go to Fräulein's with me."

"I'm not dressed for no fancy place. You better take me to the Corner Bar," he said.

My mother gave me her knowing smile. She handed me the manila envelope because she knew that's what I was going to Fräulein's to do. She knew I was wanting to grab a minute to myself and read whatever was in this envelope.

"I should be home before the kids get in from school," I said.

"Okay," she answered. "Make sure you bring Uncle Jed home, too."

"Don't worry," I said. Uncle Jed hiked his pants up even farther, spit on his hands and plastered his hair down in place. He was going out in public after all.

•

Fräulein Krista's Speisehaus is about my favorite place to eat in New Kassel. Especially because of its fattening goodies that I'm not supposed to have. I come here so that I can eat all the goodies I want without having to hide them on top of the refrigerator.

Fräulein Krista's is a big building that looks like it was magically picked up out of the Bavarian Alps and set down here in New Kassel. The interior is rugged with exposed beams. The waiters and waitresses look like adult Hansels and Gretels in their cute little knicker outfits, and the big stuffed brown bear that sits at the end of the bar only adds to the atmosphere. The bear, whom we affectionately named Sylvia, is a recent addition in the last six months. It's sort of become the town's mascot.

I sat in a booth eating a pastry that I could not pronounce and drinking a cup of hot tea, relaxing before the influx of my father's side of the family. I knew that I would not get one spare moment to myself once the week's festivities got underway. And they would start arriving today.

As my mother had known, I wanted to read the contents of that mysterious manila envelope. The package had no return address on it and the handwritten letter on the inside was not signed.

The letter was short and to the point. *Were you aware of this?* was all it said.

Inside were copies of newspaper articles. Newspaper articles from a hot August day in 1948 in Partut County.

LOCAL MAN SHOT TO DEATH ON FRONT PORCH

Nathaniel Ulysses Keith, 72, of Pine Branch, was shot to death on his front porch while his family was trapped inside the house. Authorities have no suspects at this time.

What the heck? I looked around the restaurant, uncomfortable. Unless there was more than one Nathaniel Ulysses Keith who was seventy-two years old in 1948 and lived in Pine Branch, this article was about my great-grandfather. Pine Branch was a community with a church, later a gas station and about 102 residents. There was only one Nathaniel Ulysses Keith.

I scanned the next article. If I had any doubt that this article was about my great-grandfather, this article squelched it. There was a photo of my great-grandparents' front porch, with a bloodstain on it that ran down the steps and into the flower bed. I remembered this porch. My grandfather, John Robert Keith, inherited this house from his father when he died. This was the house that my father grew up in. He was eight when his parents moved in there.

When I was a kid there was a big throw rug on the porch right where that bloodstain was. I used to sit on it and try to embroider, much to my grandmother's amusement. I was not a very crafty child.

The article gave my great-grandmother's statement. They called her by her full name, Della Ruth. Not just Della or Mrs. Keith, but Della Ruth. Her statement said that they heard gunfire and that a few hours later somebody came by, knocked on her door and told her that her husband was on the front porch dead. She was unaware that the gunfire had been that close and that anybody was on her front porch.

That totally undid the first article, which said the family was "trapped inside." Strange, though, that the journalist did not mention that.

Goosebumps traveled down my arms and back. How could this be? My great-grandpa Keith died in a hunting accident. *Everybody* knew that.

I took a sip of my tea and tried to remember how I knew that. I received Nathaniel Keith's death certificate back in the eighties. The cause of death said gunshot wound. I remember that clearly because for a moment I was stunned. Who did I call? Who had I called the first time and asked how Great-Grandpa Keith died?

Who had told me the lie?

It wasn't my father, although I do know that I discussed this "hunting accident" with more than one person in the family and with my father on occasion. I think it was Aunt Ruth that I called first and she had said, yes, he died of a gunshot wound during a hunting accident. I never questioned her story. Why would I? She was my aunt. I never expected her to lie to me. It never occurred to me that the man was murdered and that she'd *need* to lie to me. But why would she need to lie to me? Why the secrecy? Why hadn't this information been part of our family folklore? Why had all my aunts and uncles, and my father included, gone along with her story?

I couldn't help but wonder, sitting there in my favorite restaurant, did Aunt Ruth actually lie to me or was this what she was told too? She would have been twenty-four years old when this happened. Was it possible that she didn't know the truth?

I drank the last of my tea and browsed through the other articles. The last one said that six months later the case was closed unsolved.

This was not possible. Maybe somebody was playing a really ugly prank. I would, first chance, go and look at the original newspapers. There was always the chance that for whatever sick reason I couldn't even dream of coming up with, somebody made these up to look real. That had to be what it was, even though any logical reason escaped me. I didn't have enemies. Not like this anyway. Eleanore Murdoch liked to get the best of me whenever she could, but she wouldn't stoop to something like this. The coincidence of the timing of this "present" did not escape me. My dad's entire family would be here sometime this week.

I scrounged around in my change purse for a couple of bucks in change and set it on the table next to the salt and pepper shakers.

I sat there for a minute unable to move. If these articles were real, this was a betrayal unlike any I had ever known. To suddenly realize that I'd been lied to by the people I loved and trusted was too much to comprehend. Maybe they figured that it was none of my business, and who's to say they aren't correct, but to out and out lie to me when I asked how the man died?

First I would find out if the articles were genuine and then I'd ask my father about it. Maybe I'd ask my mother what to do, since my father could get really riled up about things. I looked at my watch. Three-fifteen. Rachel and Mary would be home in about fifteen minutes. I got up and left Fräulein Krista's with the manila envelope clutched to my breast.

Three

About thirty people wandered in and out of the rooms of my house. It was Monday, the official kick-off day, and the people who were here today would help me decorate our Christmas tree. Just as soon as Uncle Jed, my father and Uncle Melvin got back with the Christmas tree. Poor Rudy couldn't go with them to chop down a tree because he was outside braving the cold, barbecuing.

Rachel sat in a green velvet dress on the corner of the piano bench separating the red Christmas bulbs from the blue ones. She felt that this was important. She looked up at me and smiled automatically, changing the features on her serious face. When had she turned eight? I mean, I knew *when* her birthday was, but jeez, suddenly she was so grown up. Now she was the one pulling her hair back and putting it in the bows she wanted to wear and the style she wanted. It was the first of several things that I used to do for her that would continue to slip away from me.

The doorbell rang and I set the lights down that I had been trying to untangle for half an hour and went to the door. Sheriff Colin Brooke towered in my doorway. I always had to refrain myself from calling him Bubba. He was a large man, early forties. "What are you doing here?" I asked. "You're not related to me."

"Thank goodness," he said. He doesn't like me much. But that's all right, I don't like him much either. We tolerate each other for my mother's sake. The reason for that is because we both love her. Of course in different ways, but it's the love for her that keeps the sheriff and me from really tearing into each other. We'd called a truce about a year ago. I'd admitted that he wasn't an ax murderer or anything like that. I guess one can call that a truce.

"Are you going to ask me in?" he asked.

"Are you going to tell me why you're here?" I said.

"Torie, you know I'm here to see your mother," he said.

"I know," I said and let him in the house. "I just like to make you say it."

He took his hat off as soon as he entered the house. He was in official uniform today, which is a rarity. Even when he's on duty sometimes, he's in jeans and a T-shirt. He looked around the living room, amazed at all the people.

"She's in the kitchen," I said, above Aunt Charlotte's voice, who was telling the story about the outhouse again. It was a funny story but by the sixth time you've heard it, it's not funny anymore. I led him to the kitchen, basically because I was thirsty and wanted something to drink.

I walked in. "Mom, the sheriff's here," I said and went to the refrigerator. I kept my back to them and got out a can of Dr Pepper, trying not to look their way because they always gawked at each other the first ten minutes that they saw each other. Made me want to barf. Did I mention the sheriff is about ten years younger than my mother?

I turned around just in time to see the sheriff kiss her lightly on the lips. "Oh yuk, you guys," I said.

"What?" my mother asked. "You and Rudy kiss all the time."

"I know that," I said. "That's different. You're my *mother*." Just when I thought I was okay with this relationship something like this would happen and I'd get irritated all over again. I think it was because I couldn't get my way. I couldn't convince her early on that the sheriff was a jerk. He arrested me once and she didn't seem to give a darn. That irked me no end. God, was I really just stomping my foot and acting like a teenager?

I thought of something else quickly, before my little voice had a chance to answer that question. "So," I said. "You coming to the big dinner next Saturday?"

"I don't think so," the sheriff said.

"We're renting out the KC hall," I said.

"Colin and I have tickets to go see the *Nutcracker* at the Fox," Mom said.

Sheriff Brooke seeing the *Nutcracker*? The only nutcracker he was familiar with was the one that sat in the bowl on his coffee table. "You mean you're not going to be there either?" I asked my mother, incredulous.

"We had the tickets long before we knew what day the big dinner was on," she explained.

"But, but you *always* come to the reunion dinners," I said.

Just then my younger daughter, Mary, came walking in with a stream of Christmas lights trailing behind her. She was a full-grown kindergartener now. Her little round face was serious, her eyebrows knit together. "They won't turn on, Mommy," she said.

"Are they plugged in?" I asked.

She nodded her head yes but answered, "No."

I sat down in the kitchen chair and took the strand from her. "Are they plugged in or aren't they?" I asked, trying to shake off the irritation I had just felt with my mother.

"They were. And they didn't work," she said. "Now they aren't."

"Well, have Rachel plug them back in for you and you have to go down each light bulb and tighten them up. If there's one loose, the whole strand goes out," I said.

"Oh," she said. She looked over to my mom and the sheriff. She waved. "Hi, Sheriff," she said. He waved back and she left the room.

I had forgotten where the conversation had been interrupted

and took a second to remember. "Mom, you always come to the reunion dinner."

"You know," she began. "It's not my family. I've been divorced from that family a long time. It won't hurt me to miss one dinner."

"You are not divorced from the family. You are divorced from my father. His family has never considered you anything but family," I explained. I didn't have to explain. She knew this. "If anything they would get rid of my father and keep you."

"Victory," she said in that tone. I hate that tone. I had my own tone that I used with my daughters and they probably hated it as much as I hated the one that my mother used with me. It was just the same as saying, Hang it up, you've lost the argument.

"Well, that's fine," I said. "You don't have to go. I just thought that you'd be there. Because you're always there, but that's okay that you won't be."

I felt sick to my stomach. I wasn't sure why. I couldn't remember eating anything unusual today, but suddenly I felt a little queasy. I popped open the tab on my Dr Pepper and took a drink. I didn't normally drink out of the can, but I wanted out of the kitchen and didn't want to spend any more time getting a glass and ice. "I'm going to go outside and see if Rudy needs anything. Like a parka," I said.

As I went out the door I was nearly run over by my twin cousins. We called them the Doublemint twins because they were seven-year-old girls with perfect white teeth, perfect blond hair and enormous blue eyes. Their names were Kristen and Kimberly Brite. They were just too cute not to be made fun of.

They ran around me in a flurry, giggling, then I was nearly knocked over by the three boy cousins who had been chasing them. Finally, I stood alone on my doorstep, my husband Rudy within a hundred feet of me. My sanctuary. My hero.

"Hi," I said and walked over quickly. "You need anything out here?"

"I don't think so," he said. "It's *brr* cold, though."

"Yeah," I said and looked up at the sky. "If only it would snow."

Rudy growled.

"What?" I asked.

"You're like the only grownup that actually *wants* it to snow," he said.

"Nuh uh, Wilma loves it when it snows. She's a grown-up."

He looked at me with skepticism evident on his long face. All of us in New Kassel were beginning to wonder if maybe Wilma wasn't slipping into senility in the past year or so. She'd started forgetting things, like putting her hair up in braids.

"Be sure to take Fritz in with you when you go," he said and pointed to our wiener dog, that lay under the beat-up picnic table. "He's been out here awhile."

"All the people are scaring him," I said.

"Yeah, you had to know that was going to happen."

I nodded my head and hugged myself to ward off the cold. I glanced around my backyard imagining what the swingset and everything would look like with snow on it. It's not like it hadn't snowed before, but it had been a whole year! The chicken coop was exceptionally quiet today. Rudy had run electricity into the coop and we kept a light on in there so that it wouldn't get too cold.

"Are you all right?" Rudy asked.

I looked at him, questioning. This was one of the reasons I loved my husband. One of the many. He instinctively knew that there was either something wrong with me or something was bothering me. All I had to do was give a look.

"I'm fine," I said.

"You look really tired."

"I am tired," I said. "I think I might have mono."

"Mono? Why would you think that?" he asked and lifted the lid on the gas grill. The smell of chicken grilled in Rudy's special seasonings wafted up and out into the neighborhood. Maybe that's why the chickens in the chicken coop were exceptionally quiet.

We didn't slaughter our chickens, they were for eggs. And because I have this thing for all creatures furry, fuzzy or feathery. We bought the chicken from the grocery store. Still, I couldn't help but wonder if the chickens could tell what it was we were cooking.

"I don't know. Mono was going around at the school. Maybe I drank out of a water fountain that somebody else drank out of."

"Do you feel bad?"

"Well, sort of. I'm tired and I feel just real out of sorts. I think I'll go to the doctor tomorrow," I said. "I'm going to go by the library, too."

Rudy smiled at me, his brown eyes crinkling in the corners. "The library? There are no doctors at the library." He turned each piece of chicken over one by one with absolute precision.

"I know," I said and smiled back. "I got some newspaper articles sent to me and I'm not so sure they're authentic. So I want to go look them up at the library and make sure they're real before I say anything to anybody."

Rudy's face drew serious and he stopped turning the chicken. "You? Victory Keith O'Shea. You are actually waiting for proof of something before blazing away with both barrels cocked? You do need to see a doctor," he said. "You're not acting like yourself at all."

"Ha ha ha, you're just so funny," I said. I couldn't help but laugh though, because he was right. But this was very different. This dealt with my father and his family personally. I really did have to be careful and walk on eggs.

"Come on, Fritz," I said and snapped my fingers. He jumped right up and came over to me. I turned to walk back in the house and saw my cousin Jolene Liebowsky walk out my back door. She was Aunt Sissy's youngest daughter. Jolene was tall with long silky black hair and a huge belly. I ran over to her, "My God, Jolene, when did you get married?" I asked her and placed my hands on her obvious third-trimester tummy.

She smiled, full red lips parting to reveal big white teeth. She hugged me and said, "I didn't get married, I'm just pregnant."

Gee. You never know what to say or do when you make a faux pas as big as that one. I smiled since she seemed to be comfortable with it. "Oops," I said.

"That's okay," she said. "I figure I'm going to be answering that a lot this week."

"When are you due?" I asked.

"About six weeks. It's a boy."

"Oh, that is wonderful," I said. "You're number four."

Her eyes grew wide. "No way," she said. "There are four of us pregnant? It happens every year," she said. "This is scary. Who's number five?"

"Not everybody's here yet," I said. "If there isn't a number five this will be the first time in ten years."

Four

Aunt Charlotte, affectionately called Charlie, was built like most of the women in my father's family. She was about five foot five and there was a certain pear shape to her, really narrow through the shoulders with hips twice the size. My mother's family tends to be narrow through the hips and top heavy, so I got lucky and came out somewhere in between.

Aunt Charlotte stood in my living room hanging my antique Christmas ornaments that my grandmother, her mother, had given me years ago. The reason she had given them to me is because she had bought them the year my father was born. I started putting them on the tree only in the last few years because with toddlers it wasn't a smart thing to do. The girls were old enough now, so there was no need for that sort of caution.

Aunt Ruth had not arrived yet and, Uncle Jed, my father and Uncle Melvin were all down in the basement, doing what else? Playing music. Uncle Isaac and Aunt Sissy, whose real name is Felicity, had not arrived either. It was too much of an opportune moment not to say something to Aunt Charlotte about Nathaniel Keith, her grandfather. I wasn't about to say anything about the newspaper articles, I just wanted to get the story from her on how he had died. Or how she'd been told that he had died.

Mary was still trying to get that one strand of lights to work. I considered this a miracle, because Mary is my flighty, rambunctious child and usually does not have the patience for this sort of thing. There were about ten kids in the living room, and at least five of my cousins who were older than me, in their late thirties. I was fairly safe to bring up this subject.

"Charlie," I began.

"Yes?" she said. She hummed along to the Gene Autry Christmas album that I'd had since I was a kid, the one with Rosemary Clooney on it.

"I've recently dusted off my genealogy cap, and started working on my family tree again," I said.

"I thought you always did do that stuff," she answered.

"Well, for other people, but I haven't worked on mine in years. It's really weird getting reacquainted with all of the information. There was so much stuff I had forgotten or things that I got mixed up."

I placed a ceramic angel in an open spot on the tree. Rachel tied little red velvet bows on the ends of some of the branches. My mother and the sheriff were in the kitchen popping corn and then they were going to start stringing it for us. I preferred popcorn or beads on the tree to that garland stuff.

I ventured further. "Now, who was it, which one was it that died in the hunting accident?"

Anybody that knew me fairly well would know that I would not get something like that confused. Hopefully though, that particular character trait of mine would get by Aunt Charlie.

She looked over at me from the coffee table where she was putting a hook on one of the ornaments. She wore Coke bottle glasses so her brown eyes seemed huge against a rather small-boned face. She had turned sixty-eight this year, and was the best quilter in the state to come along since my grandma. My opinion of course.

"How could you forget that?" she asked.

"Well, some of my records are all mixed up," I said.

"It was Nathaniel Keith, my grandfather, your great-grandfather," she said and walked over to the Christmas tree and began searching for the perfect place for the ornament she had chosen. She wore a handmade quilted vest with Christmas ornaments all over a deep blue background.

"That's what I thought," I said.

My cousin Wendy, Uncle Isaac's daughter and the mother of the Brite twins peeked her head from around the back of the tree. "Torie, you can just talk about dead people at any time, can't you?"

"Well, yeah," I said.

Wendy rolled her blue eyes. We were the same age and she had plopped out five children in six years. She was a Girl Scout leader, Brownie leader, room mother for all five children, and she made miniatures for a living. The little dollhouse furniture and stuff that you see in craft stores she made with the patience that God gave Job, and totally neglected to give to me. Two of her children were gifted musicians already and one of the boys looked as if he'd be headed to the Olympics in a few years as a swimmer. These kinds of women really do exist. She stood behind my Christmas tree to prove it.

"It's not like I'm talking about blood and guts, Wen. I'm just talking about our ancestors who have died," I said. I hoped it didn't sound like I was trying to stick up for myself too much. I got a little touchy over this sort of thing. I used to take a picnic lunch and eat it in the middle of the cemetery with the dead people when I compiled the cemetery information for publication. The folks in my family thought I was a bit strange and didn't hesitate to tell me so. Now I'm a little sensitive over it.

"It's just that even at Christmas you still have to talk about dead people," Wendy went on. Her blond hair bounced around her face, reminding me of those old Prell commercials.

"Well, if they were alive I wouldn't have to talk about them, I'd just go talk *to* them," I said. Okay, maybe the situation wasn't so ideal to bring this up after all. Somebody's child came running through my living room and skidded into the wall. My record player skipped and Gene Autry went from "Rudolph" to "Here Comes Santa Claus." I cringed. I really needed to buy this on CD. The boy smiled all precocious-like and took off into the other room.

"Whose kid was that?" I asked with my hand on my hip.

"Looked like one of Lester and Joanie's kids," Aunt Charlie said.

"I didn't even know they were here," I answered. I swallowed my irritation and hung another ornament. The popcorn smell from the kitchen was almost more than I could bear. There was a reason I put my mother in charge of that sort of thing. I always ate more than I strung. And when I picked strawberries at my grandma's, I always ate one for every three that I picked. "So anyway, Aunt Charlie. That hunting accident was 1948," I said. "Do you remember it?"

Of course she would remember it, she would have been about eighteen years old.

"Yeah," she said. "Course I remember it. Grandpa had gone out hunting with his two sons Uncle Granville and my dad. Jed went along, too."

"And . . . what happened?" I asked.

"Torie!" Wendy said and stuck her head out from under the tree this time. Just what was she doing anyway?

"Oh hush, Wendy. I want to know what happened."

"I don't really know. I was in town," Aunt Charlie said and pushed her thick glasses up on her nose. "Go ask Uncle Jed. He can tell you. Far as I know they went hunting and they got lost, got turned around or something like that. Grandpa Nate refused to go the way the others wanted to go and he went the other way. He tripped and shot himself with his own gun."

"Oh," I said. "How awful."

"Yeah, it's an awful way to go." She didn't talk about it as if she was telling a big lie. But then, if she'd been telling it since 1948 she'd have the story down pat. She didn't seem nervous and her mannerisms didn't change when she told the story.

"Can we change the subject now?" Wendy said. She was back behind the tree again.

"Wendy, what are you doing back there?" I asked.

"I'm hiding all the wires from the lights so that it looks like the lights are just setting on the branches."

"Oh," I said. That would never have occurred to me.

One of Wendy's sons came in and sat down at the piano.

"Oh, Kevin honey, why don't you play us some music?" Wendy said and walked over and turned off my Gene Autry album without asking. I checked the notion to punch her a good one and smiled. I'd wanted to punch Wendy plenty of times as a kid, and this was no different. Two hours around her and that same insecure little girl surfaced at the hands of my incredibly gifted, patient, multitalented, albeit rude, cousin.

Kevin, who was about ten years old rolled his eyes. He really didn't want to play. He'd just sat down on the piano bench because the couch and chairs were all covered with glass ornaments waiting to be put on the tree. "He doesn't want to play," I said. "Turn my record back on."

"Oh, sure he does," Wendy said. "Don't you, Kev. Come on, play something."

"You know 'The First Noel?' " Rachel asked.

Kevin broke into one of the more recognizable Preludes by Chopin. Wendy smiled and played with the hair at the nape of her son's neck, pleased at his selection.

"That's not 'The First Noel,' " Rachel said with her nose puckered in dislike. "That's not anything."

THE NEW KASSEL GAZETTE

The News You Might Miss

by Eleanore Murdoch

The Christmas season is fully underway here in New Kassel. It's December and no snow as of yet, so if you guessed the first snow would be in November you were wrong.

The Boys Choir of Santa Lucia is having their annual Christmas play and concert this coming Tuesday night. Oscar wanted me to mention that there are a few girls in the choir because Father Bingham couldn't get enough boys to sing the first soprano part.

The Lick-a-pot Candy Shoppe is hosting a Snowman Contest this year. A pound of chocolate fudge will go to the winner. No adults please.

And ignore any strange noises coming from the O'Shea residence this week. They are hosting a family reunion. Remember the lake? 1991? Those same people.

Until next time,

Eleanore

Five

I drove along Clayton Road in St. Louis County on my way to the library. I wasn't going to the main public library downtown, I was going to the county headquarters. I passed the Mormon church and the Mormon library on Clayton road, then passed Braun Antiques on my left, then made a right on Lindbergh.

The library was just about a quarter of mile, if that, on my left. I went inside and through the octagon entrance into the main part of the library. I had a doctor's appointment at two, so I couldn't spend too long here. I went around to the right and up the open staircase to a loft type of area, then up another flight of steps to the top floor, which housed the genealogical records. They had a few newspapers on file for some of the areas in Missouri and I knew that Partut County was one of them, because I had checked them before.

I signed in for a microfilm machine and opened one of the big drawers with the microfilm. I grabbed the one I needed and sat down to feed the machine. It's a little tricky working the microfilm machine but once you get it down pat, you can usually work all the different kinds. The newspaper began in January 1948. I hit the Forward button and watched as the papers zoomed by so fast it made me sick to my stomach. I stopped the microfilm. May. I zoomed it again and stopped. August. I inched it forward until I had the right day. And the right headline.

LOCAL MAN SHOT TO DEATH ON FRONT PORCH.

It was real. I had half expected this to be a prank, so the reality of it got me right in the gut. I sat back and ran my fingers through my shoulder-length hair and breathed in a deep cleansing breath. It was real. This was not a prank.

Now I was not only faced with the fact that I'd been lied to my whole life, we'd all been lied to. I had to deal with the fact that this was *unsolved*. And that somebody desperately wanted me to know about it. They wanted me to know about it in time for the family reunion so that I could question everybody. It had to be a member of the family that had sent me these clippings. Who else would have done it? Who else would have known about it?

There was also the fact that somebody had actually killed my great-grandfather. It was unsettling to think that somebody didn't like my ancestor enough to kill him. Don't ask me why, there was no logical reason that I felt this way. I just did. Even though I knew that my ancestors weren't angels. In no way, shape, or form. I even had a murderer in the family tree, way back there. Maybe it was because my great-grandfather was alive in this century. It made him more real to me.

I had pictures of this man. I had pictures of this man sitting on my mantel with my great-grandmother, his wife, Della Ruth.

I rewound the microfilm and put it away. I stopped on the way out and checked out a book on how to quilt. I'd been wanting to try my hand at it for a while, and even though we didn't live in St. Louis County, I could have a library card if I paid for it.

I was on Lindbergh and made a left back on to Clayton. I followed Clayton all the way down to Ballas, watching all the beautiful estates outside my window. Big red bows and wreaths hung from the large doors. This was the neighborhood of money. I made a right on to Ballas and then up to St. John's Hospital for my doctor's appointment.

My doctor was in the office building connected to the hospital. I went in, reported that I was there, took a seat and began thumbing through one of the books that I had checked out. Christmas music was piped in through the little round speaker in the ceiling above me. Watercolors in cheap metal frames hung on two walls and the usual rack of health-related pamphlets hung next to the office window.

The nurse came out and called my name. Of course she said Victoria, instead of Victory. Nobody ever gets that right.

My doctor was a small, sweaty man with big nostrils and a bald head. He had a great sense of humor and had never failed to correctly diagnose what was wrong with me. Well, at least not that I knew of.

"What's the problem today, Torie?" he asked. He tapped me on the knee with my file folder and smiled, his stethoscope hanging loosely around his neck.

"I think I might have mono," I said. "It was going around the school and I have felt really run down and tired and just not myself lately." It was a prepared statement. I always did that when I went to the doctor. I rehearsed before going in, practicing exactly what it was I wanted to say.

"Sore throat?" he asked.

"No, not really," I said.

"Swollen glands?"

"I can't tell," I said.

He felt my neck and made me say *aaah* with one of those popsicle stick things, which of course I gagged on. "Fever?"

"No, not really," I said.

He reached in a cabinet, pulled out a box and removed a stick covered in plastic. He handed it to me. "Go pee on this."

I looked at him like he was crazy.

"Go on," he said. "And then come back in here. I'll be waiting for you."

I did what he said. As I was walking back to his office I noticed that the stick had turned blue. I gave it to him as I walked back in and sat down on the examining table again.

"You're pregnant," he said.

"Yeah, right," I said and laughed. I continued to laugh until I noticed that he was not laughing. "You . . . you can't be serious."

"Yes," he stated.

"That's not possible."

"That's what everybody says."

"No, really, Doc. That's not possible. Rudy and I are very careful."

"Obviously not careful enough."

I did not believe him. Even though he was standing there with one hand on his hip and my blue stick in the other hand, I still didn't believe him. "You told me to pee on a stick," I said. "And that's supposed to prove something?"

"It means you're pregnant. You don't have mono."

"How do you know I don't have mono?" I asked. The blood had drained from my face, I could feel it.

"I can test you for it if you want, but you don't have swollen glands, fever or sore throat. What you do have is symptoms of feeling run down and being tired and one blue stick that says you're pregnant," he said, all chipper. "A lot of women mistake early symptoms of pregnancy with the flu or mono."

I sat there perfectly still. The other two times I found out I was pregnant I was at my OB's office, not my regular doctor. They made me pee in a cup and I didn't see what kind of test they used. Plus, we'd been trying so I was expecting it. This came out of left field and I was not prepared for it at all. It never even occurred to me. This just could not be. I was pregnant? I was going to have a baby? The last time I had a baby Rachel threatened to make it sleep in the street if it was a boy. Thank goodness it was a girl.

Tears welled in my eyes. I wasn't ready for another baby. There weren't supposed to be any more. What was I going to do with another baby? Where would I put it?

"You're sure?" I asked.

"There are other things that can make you tired, but before poking your veins for blood, I thought we'd go this route first. I was right. When was your last period?"

I thought about it for a minute. I was so wrapped up in this whole reunion thing that I hadn't even realized that I was . . . five weeks. I counted it on my fingers. Five weeks. It was five weeks ago. And the blue stick said I was pregnant.

"Oh my god," I said. "I'm pregnant."

"Told ya," he said and smiled.

"Don't smile like that," I said, all serious.

"What?" he asked. "This isn't good news?"

"I don't know yet," I said. "I have no idea what Rudy will say. My mother will probably have a stroke. Sylvia will go ballistic. None of the dresses will fit. Oh, man."

"Do you want me to call somebody to come and get you? Are you so upset that you can't drive yourself home?" he asked.

I barely heard his words echoing around in my head. I was off on another planet somewhere. "When?" I asked. "When is it due?"

"August sometime," he said. "You need to make an appointment with your OB."

"Yeah," I said. "You're absolutely right."

Pregnant. I got off the examining table, picked up my purse and book and headed out the door. Pregnant. Baby. Baby. Pregnant. My head hurt.

Six

There's nothing like having a really big secret and not being able to tell it to anybody. Which is why most secrets don't make it as secrets very long, I would presume. I let the whole evening pass and didn't say one word about that blue stick at the doctor's office. Not one. On one hand it took every ounce of self-restraint that I had, and God knows that ain't much. On the other hand I was actually afraid to bring up the subject. This wasn't something that had even been discussed. Rudy and I had our two kids and never talked about what we would do if this sort of thing happened. I was clueless as to how anybody would react.

I stood by the refrigerator drinking a glass of milk. Mary's newest artwork was hanging from a magnet of a pig that said Pig Out. The drawing was of our house and it had people coming out of all of the windows and doors, even the chimney. I think she was trying to tell me something.

My father walked up the basement steps and surprised me. I jumped. It was late, almost midnight, and everybody was in bed or off to their hotel, bed and breakfast or whatever it was they were doing. I gave a small jump when my dad came in the kitchen.

"Scare you?" he asked and sat down. He wore his hair in the same fashion that he'd worn when he was eighteen. The Elvis pompadour thing, even though he wasn't much of a fan of Elvis. He wore a red work cap with marble dust splatters on it, cocked to one side so that his pompadour wouldn't get too smashed. His hair used to be so black it was nearly blue, but now it was turning gray around the edges.

"Yeah," I said. "You scared me."

"Sorry. Got any coffee made?" he asked.

"I think there's some sludge in the bottom of the pot," I answered.

He got up and filled his giant, filthy QT mug with my wonderful sludge and sat back down. He lit up a cigarette and I handed him a saucer.

"Wish you people would get ashtrays around here," he grumbled as he took the saucer from me.

"None of us smoke," I said. "It just never occurs to us to get an ashtray." I walked over to the table and sat down with my half full glass of milk. "Uncle Melvin go home?"

"Yeah, I'm about ready to head out myself."

"Before you go," I ventured, "I was wondering. How exactly was it that Great-grandpa Keith died again?"

He looked at me strangely and raised an eyebrow. My father hated it when I knew something about his family that he did not. He felt like it was his family, he knew them before I did and so he should know everything first.

"Why?" he asked.

"Just tell me how he died."

"Why?"

"Come on, Pop, just humor me."

"Well," he said and took a drink of the sludge. He actually grimaced but took another sip anyway. "It was August."

"What's in season in August?"

"This was the forties, in the country. You can hunt whatever you want," he said, irritated. "They were hunting squirrel, though, I imagine."

"Okay," I said.

"It was August and Grandpa Nate took his son, Uncle Gran—"

"You mean Granville?"

"Uncle Granville," he said. "And my dad and Jed along with him. I heard they'd been drinking a little, because it was so hot and everything."

These particular ancestors of mine didn't need the excuse of the heat to be drinking, but I thought it best not to express my opinion on this. Dad continued.

"Anyway, they got turned around in the woods and couldn't figure out where they were—"

"Why would they go so far in the woods if they were just hunting squirrels? You could practically find them in the backyard," I said.

"Are you gonna let me tell this damn story or not?" he asked. He was slightly annoyed. Ticked would be more like it.

"Sorry," I said all sheepish.

"So, anyway, Uncle Jed suggested that they just go in the opposite direction of the sun and eventually they'd run into the river because they'd be heading east," he said. "Grandpa Nate wouldn't hear anything of it. He wasn't going to listen to no snot-nosed grandkid tell him which way to go in the woods. He knew those woods like the back of his hand."

"Even though this snot-nosed grandkid was twenty-eight years old?" I asked.

Dad gave me the eyebrow again and I shut up.

"Anyway, so Jed decided he was just going to head for the river. He didn't really care what Grandpa thought. So, him and Dad, which was your grandpa, headed for the river. Well, Uncle Gran decided about five minutes later that his dad was being foolish and that yes, he was going to go with Jed. Well, about ten minutes after they were headed to the river, they heard a gunshot."

He stopped talking and looked at me as if I was going to butt in. I shrugged my shoulders that I didn't have anything to say, really, and he went on.

"They ran back and found Grandpa Nate. They said that he'd tripped and shot himself with his own gun," he said and took another drink from his QT cup.

"First of all," I said, "how could four grown men who grew up in that area, who grew up in the woods, get lost in broad daylight?"

"The woods are thick and I guess when you're drinking it can all begin to look alike," Dad said.

"Why would they go off and leave him?" I asked. "Why would they just decide to leave a seventy-eight-year-old man alone in the woods to find his way home?"

"He was being stubborn as a mule," my dad said. "Jed said that they couldn't get him to do anything, so they just left him."

I didn't buy it. And I had proof that was not how he died, anyway. But, even without that proof, I couldn't figure out why they would go off and leave an old man in the woods. Didn't anybody question that? I just found that hard to believe, although I did realize that my uncles and such were ornery.

"Well, Dad," I said. I got up and put my glass in the sink and reached up on top of the refrigerator to get the manila envelope. I set it down in front of him. "Somebody sent these to me, anonymously, I might add. I checked them out at the library and they are the real thing. I'm not saying that you're lying to me, but I am saying that what you're repeating is a lie."

My father looked at the newspaper articles with no expression whatsoever. He read them silently and then set them down. "That's just bullsh—"

"No, it isn't," I said. "I looked for myself. They are real. Look at that porch. That's the porch you grew up on and I did, too. Della Ruth was his wife . . . it is real."

"Who have you told?" he asked.

"Nobody. You're the first," I said.

He picked the articles up again and after about a minute shoved them back into the manila envelope. "What are you going to do?" he asked.

"I'm going to find out why this investigation was dropped. It's classified as unsolved. I don't know if I can ever find out who killed him or why, it being so old a case," I said.

"Why?" he asked. "What does it matter to you?"

"It matters," I said.

"Why?"

"He was my great-grandfather."

"You never knew him," he said.

"His blood still runs through my veins and I want to know who killed him. Don't you?" I asked.

"Not really."

"It doesn't bother you at all that, number one, you've been lied to your whole life? You obviously believed the hunting story," I said. My father only shrugged his shoulders and lit up another cigarette. "Number two, you knew this man and it doesn't bother you that somebody just killed him? Killed him violently and left him on his front porch for his wife, your grandmother, to find?"

"You don't know what you could be stirring up," he said. "This is people's lives we're talking about."

"Your grandmother lied to you, your parents lied to you," I said. "I don't know about you, but I would want to know just what the big secret was that they had to lie about it."

My father stood and dumped the cigarette butts into my trash can, then placed the saucer in the sink. He looked at me for a second with an expression I don't think I've ever seen before. I couldn't begin to name the emotion that was running through him or just what the look meant. "Keep it quiet," he said. "You don't know when you might be talking to the person who did it."

My breath caught in my throat as I realized what exactly it was that he was saying. Tears welled in my eyes and I had to remind myself that it could be just hormones that was causing such a strong reaction. When I was pregnant with Mary I cried over toothpaste commercials, after all.

"It could be any of your aunts and uncles that did that," he said and pointed to the envelope on the table. "Could have been either one of your grandparents, could have been anybody."

The thought of my beloved grandparents being murderers made me sick to my stomach. I didn't believe that. And if one of them had pulled the trigger there would have been a really good explanation. I just knew it. I hoped. What if I were wrong, though? I began to see just what he was getting at. If my Aunt Charlie, for example, was a murderess it would disrupt the lives of her two children and grandchildren. Was I willing to take that chance? But was it okay to let a murderer get by with it?

I just looked at my father with a really confused look on my face, I know, because I was really confused.

"See you tomorrow," he said. "And if you see Aunt Ruth, don't mention this."

"Why?"

"Because she gets really upset over things. She's convinced herself that she's Donna Reed. Don't go making her think otherwise," he advised me.

"Okay," I said. "Good night, Dad."

"Good night, Torie."

He shut the door and left me to wrestle with my own conscience about what to do. If I found out who murdered Nathaniel Ulysses Keith, I didn't necessarily have to tell anybody, right? Besides, somebody wanted me to know about it. It had to be a family member. I decided that before I went to bed I would make a list of all the family I had that lived in St. Louis. That was where the postmark was from on the envelope. I needed an ally in this.

Seven

The next day I was driving down River Point Road and was going to make a right down by the Old Mill Stream restaurant and head out of town. I was on my way to see the sheriff. On my own accord, without being coerced. I did want something from him, though.

The radio said that there would be snow tonight for sure, and I felt my heart give a little leap. *Snow.* I couldn't wait and I hoped with all my heart that this wasn't another false alarm. Just as I was daydreaming about playing in the snow with all of my cousins, as I used to do when I was a kid, this large figure stepped out in front of me. I slammed on the brakes. Luckily I was doing but twenty miles an hour.

Eleanore Murdoch stood in front of my car with her hands on her hips, her big plastic Christmas tree earrings swaying in the wind. A green crocheted hat was pulled down to her eyebrows, making her look like one of those craft dolls with the big eyes and no hair under the hat. She was a very top-heavy woman and her brown wool cloak resembled a small tent.

My purse, notebook and envelope that were sitting on the seat next to me went flying into the floorboard when I'd slammed on the brakes. I honked my horn at her for no other reason than being just fuming angry.

I rolled down my window as she headed for my side of the car. "What in blazes is wrong with you, woman?"

"I wanted to talk with you," she said with her nose raised in the air. Eleanore was *the* town gossip. She and her husband, Oscar, owned the bed and breakfast in town, called the Murdoch Inn. She was booked this week with lots of my family. She also had a small, one-page article in the *New Kassel Gazette*, and thought she was the up-and-coming star of journalism. She was also a snoop. Of course, so was I, but I didn't seem to be so blasted annoying with it.

"Can't you call me or knock on my door?" I asked. "Do you have to run out in front of my car? I could have hit you!" The damage would have most likely been to my car, but I kept that part to myself.

"I wanted to talk with you right now this minute," she said. "It couldn't wait. I saw you coming down the street and decided to flag you down."

"What is it?" I asked, checking my temper.

"It's your cousins."

"Which ones, Eleanore?"

"You know," she said and looked around self-consciously.

"I have twenty first cousins and forty-three first cousins once removed with four new ones on the way. I can't even begin to tell you how many second cousins I have. Which of the masses are you referring to?" I asked.

"You don't have to get snotty, Torie," she said.

"You don't have to be so vague, Eleanore."

"I am speaking of Larry Keith and his . . . his . . . *friend*," she said finally.

"You mean Tommy?"

"Yes," she said. The end of her nose was beginning to turn red from the cold and she had started the "cold dance," rocking back and forth to try and stay warm.

"What about them?" I asked and threw the car into park. I knew what about them. They were gay.

"I think," she began and then stopped. Was Eleanore actually showing some finesse? "I think there is something not right with them."

"How so?" I asked.

"I think . . . I think that they are, you know," she said and then leaned into my window and whispered, "gay."

"Oh, that," I said.

She gasped and straightened herself up quickly. "You mean they *are*?"

"Yes," I said. "What's the problem?"

"I can't have gay people in my bed and breakfast," she said haughtily.

"Why not?" I asked. "Are you getting complaints about public displays of affection?"

"Well, no," she said.

"Are they carrying around banners trying to persuade people to join them?"

"Of course not."

"Then what's the problem?" I asked.

"Well, you can tell that they are, you know, gay. And what will that do for my business?" she asked.

"It will do wonders for your business," I said. "The only people in the bed and breakfast this week are my family anyway, and we all know that they are gay. Just leave them be, Eleanore, and they won't bother you."

"I didn't say they were bothering me," Eleanore said, suddenly dignified. "I'm an open-minded individual, after all. I just thought it might be bad for business."

I gave her the you-should-be-ashamed-of-yourself look. "If somebody starts tearing up furniture or being noisy, call me," I said. "And I'll do something about it."

A car came up behind me on the road and honked. After all, I was in the middle of the road in my huge station wagon. I waved them on around me and they went around. It was Tobias Thorley, our accordion player. He waved as he went by and Eleanore and I waved back.

"If all they are doing is just *looking* gay, I can't do anything about that, and won't do anything about that," I said. I put my car back in drive but held the breaks on still. "Is there anything else?" I asked. Eleanore looked at me as if I was speaking Martian. "Look, Eleanore, Larry is my cousin. I played with him as a kid. I love him. He's not hurting anybody."

She just looked at me. As I drove away I yelled out the window, "When my cousin Danielle checks in, her husband is full-blooded Indian," I yelled. "Just in case you got something against Indians."

I left her standing in the middle of the street, my temples throbbing. I looked in the rearview mirror and her hands were back on her hips. I was happy with myself the way I handled that, but knew that it was wasted on her. Instead of her realizing how petty she was being, she was now probably worrying over when the Indian would arrive.

I headed out of town on New Kassel Outer Road. It was a two-lane blacktop that wound around the small undulating hills that made up the landscape between New Kassel and Wisteria. The trees were bare, the sky a gray swish of an artist's brush and everything was asleep for the winter.

I passed my Aunt Emily's farm—she was my mother's sister—and then passed the intersection for Highway P. New Kassel Outer Road became Main Street once I was in Wisteria. I was accosted with signs for every fast food place imaginable. Wisteria is a small town by the country's standards, but it was the largest town within ten miles so it had all the fast food places that you wouldn't find until you got up to Arnold.

I passed by Rally's, Burger King, Long John Silver's and then finally came to the stoplight in the middle of all of this food heaven. I turned left up a hill and stopped my car in front of the Sheriff's Department.

As soon as I was out of the car, the biting wind struck me square in the face. It must have dropped ten degrees in the last two hours. I ran into the office and found the sheriff sitting back in his chair with his feet up on the desk, reading a magazine.

Awards and such in thin black frames hung as crooked as a dog's hind leg on the wall behind him. The one thing in the office that was in a really nice frame and hanging completely straight was a big 18 × 24-inch picture of all the NFL football helmets.

As soon as he saw me he removed his feet from the desk as if a spider had just crawled across his leg. "Torie," he said.

"Sheriff Brooke," I said and walked over to him holding the manila envelope under my arm. I unbuttoned my coat and threw my hat on the top of his desk. It landed right next to a picture of him and my mother taken at last year's Octoberfest. "Working hard?"

"I was just finishing up paperwork and stuff. My lunch hour," he said.

"Oh," I said.

"Got two deputies out in cars today and one is on vacation."

"Oh," I said again. "I was wondering if you could help me out on a little project."

A blank look crossed his face and I knew that I was going to have to fight him to get him to do what I wanted. That expression was complete mental shutdown, no breaking through it, he wasn't listening to me at all. He leaned back in his chair again. "What?"

I handed him the envelope. He didn't open it, he just looked at me.

"I received this a few days ago with no return address. No signature on the letter. I went to the library to make sure they were authentic and they are," I explained slowly.

Now he opened the envelope and pulled the contents out. He scanned quickly, reading only the headlines. "What's this about?"

"The man shot to death on the front porch is my great-grandfather, Nathaniel Keith," I said.

"Oh, great," he said and rubbed his eyes and pinched the bridge of his nose.

"Don't start until you hear me out," I said.

The sheriff threw his hands up in surrender. "I'm listening."

"The articles say that it was unsolved, no real suspects, all that good stuff," I said.

"But you know different?"

"No. I have no clue as to what happened. The problem I have with this is that we were all told he died in a hunting accident," I said. "It just bugs me that somebody thought there was something worth hiding enough to make up a lie for their children."

"I can see how that would bother you," he said.

I looked at him surprised. He never agreed with me. But if he did he wouldn't usually say so. Not out loud, at least. His blue eyes showed no emotion other than irritation, but at least he had agreed that he understood.

"Thank you," I said. "It also bothers me that somebody, who I am fairly safe in saying is a family member, brought this to my attention, but didn't want me to know who they were."

The sheriff shrugged. He got up and poured himself a cup of coffee from the automatic coffee maker in the corner of the room. The phone rang. "Just a minute, Torie," he said. "Dispatcher is out for lunch."

He picked up the phone and I looked outside watching the traffic go up and down Main Street. I could see the bags and packages in people's cars. There were only about fifteen days left to shop.

"Well, Tobias, I don't know what to tell you. Just calm down, that cat will come down when it gets hungry enough," he said. "I can't leave my office to come and get a cat off of your roof. No, no, Tobias, I have other things to do. Well, if you want to take a hose to it, that's your business. Hope you can live with yourself, though, since it's about twenty degrees outside." He slammed the phone down and cussed at it.

"So, what do you want me to do about this?" Sheriff Brooke asked.

"I was wondering if you could find the investigating officer of the crime—"

"Oh no," he said. "No."

"I just want to know, if he's alive that is, if he would just talk to me about it. If he won't talk to me, talk to you. I know that there was evidence and things kept out of the papers, there always is. That's it. He's got to be retired if he's still alive, and the case is long closed. What can it hurt?" I asked.

"Does your father know?" he asked.

"Yeah, I talked to him about it last night. I think he wants me to find out who it is as long as I don't find out who it is."

"Huh?" he asked.

"I think he's afraid I might find out it's one of his brothers or sisters or his parents or something."

"He could be right," Sheriff Brooke said. "You willing to take that risk?"

"I'm not saying I want this case solved, I would just like to know more about it, and why we were fed a huge lie about it," I said. "That's all."

Sheriff Brooke took a drink of his coffee and looked at me blankly. He was waiting for me to say something else.

"I just want to know who the suspects were."

Still the blank expression.

"And the motive. Why would somebody kill my great-grandfather?"

He took another drink of coffee.

"Please," I said.

"I'll see what I can do," he said like magic. "I'm sure it won't hurt to just talk to him about it. He may be dead," he said.

"I realize that, and if he is, well . . . I'm not sure what I'll do then." I tried hard not to let him see how happy I was that he was going to at least try to find the guy. "His name is Hubert McCarthy," I added and pointed to the papers.

The sheriff took the papers over to his copy machine and made copies of everything and then handed them back to me. "I am not going to investigate this," he said. "I'm just going to take you to talk to him if he is willing. That's it. I've got other things to do."

"That's fine," I said. "Actually, that's wonderful."

I put my hat back on my head and buttoned my coat. It was a little strange that I didn't have to beg, plead and do a polka for him to grant me this one little wish. Why was he being so nice to me?

"Thank you," I said. "Very much."

He just nodded to me and I left. As I stepped outside I felt something wet on my face. I looked up at my car and saw tiny snowflakes blowing on the hood. The sheriff was going to find Hubert McCarthy for me and it was snowing. It almost made me forget that I still had to tell my husband about that blue stick at the doctor's office.

Eight

New Kassel Lake is situated about a mile out of town. It was frozen over completely solid. It wasn't a large lake, but it was too large to be considered a pond. Fishing was tolerable in the summer, but mostly the lake was used for swimming by the local teenagers. I stood in my ice skates on the edge, waiting for Mary to get her skates laced up. It was about eight o'clock at night and a large portion of my reunion-going family were in attendance skating or sitting on the sidelines by the bonfire talking.

The snow fell lightly, just giving the trees a dusting. This wasn't a serious snow, yet. The lights around the lake turned the snowflakes a bluish color as they came down out of the sky.

The sheriff sat under an awning that the Rotary Club had built the spring before last, with my mother right next to him. He wouldn't be caught dead ice skating. At least he had come to watch, though. I looked down at Mary. Her coat was Christmas red, and her mittens were white. Well, they were white when I bought them. She looked up and smiled at me, her cheeks nearly as red as the hood on the coat.

She was a much better skater than I was, but then she took lessons once a week and I rarely skated. I'd had an accident on my grandparents' farm when I was about six. We thought the ice was frozen, but it wasn't and it broke, plunging me into the muddy abyss below. My cousins, who were also only about five or six just stood there frozen in shock as I bobbed up and down. There was no time to yell; every time I surfaced I gulped another breath in time to sink again. Eventually the mud and muck just sucked me down farther. The only thing that saved me was that my father, who happened to be outside chopping wood for his mom and dad, came around the corner of the house and saw what was happening. I remember this very large hand appearing out of nowhere and raising me out of the muck and saving my life. Those same hands then beat the living tar out of my cousins.

So, needless to say, frozen ponds hold a certain level of fear for me, but I try not to pass on my fears to my children. I figure they're going to come up with their own set of fears and phobias, why should I add to them. So, here I was, standing on a frozen body of water ready to ice skate.

Rudy and Rachel were already on the ice. They waved at me from the middle of the lake. Mary stood, ready to skate. We moved out onto the ice, and Mary and Rachel instantly started some sort of romantic make-believe stuff on ice.

Damon Sneed, my favorite male cousin, came swooshing by and nearly spun me around with his g-force, he was skating so fast. "You think you're something," I said to him with my hands on my hips. He did a little flip thingy, an axel of some sort, and then came over by me.

"Wow, Damon," I said, impressed. "When did you learn to skate like that?"

"That is the result of two years in Canada," he said. "My wife and I skated every weekend."

"Cool," I said. I loved Damon. When we were kids I used to call him Demon Seed, instead of Damon Sneed. God he hated that. He was always trying to come up with something to get back at me with, and it was just never as good. He was tall and slender, with black hair and syrupy brown eyes. His complexion was olive and he definitely took after our grandmother, who was French.

"You got a great town, Torie," he said. "I've been here two days and I don't think I've ever had this much fun."

"Well, it's not my town," I answered him and fumbled on a bump in the ice. "I just live here."

"You do much more than just live here," he said and smiled. "Wish I could have come back in ninety-one."

"Yeah, where were you again?"

"That was when we were in Canada."

"Oh, yeah," I said. Damon lived in Arizona now and I'd gone to visit him once. Couldn't believe it could be so hot and not have one mosquito.

"Hey Damon," I said. "What do you know about our great-grandpa?"

"Not much," he said. He was Aunt Charlotte's son, so I knew that what information he had would come filtered down through his mother. "My dad never liked him too much."

"Really?" I asked. "Why is that?" I was surprised by this. People never went around praising Nathaniel Keith, but I can't say that I actually heard anybody put him down either.

Damon shrugged his shoulders. "Can't think of anything specific," he said. "Just that he was a drunk and that he liked to chase women."

"Well, that's pretty specific if you ask me," I said. His words didn't really mean too much to me, because getting drunk and being a womanizer seems to be the thing that people of days gone by tacked on to anybody that they didn't like.

"I don't know," he said and shrugged again. "Why do you ask?" He turned around backward on his skates and skated in front of me, facing me.

"I'm working on a scrapbook type of thing and wanted little anecdotes or personality traits to put with each ancestor," I said.

"Oh," he said. "Then you don't want the bad stuff." He looked around his shoulder to see if he was going to run into anybody else on the ice. I was having difficulty in keeping up with him. He was a flawless skater and I was having to work at every stroke.

"If that's what he was, then that's what I'll put in the scrapbook," I said. I was lying, of course, about the scrapbook. I seemed to do that a lot lately.

"Let me see if I can think of anything that I've heard that was good," he said. "You should really ask Uncle Jed or Aunt Ruth, even Uncle Isaac. They were adults when he died. All I can give you is secondhand stuff."

"I'm going to," I said.

"Um," he said and stroked his chin, deep in thought. "I think I heard my mother say something one time about him being in a swimming accident . . ."

"Hunting accident," I corrected.

"No, swimming. He was a young man and saved some boy's life—from drowning or something like that," he said.

"Oh," I answered. I hadn't heard that one. "Do you know how he died?"

"No," he said. "How did he die? Wouldn't you, Miss Genealogist, already know that?"

"Oh, I know," I said. "I just thought I'd see what you knew about it."

"I don't know anything," he said. "How did he die?"

"Hunting accident," I said. My nose was numb from the cold and my lips moved slower than normal. Which I'm sure was a relief to Damon. I outtalk most anybody. There was a shirt at the mall I was thinking about buying for myself. It said HELP, I'VE STARTED TALKING AND I CAN'T SHUT UP. Anybody who knows me in the least knows that is perfect for me.

The Doublemint twins skated by, each one holding on to the other one for dear life. That made me feel better. They were Wendy's kids and not perfect at something. Damon winked at me and went off to chase the twins. Their squeals could be heard all the way into town, I'm sure.

Rudy skated over to me and grabbed my hand. "How are you doing?" he asked.

"Oh, fine," I said. I really needed to tell him about that blue stick at the doctor's office. He smiled at me and gave me his cutesy look. The one that declared that he was lovable and that I couldn't resist him in the least. He wore a brown leather coat and one of those toboggan hats that had a ball of fringe at the very end of the yard of material. His hat literally came down to his butt. It looked like one of those long turn-of-the-century sleeping hats. He was just too cute for words.

"Hey," he said. "How'd your doctor's appointment go? Do you have mono?"

"No, I don't have mono," I said in a vague tone of voice.

"Oh that's good," he said. Suddenly a serious look crossed his face. I guess he just thought that maybe I had something worse than mono. I suppose, depending on the angle you took, being pregnant could be worse than mono. I had a cousin once who wished for a tumor when she thought she was pregnant. She was pregnant.

"It's nothing real serious," I said to appease his sudden uneasiness. "Well, I guess that depends."

"What?" he asked. We had made it to the side of the lake where my mother and the sheriff were. They waved to me and I waved back feeling like I was eight years old.

"Well, see . . ." I began. "There was this blue stick at the doctor's office—well, actually it was white when it began but it turned blue halfway through it—"

"What are you talking about?" he asked and laughed. "Sometimes I think you deliberately think of the most difficult way to say something just so you have more time at talking."

"I'm pregnant."

At that Rudy fell face first on the ice. He yelled out in agony as I heard him go thunk. "Oh my God, Rudy," I said. I looked down and then I saw the ice turn red. Rudy came up holding his nose, blood soaking his gloves. He gave a real low painful-sounding moan and his eyes watered.

"You're what?" he said through the glove. "You're pr . . . pr . . . did you say you were pregnant?"

"God, Rudy. Shut up and get over here and sit down."

The sheriff came walking out onto the ice and all of my family started to gather around. Rudy's wide-eyed stare never left my face as the sheriff and I helped him walk off the ice. Every now and then his eyes would involuntarily cross. God, that must have hurt.

He sat down on one of the bleachers and immediately put his head backward. "Oh, don't do that," I said. "You want to lean forward a little. Not too much, though."

"Thought I was supposed to put my head back," he said and moaned in agony again.

"No, it's forward."

"No, I'm pretty sure it's back."

"Fine, stubborn," I said. "Put it back and see what happens."

He put his head back and left it that way for a few seconds. He abruptly gagged and put his head forward. I took his toboggan hat off his head and folded it and stuck it under his nose. There was nothing else for me to use.

"The blood ran down the back of your throat, didn't it?" I asked.

He just waved a hand at me. Yeah, yeah, I was the wife and I was right, no use in actually declaring it. Suddenly his head snapped back up. "Did you say—"

"Hush," I said. I didn't want the sheriff and the umpteen cousins that had gathered around to hear this way that I was pregnant.

Sheriff Brooke had remained quiet until now. Rachel and Mary made it off the ice and were walking over to the bleachers through the grass that was slowly but surely turning white from the snow.

"Did you trip on your lace?" Sheriff Brooke asked.

Rudy just glared at him.

"We need to get you over to Wisteria General," the sheriff added. "You could have broken it."

Now Rudy glared at me.

"What?" I asked Rudy. "I didn't do anything."

"You could have waited until we were in front of a cozy fireplace or something," he said through the toboggan hat. "Did you have to tell me that then? Right then and there?"

"Well, you asked," I said. "And I've known for a day or so and I was beginning to feel guilty keeping it from you. You asked."

His glare grew more intense. Just as I was about ready to fear for the longevity of my marriage, his eyes crossed again and I cracked up laughing. I stopped fairly quickly, though. He was clearly not a happy man.

"If I hadn't told you, you would have thought the worst—"

"This is the worst!" he yelled.

"Or you would have just badgered me until I told you anyway. I wasn't planning on telling you on the ice. You asked me."

"Asked what?" Sheriff Brooke asked.

Rudy and I simultaneously said, "Nothing!"

"Fine," the sheriff said and held up his hands. "Rudy, you need to get over to the hospital."

"I don't think it's broken," he said.

"How would you know?" I asked. "Did it make a crunch sound?"

"Of course it made a crunch sound. I landed on my nose on the ice."

The sheriff and I looked at each other. "It's broken," I said.

"Look," Rudy said and held his hat out. "It's already stopped bleeding." Blood had run all the way down to his chin and when he tried to smile at me, I could see the blood gathered in between his teeth. It made me a little queasy.

"Yeah, but that doesn't mean it ain't broke," the sheriff said.

"Daddy, Daddy," the girls yelled. Rachel immediately stopped short when she saw all the blood and scrunched her nose up, distorting her face. "Ooooh that is just so gross, Dad," she declared.

"Thanks, Rachel," he said.

Mary, of course, went right up to him. "Neato," she said. "You're going to have to wash your hat now."

"What happened?" Rachel asked, her face still distorted in disgust.

"Your dad fell on the ice, I think he broke his nose," I said.

Rachel gave a little giggle, then Mary began laughing out loud. Rudy's irritation at their obvious insensitivity to his situation was evident on his face. It didn't seem to bother the girls, though. They continued to laugh.

"Sheriff," I said. "Would you make sure that my kids get home okay with my mother? I'm going to take Rudy to the hospital for an X ray."

"Sure thing," he said. "Not a problem. Be careful, though. I think the snow is coming down a little harder."

Why was he being so nice to me? Normally he'd be wishing that I would hit a patch of ice.

"Okay," I said. "Come on, Rudy. Let's get you to the hospital."

He stood up and looked down at me. "Are you really . . . you know?"

"The blue stick says I am."

"Wow," he said. He followed behind me like a little lost puppy in total silence as we walked to the car. About an inch and a half of snow now covered the grass and it crunched beneath our feet. It was the only noise I heard, except the distant skaters and the occasional moan that Rudy would make.

I unlocked the door for him and went around to my side of the car. He spoke to me over the hood. "Really. You're really pregnant."

"Yes."

"Cool," he said, his attitude changing abruptly. "I'll get my boy after all. I will no longer be outnumbered! I'll have somebody that will help me fight for the bathroom!" Evidently his head started throbbing or some kind of pain in his nose seized him because he winced, shut up and went back to moaning.

If he hadn't just busted his nose himself, I would have busted it for him.

Nine

Aunt Sissy!" I cried. My favorite aunt in the whole wide world came walking up my front drive with her specialty perched in her very capable hands: red velvet cake. If it weren't for the fact that I might damage the red velvet cake, I would have jumped into her arms just like I did when I was a kid. I was so excited to see her, I stood there on my front porch giddy as a schoolgirl.

"I can't believe you're really here," I said as she stepped up on the front porch. Aunt Sissy lived in Minnesota and rarely drove in for these functions. The reason she is called Sissy is because my dad couldn't say Felicity, it came out Sissity. So they just called her Sissy.

"I'm here, dammit," she said. "With your favorite cake." Aunt Sissy wore her characteristic jeans cut off at the shins, a sweater with different color patches all over it and her yellow Converse sneakers. I'll admit, that's who I learned to wear my Converse hightops from. She was the most unique and free-spirited person in the family. Well, other than Uncle Jed. He's so weird, we almost don't claim him, though.

"This is so cool," I said. "You won't recognize my girls, they've grown so much since we were in Minnesota last."

"I hardly recognize you," she said. "When did you sleep last?"

"Where's Uncle Joe?" I asked, to avert her question.

"He's flying in," she said. "Had business to attend to."

We walked in the door and Rudy greeted us. His nose was not broken, but he sure banged it a good one. We spent two hours in the hospital yesterday during which they asked him all kinds of questions. I think they thought we'd been fighting and that I hit him with something. A swollen nose and slightly bruised eyes were the only damage. Well, aside from that pride of his.

"Egads, Rudy. Did Torie beat you up?" she asked.

"Yup," he said.

"It's about damn time," she said and walked right on by Rudy and into my kitchen. "Hello, Jalena," she said to my mother. "Still as beautiful as ever, I see." She spoke the words almost as if it were a sin for my mother to be beautiful. She had such a brusque and matter-of-fact tone to her voice and her manner of speaking that unless she was in her herb garden or, like all my other aunts, quilting, she always spoke like she was giving a business dissertation of some sort.

"Thank you, Sissy," my mother said. "I was just going out on the porch."

"Oh yeah," Aunt Sissy said. "Go on. You can't wait to get away from me."

My mother just smiled and went on out to the porch. This was typical for Aunt Sissy. I can't explain why I like this woman so much, I just do. I took the cake from her and put it on the counter next to the mincemeat pie that somebody brought. I couldn't even begin to remember who it was.

Wendy came into the room. "Aunt Sissy," she said. She walked over and did one of those air kisses that you see in Hollywood. "I've missed you so much." The syrupy sugar just dripped from her lips.

"Yeah," Aunt Sissy said with about as much enthusiasm as one would have watching a snail crawl across the porch. "Missed you, too."

"Torie, my mother said you had a blender we could use to make daiquiris," Wendy said.

"Yeah, up there in that top cabinet. Be careful, though. The deep fryer likes to fall out on people's heads," I said.

"Okay," she said. She pulled a chair over and got the blender down, and sure enough the fryer came flying out, but she was ready for it and caught it and shoved it back in. "Thanks," she said and put the chair back. She straightened her blouse down over her skirt so that there were no wrinkles, left the blender on the counter and then left the room.

"I hate that girl," Aunt Sissy said.

I just smiled.

"So, Ike is here," Aunt Sissy declared.

"Evidently," I said. She was speaking of her brother Isaac who was Wendy's father. "I didn't see him arrive, but it would seem that he and Aunt Nancy are here, based on what Wendy just said."

"And my other rotten no-good brother?"

"Which one?"

"All of them."

"Actually, they are all here. Or at least somewhere in town. The only one we are waiting on is Aunt Ruth, now that you are here."

"So when you people gonna get some snow?" she asked.

"It snowed last night."

"You call that snow?" She made some dismissive noise and then said, "That's just the clouds shaking off dust."

"Well, up there in Minnesota things get a little ridiculous. Fifty feet of snow is a little overboard."

"Well," she said, "maybe since I'm here the snow will follow me and you people will get more than a dusting."

"What's with all this 'you people' crap? Did you forget you've only lived in Minnesota for ten years? We are *your* people."

She made that noise again. "Oh, I brought you something." she said. "I brought you a big box of scrap material so you can make a quilt."

"Aunt Sissy, I don't quilt," I said, even though I had checked a book out on it. She knew I didn't quilt. We'd had this discussion many times and it always ended with her being thoroughly disappointed in me.

"As much as quilting runs in your veins, you should quilt. I don't care if it's ugly and none of your points meet, you should be doing it."

I took her coat that she had folded across her arm. Coat was not the word for it. It was more like a jacket. Guess if this wasn't real cold down here either. "Aunt Sissy—"

"Don't. Just hush," she said and held up her hand. "I also brought you a box of stuff that was Mom's."

I looked at her for a moment. Why would she bring me a box of Grandma's things when she had children of her own to give it to? "What things?" I asked, curious but cautious.

"It's just a box of things. Some letters, cards, a few old buttons, a handkerchief or two, some matchbooks. You know, the kind of stuff you'd get out of somebody's junk drawer," she explained. "Let me go out to the car and get them."

"Wait," I said. "Why would you bring them to me?" She could cause some hurt feelings among the other cousins. She just looked at me. That look made me think that maybe she *wanted* to stir up trouble.

She escaped through the living room and out to her car. Wendy came back into the kitchen with a bottle of rum ready to make daiquiris. "I hate that woman," she said about Aunt Sissy. I could have told her that the feeling was mutual but decided not to. She went to my freezer and got out frozen strawberries and the lime juice and went about making the daiquiris. I decided to meet Aunt Sissy on the way in, because I didn't want her to come back into the kitchen with the stuff and take a chance on Wendy seeing it.

Rudy smiled at me from his favorite chair as I entered the living room. He and a bunch of my cousins were watching some sport activity. It seems that after he'd had a chance to think about this baby thing, he is actually quite excited about it. Which not only worries me but scares me. I on the other hand, was still wrestling with the idea that I had a baby, a little creature that was going to grow up and scream at me, growing within me at this very moment. It just didn't seem real. We hadn't told anybody else. It's sort of hectic and we thought we'd just announce it at the dinner on Sunday when everybody would be in attendance.

I met Aunt Sissy at the door. She was carrying two boxes. "Let's take these upstairs," I said and took a box from her. She followed me up to my office and the bedroom that Rudy and I shared. Our upstairs used to be just all one attic, but before we bought the house the owners sectioned it off. So the steps were the divider between my office and our bedroom with the bathroom directly in front of the steps. There was no real wall to separate my office from the bedroom.

I had just redecorated our room in blue gingham. My pinewood floors were the perfect accent against pale blue walls, with dark blue checked border and similar curtains. I set one of the boxes on the bed and Aunt Sissy sat her box in the floor.

"Where'd you get that quilt?" she asked, looking at the mauve Lonestar on my bed.

"Oh," I said, "an old lady left that to me in her will. Only met her once, but she took a liking to me, I suppose."

She pointed to the box that I was holding. "There are scraps in there that are twenty-five years old," she said.

"Oh, good. So then I should have a lot of polyester and paisley." I opened the box and was immediately struck by what she had said. I recognized pieces of fabric that my grandmother had used on the aprons she made for herself. I also noted a few fabrics that had been dresses my grandmother had made for me when I was about five or six.

"Some of Dad's old shirts in there, too," she said. "Know how crazy you were about him."

I was speechless. Not only speechless but touched. My throat constricted and I was surprised by the fact that this gesture nearly brought me to tears. It was as if she'd gone through her scrap collection and picked this stuff out just for me.

"I went through my scrap collection, which is about ready to take over the house, and picked those out just for you," she said.

I love Aunt Sissy. There is no subtlety here. No guessing what she means or if she's sincere. She just lays it out there for you.

"I don't quilt, Aunt Sissy."

"Now you can," she said.

"What if I screw up on the scraps that you gave me? I would never forgive myself."

"Then don't screw up."

"I don't know what to say."

"I don't want you to say anything. I want you to make a quilt."

"All right," I said. "I'll try."

"Good. I'm going in to town. Gonna find that good-for-nothing brother of mine."

"Which one?"

"Jed. Haven't seen him in years."

"He's probably at the Corner Bar."

"I know exactly where he is," she said. "I'll be back in time for dinner."

With that she just turned and disappeared down my steps and into the craziness of the room below. I went into my office and found the book on quilts that I had checked out at the library. I brought it back into my bedroom and sat down on the bed, next to the box of scraps. I flipped through the book and got to the part that had patterns especially for scrap quilts. Quilts that you could make with small pieces of material. There was one that caught my eye. It was called the Indian Hatchet. Part of the reason that I was struck by this was that in the middle of each square was a diagonal piece of white material that people signed. It was a signature quilt or friendship quilt.

What better way to get samples of people's handwriting to

match to the note that I received with the newspaper articles? I would have everybody in attendance sign one of these squares. Then I could get samples of their handwriting and have a keepsake made out of keepsake material. I looked over at the box on the floor. I'd tackle that tomorrow. Right now it was enough to feel happy with my plan to find out who sent me those articles.

THE NEW KASSEL GAZETTE

The News You Might Miss

by Eleanore Murdoch

Our Honorable Mayor, Bill Castlereagh, won the first-snow contest. He correctly predicted when we would get the first inch of snow. He wins four baseball tickets to the Cardinals game of his choice in the spring. Elmer Kolbe stated that the lake has been skatable for about a week now. Put on your skates and go on out to the lake for good clean fun.

In case you see Rudy O'Shea around town and wonder where he got the black eyes and swollen nose, they were the result of a serious skating accident. He swears that it was not the result of marital miscommunication.

And if you don't live in this town, please be respectful of other people's property. Elmer says if he finds out who stuck cigars in his garden nymphs' mouths, he's going to stick them up your nose.

Until next time,

Eleanore

Ten

I found Hubert McCarthy," Sheriff Brooke said. I held the phone in one hand and decorated sugar cookies with the other. Mary danced on one of the kitchen chairs, Uncle Jed ate the cookies faster than I could decorate them, and Aunt Charlotte stirred fudge over the stove. My mother had barricaded herself in her room around three in the afternoon and I hadn't seen her in about two hours.

"You're kidding," I said in response to his news. "Dead or alive?" It would be just like the sheriff to call me up and say he'd found Hubert and that he was actually in a grave somewhere.

"Kinda in between," the sheriff answered.

"What?" I asked. "Mary, get off the chair, you're going to fall." She gave me that you-don't-know-what-you're-talking-about look and continued to dance. I came around to the side of the table to get her and my phone cord caught the can of sprinkle stuff and knocked it over. I now had two sugar cookies smothered in red sprinkles. It's a good thing I had the red tablecloth on the table. I shook the two cookies to try and get as much of the stuff off as I possibly could. "You're in so much trouble," I said to her.

"I said I would find him and I did," the sheriff said.

"No, I was talking to Mary," I said and snapped my fingers at her. I tried my best to look menacing, but she knew I couldn't reach her and she just kept dancing on the chair. It's times like these you just want to say, Fine, go ahead and break your neck. But as a parent you'll never say those words because if it happened you could never live with yourself. So I tried to stretch farther across the table.

"What do you mean by kinda in between?" I asked the sheriff.

"He's alive, but he's not in real great shape. He's about eighty-five and lives with his son, Roger," he explained.

I snapped my fingers at Mary again. Still, she danced. I looked over and saw Uncle Jed shoving cookies in his mouth, laughing heartily at me snapping at Mary. "Really, Uncle Jed, don't encourage her." He just kept on laughing and gumming those cookies like there was no tomorrow. Amazing how well he could eat with no teeth. Maybe that was why he was eating them warm, so they'd be softer.

"So can I go talk to him or not?" I asked.

"His son said that it was okay with him if we came and talked to his dad. He said he remembered the case, he was about ten years old when it happened."

"When can I talk to him?" I asked.

"Anytime."

"How about this evening, after dinner?"

"That soon?" the sheriff asked. I could hear the speculation in his voice. "I don't know what the guy would say to that."

I forgot about Mary for the moment and tried to walk into the little alcove by the basement steps so that nobody would hear me. "Look, Sheriff, if I don't get some answers really really fast, my family will be gone. I'm down to like three of four days before people start leaving. It won't hurt to ask. If he says no, he says no."

I walked back to the main part of the kitchen. "Hang on," I said to him. As soon as I put the phone down, Mary took off, running into the living room. She thought she'd been had. What she didn't realize was that I was after a piece of paper and pen. I came back to the phone and picked it up. "Okay, his name was what again? Roger McCarthy?" I wrote it down. I scribbled *H's son* underneath it.

"Yeah, Roger McCarthy," he answered. "He lives up in Southwest St. Louis, near Kingshighway and Chippewa."

"Okay," I said and wrote it down. "Call him and see if I can head up there this evening and call me back with the exact address." I almost hung up the phone without thanking him.

"Thanks, Colin," I said. "I appreciate this."

"I'll call you right back."

I hung up the phone. "Mary!" I yelled. I went into the living room to find her but she was nowhere to be found. I found Rachel and stopped her. She was playing jump rope with four other girls. In my living room. "Downstairs in the basement with that," I said. "Or go outside."

"Mom," she said and stomped her foot. "It's cold outside."

"Then go down to the basement, now," I said. She gave me that look that said I was totally unfair and uncool. "Where's Mary?" I asked before she headed into the kitchen to the basement steps.

"Under the couch," she said, still in that pouty voice. Her ponytail flopped all around in response to the exaggerated way she walked through the kitchen.

With that Mary crawled out from under the couch and ran to the front door and outside before I could get within two feet of her. With no coat. "Rudy!" I yelled.

"What?" I heard him yell from somewhere in the house. "Get Mary," I yelled. "She went outside without a coat!"

I was so irritated I could have just spit. I walked back into the kitchen, and the piece of paper with Roger McCarthy's name on that I'd left on the table by the pile of red sprinkle stuff was nowhere to be seen.

I looked around the kitchen. Uncle Jed was gone and Aunt

Charlotte still stirred fudge. I didn't want to ask her outright if she had seen who took it or where it had walked off to. I checked over by the countertop, nothing. "Huh," I said with my hands on my hips. Either Uncle Jed or Aunt Charlotte swiped that piece of paper while I was looking for Mary or somebody else walked through the kitchen and snatched it. This did not bode well.

The phone rang and I walked over and jerked the receiver off the wall. "Hello," I spat.

"This evening as long as it's before eight o'clock because his father gets his bath then and goes to bed." The sheriff's voice carried that message with much caution.

"I'll be there at . . ." I looked over at the clock on the wall. It was five-forty. That didn't leave me much time. It took a half-hour just to drive up there. "I'll be there by seven," I said. "You going with me?"

"If you think I'm going to let you go alone, you're nuts," he answered.

"Fine," I said. "Be here no later than six-thirty. Better yet, meet me at the McDonald's in Arnold. If you come here I'm going to have to answer a million questions I'm not ready to answer."

"McDonalds, in Arnold at six-thirty. Is that Arnold proper or the one at Richardson Road in Arnold?" he asked.

I forgot they now had two McDonald's in that town. "Arnold proper. You know the one at 141."

"Okay," he said. "See you then."

Eleven

I pulled in to the McDonald's and to my surprise found the sheriff leaning up against his Festiva waiting for me. I pulled up next to him and rolled down my window. "Aren't you cold?" I asked.

"My heater doesn't work in the car, so I can't tell much difference between inside and out," he answered.

"Well, in that case, I'm driving," I said. "Get in."

He got in to the car and we made small talk all the way up Highway 55, basically about the fact that he had the money to fix his heater but he just kept forgetting to do it, and all the reasons why he kept forgetting to do it.

We reached Loughborough and I got off the highway. We passed by one of my favorite neighborhoods in St. Louis. Older brick houses with stained glass windows sat comfortably on large lawns. These houses were built from real wood and real brick and not these shake-'n-bake plasterboard things that you see in all the new subdivisions. You can't get new houses made like the old ones.

During the day you could see the big trees that lined the sidewalks. It was dark now, though, and you could only see shadows of the trees highlighted with the dust of snow or Christmas lights. Many of the houses had candles in the windows and Christmas lights around their roofs. Having done that last year, I knew how dangerous teetering on a twelve-foot ladder in the freezing cold could be. We did not hang lights around the house this year.

I took the little jog on Gravois, and I mean little. It's not even a full block's worth of a road. It has a clock on the southbound side of the street that is perpetually set at eleven minutes till six. It's been like that for years. I made a left on Kingshighway and then followed it up ten or fifteen blocks until I reached the McCarthys' street. They were just west of Kingshighway in a two-family flat. In south St. Louis the two-and four-family flats were all basically the same. Red brick, hardwood floors and small, stained-glass windows somewhere in the living room or hallway. They also had ancient plumbing and kitchens without countertops, which sort of took away from the charm of the hardwood floors and stained-glass windows.

This area was just a few blocks south of the neighborhood known as the Hill, which was the Italian community. Talk about good food. No place better to eat Italian food than in an Italian-owned restaurant. At the turn of the century there were clay mines near this area and the newly arrived Italians found ready work. Joe Garigiola and Yogi Berra grew up on Elizabeth Street on the Hill.

I parallel parked—I think I impressed the sheriff, by the way—and we walked up to the cement front porch and rang the bell.

A man about sixty years old answered the door. He wore a plaid flannel shirt and a gray dickie, with slippers on his feet. A chain hung from his glasses, so that he could hang them around his neck if he wanted to. His eyes were a silver blue and his demeanor was calm.

"Hello, Mr. McCarthy," the sheriff began. I'd learned to let the sheriff do the introductions. "I'm Sheriff Colin Brooke, and this is Torie O'Shea, the woman I told you about on the phone."

Mr. McCarthy shook the sheriff's hand and then mine. "Come in," he said.

I no longer felt guilty about all the clutter in my house once I stepped foot into his. He had large area rugs to keep the cold of a hardwood floor from invading his cozy living room. Shelves hung on the walls with knickknacks and doohickeys galore. An eighteen-inch Christmas tree stood on top of his television, with one strand of blinking lights and seven ornaments. There was no topper because it probably would have toppled the thing over.

Photographs, I assumed of family members, hung on the walls and one corner table seemed to be infested with picture frames. One photograph was a man in uniform. I assumed it was his father, Hubert, judging by the age of the photograph.

"It's so good of you to see us," I said. The smell of fruitcake was thick in the air. I hadn't had fruitcake since Wilma accidentally made forty of them five years back. She thought Sylvia said to make forty, when Sylvia had said fourteen. We all got fruitcake that year.

"Sit down," he said and gestured to his couch, which was covered with a busy little paisley print.

The sheriff and I sat down.

"Can I offer you anything to drink?" he asked.

"No, thank you," I said. The sheriff shook his head.

"I'm going to get me a glass of water, if you don't mind," Roger McCarthy said. We nodded and he went in to the kitchen.

An orange tabby cat came walking casually out of the kitchen into the living room. Sheriff Brooke instantly stiffened. "What's the matter with you?" I asked.

"I don't like cats," he said.

"Aw, you're not afraid of a little old kitty, are you?" I rubbed my fingers together and made a meow sound. The cat walked over to me and jumped right up on my lap. "Say hi to the nice sheriff," I said, taking his paw and pretending I was going to touch the sheriff's arm with it.

"You touch me with that cat, and I'll throw it across the room." His voice was calm but there was a definite edge to it. He meant business. I found this exceptionally humorous.

"Did you hear that?" I asked the cat. "Big old mean sheriff."

Roger came back in and said, "Oh, I see you've found William."

"He found me," I said. "Which is the normal way things are done with cats."

"That is so true," he said. He gave a big sigh. "So, you want to talk to Dad about the Keith case."

That sounded so weird. The Keith case. There had been a case named after my great-grandfather for how many years? The Keith case. That was eerie.

"Yes," Sheriff Brooke said. "You indicated on the phone that would be all right."

"Certainly," Roger said. "I'll just go and get him."

Roger McCarthy disappeared again and I petted William some more, feeling him purr deep within his chest. The sheriff looked at me as if I had a rare disease or something. Roger came back out wheeling his father in a wheelchair.

Hubert was half stooped over in his chair with an orange and yellow afghan wrapped around his legs. When he breathed, his lungs made a swishy sound. He did not wear glasses so I could see the milky film from cataracts that covered his eyes. Brown age spots covered his hands and forehead, trailing back into his thin transparent hair.

"Mr. McCarthy," I said very loudly.

"His hearing is fine, Mrs. O'Shea," Roger said.

I blushed and cleared my throat, embarrassed by my assumption that a decrepit-looking old man wouldn't be able to hear. "I'm sorry," I said quietly.

"Mr. McCarthy," Sheriff Brooke said. "This is the great-granddaughter of Nathaniel Ulysses Keith." The sheriff looked to me to make sure that he had got my great-grandfather's name correct. "Do you remember Nathaniel Keith, from Pine Branch?"

Hubert McCarthy narrowed his eyes on me. "Which one are you?" he asked in a raspy voice.

I assumed he meant whose daughter I was. "I'm the daughter of Dwight Robert Keith. Who was the son of John Robert Keith."

"Dwight," he said. "The boy."

"Yes, the boy. He was the youngest and only about eight years old when his grandfather was killed," I said.

He made some well-that's-not-too-bad noise and rubbed his front gums together. "Why now?" he asked. "Why didn't somebody care about this twenty years ago when my mind was better? And my legs were useful."

"Well, sir," I said. "Nobody knew about it until now."

"Nobody knew about it?" he asked, incredulous. "What do you mean nobody knew about it? That's horseshit if I ever smelled it. They all knew about it."

I sat on his couch a minute and tried to let his words sink in. Unexpectedly William jumped off my lap. I let out a slight squeal and then felt completely ridiculous when I realized how on edge I was about this whole thing. "What do you mean they all knew about it? What do you mean by all of them?"

"I mean all of them. Every last one of them."

"Not my father," I said, more defensively than I intended.

"You believe that if you want to, but I interviewed him myself and he was at the house when it happened," Hubert said. "Nathaniel's son John Robert, his son Granville, John's wife Della Ruth, and all the kids. Jed, Ruth, Ike, Charlotte . . ." he snapped his fingers trying to think of Uncle Melvin's name. I knew it was Melvin because so far he'd named them in perfect order. "Oh, what was that pugnose bugger's name . . . Melvin, that's it, Sissy and Dwight," he said. "They were all there on the farm. Some were in the barn, out with the chickens, some in the house. And one of Nate's grandkids by one of his daughters was there, too."

I was amazed at how clearly he could still recount the witnesses to this fifty-year-old case. Tears threatened to bubble up but I fought them hard. I sensed the sheriff looking at me, gauging my reaction to this. My father had sat right there at my kitchen table and told me a lie, knew he was telling me a lie, knew that I would probably find out that he was telling me a lie, and still lied to me. God, I wanted to hit him right now.

"Well, sir, none of us knew about it. None of my generation. The great-grandkids. And, to be honest, we've been lied to about it all of our lives," I said. "But, I was tracing the family tree and came upon his death certificate . . . and then the newspaper articles."

Hubert smiled slightly then. "I knew it. It always comes back around. Can't do nothing in this world that it doesn't come back around in one form or another."

I looked at Roger, who hung on his father's words. "Dad moved up here to the city a few years after that case," Roger said to me when he felt me looking at him. "In 1955. My brother lives in Chicago and Momma died a few years back."

"What do you want to know?" Hubert said. "Maybe you can get to the bottom of it."

"Why would I be able to get to the bottom of it?" I asked.

"Because they all know who did it. And none of them are talking. We didn't have the technology back then like we do now. We found a shotgun in Pine Branch creek, but who's to say who it belonged to."

The sheriff, who had been quiet and noncommittal this whole time, nodded to me to go ahead and ask whatever it was I wanted to know. I took a deep breath.

"What was the motive?" I asked.

"There was three or four good motives. One was the property. There was lotsa talk then about turning that area into a resort. Making a manmade lake with fish and stuff . . ." He rubbed his gums together again. "He was one of the few that didn't want to sell. Lotta people around there that'd been farmers all their life, poor farmers doing backbreaking work, were ready to sell and get out. Nate Keith wouldn't have nothing to do with it. Said his daddy had earned it with blood he'd shed for the Union and he wasn't a-going to sell it."

"So was it the pressure to sell that was the motive or the fact that his children wanted their hands on it so they could sell it that was the motive?"

"Both," he said. "Had bad things happening to him in the years before he was killed. Barn burned, had to build a new one. Somebody set fire to a tree in his front yard, pigs were poisoned. That sorta thing. But, I also know that John and Granville and their sisters Lea and Sara were wanting their daddy to sell. They wanted out of Pine Branch."

"John?" I asked. "My grandfather? You sure you got the right son?" My grandfather never gave an indication in all his born days that he wanted out of Pine Branch. He was a country boy, loved the land he had and only left it once that I remember hearing about. That was a vacation to Florida. My grandmother had to threaten to divorce him to get him to do that.

"Oh, yeah," Hubert said and took a deep breath that was agonizing for me to watch. "Back then John was a different man. He wanted to go to Canada and live in the mountains, but couldn't never get the money to go up there and buy the ranch he wanted. He was also one of the best fiddle players in the country and I think he wanted to have a shot at playing places where he could make more money. And Lea, well, Lea just wanted out. She always thought she's better than everybody else."

Hubert gave his son a look, and Roger went to the kitchen and came back with a glass of water. Hubert took a long drink, a little of it dribbling on his chin. He swiped at it with the back of his hand.

"So it could have been his neighbors or his kids," I stated.

"Or his grandkids," he said and nodded. "I don't think that was really the motive for killing him. People hated him for plenty of other reasons. There were other motives."

"What happened to the land?" Sheriff Brooke asked. "The resort they were going to build?"

"Found out that southeast Missouri is riddled with caves underneath it. They run all over and everywhere. Tons of sinkholes down there. Well, they couldn't make a manmade lake. They tried it on a smaller scale to see what would happen. A few days would go by and the lake would drain down into the caves. Come back there'd be dead fish in the bottom of the lake and mud. No water. No resort."

The sheriff shook his head as if that meant something to him.

"What were the other motives?" I asked.

"Nate Keith was a no-account jerk, I'll just say it plainly. Had giving and loving kids, a great wife and he was no good. He nailed any woman that wasn't hairier than he was." I had to choke back a laugh at his choice of words. "Della Ruth coulda got fed up."

"At sixty-eight? My great-grandmother would have been sixty-eight years old in 1948. You think she would have cared by then?" I asked.

"I always thought Della Ruth had an agenda of her own," he stated and looked me in the eye. He didn't give me a chance to ask him just what he meant by that remark. "He was mean and his boys didn't like him none too much and his grandkids were afraid of him."

"So this could have been a crime of passion, you're saying."

"Anybody shoot a man on his own front porch and let him bleed to death, it's a crime of passion. Man lay out there for hours before he died. They can say they didn't hear anything all they want. He had to be out there begging for help. Nobody let him in."

I took a deep breath. A shiver ran along my spine and settled deep into my bones. I couldn't skirt around the fact that with every word the man said, it didn't look good for my beloved aunts, uncles and grandparents. Could I really have a murderer this close to me? I mean, I knew that I had a murderer way back there in the 1700s. My family tree had everything from horse theives to royalty. This was different. "What other motives? Are there any others?"

"When Nate was a boy, he and a couple of the neighborhood boys went swimming in the swimming hole," he said. "One of the boys drowned and died. It was always rumored that it was Nate's fault. The drowned boy's brothers swore they'd get him back for it."

"He was seventy-two years old!" I said. "You think they waited, what, sixty-five years for vengeance?"

"Never said they waited sixty-five years, Ms. O'Shea. That coulda been the final straw. You really don't know that much about your family, do you?" he asked.

"What do you mean?" I asked. My hackles were raised and the sheriff could tell it. He placed a hand on my arm to tell me to calm down. How dare Hubert tell me that I didn't know that much about my family! I knew more than anybody else did. I knew more than any of my generation. I'd worked long and hard to make sure that I knew everything I could find out about my family.

Hubert ground his gums together and then smiled at me. "This was my only unsolved case, Ms. O'Shea. In all my years in law enforcement. All because a family decided to protect somebody."

"So you're saying that you think it was a member of my family and not the surrounding property owners or the boy's family from the swimming accident?"

"One and the same, Ms. O'Shea. One and the same."

Twelve

Man oh man, why didn't I ever listen to my father?

It was about four hours after I'd left Mr. McCarthy's house in southwest St. Louis. I sat in my office at the Gaheimer House, for no other reason than I just had to get away from my family. All of them. I'd dropped the sheriff off at his car at McDonald's, came straight to the Gaheimer House, called Rudy and sat down at my desk.

I really wanted to crawl in a hole and stay there. I'd just had to know the details of Nathaniel Keith's death and now that I did, I wished I didn't. And yet, that's not entirely true either. I've always had this burning desire to know everything. *Everything*. I can't stand not to know something. It drives me crazy. My mother says that I'm just nosy. Whatever it is, I can't control it any more than I can control blinking. I can for a while but then I just have to give in.

Well, this time instead of gleaning satisfaction for myself, my nosiness has only made me more miserable. I walked out of my office and to the soda machine in the hall. I put in my fifty cents, pushed Dr Pepper and nothing happened. The temporarily-out-of-stock button flashed on my choice of beverage. The Coke and 7-Up and all the caffeine- and sugar-free junk was all in stock. Not my Dr Pepper. I punched the Dr Pepper button with my fist in case it needed stronger coercing. It didn't work. I pushed the Change button but it wouldn't give me my change. No change. No soda. I could get more change. I'd just do without.

I walked back in to my office and contemplated screaming, but then thought better of it. I paced back and forth across what floor that there was in my office and pondered just what I was going to do with the information that Mr. McCarthy had just given me. I could forget about it, or I could pursue it. Easy as that. I could smile and spread the hunting accident story to my children and their children as if I didn't know any better. Or I could try and find information on the swimming incident and maybe interview some of Granville's kids or Lea's kids. How did I know that they'd tell me what I need to know?

I didn't even know that if I pushed my father, he would finally tell me that, yes, he knew the true story as to how his grandfather had died.

I was tired of pacing so I grabbed my coat off the coat rack and headed down the hall and through the ballroom. The Christmas tree that Sylvia had decorated was absolutely gorgeous. She had bought a real tree and decorated it with small, homemade candles, a seventy-year-old chain of beads, glass ornaments ranging from the 1930s to the 1940s, ribbons and various ornaments. Even though the candles weren't lit, it looked majestic strategically placed in front of the large picture window in the ballroom. Sylvia had tried to keep the ribbons that perched on the upturned branches within the green and purple color scheme of the ballroom. She had beauty in her heart, she just usually never let you see it.

I turned off the lights, locked the door, set the alarm and stepped outside. I decided almost instantly that I didn't want to drive home. My house is only a few blocks from the Gaheimer House and Rudy's van was at the house in case of an emergency. The night was cold, but the air was heavy. I wanted to walk. I was struck by how quiet the town was. By how quiet the world was.

I would have to tell my mother about the fact that I was pregnant within the next few days, because she and the sheriff would not be at the big dinner on Sunday when we planned to tell everybody else. I honestly didn't know what her reaction would be.

I was so deep in thought that it took me a few minutes before I realized that it was snowing. I looked up at the sky and big fat wet flakes were falling to the ground. My heart skipped a beat. It was snowing. *It was snowing!* Real snow. Not just a dusting. These were big heavy flakes and they were sticking to the ground and accumulating fast. Aunt Sissy had brought that Minnesota snow with her after all.

I couldn't help but walk a little faster and when I arrived home I walked in the front door with a rush of cold air and announced at the top of my voice, "It's snowing! Everybody outside!"

Rudy sat in his easy chair all comfortable and warm with his feet propped up watching a *Seinfeld* rerun or something like that. Aunt Sissy sat on the floor doing her yoga, my cousin Damon and his wife, Tillie, and their son two daughters were all in the kitchen talking with my mother.

Disappointment filled my heart when nobody leapt up to go outside.

"What's the matter with you people? Get up, get on your coats, mittens, gloves, hats, scarves, whatever you've got. Outside!" I yelled.

Aunt Sissy opened one eye from her yoga and then uncrossed her legs and stood up. "Well, come on everybody," she said. "Let's do as she says. Rudy turn that idiot box off and get your shoes on."

Rudy looked at her with a pained expression but he finally sat up. I walked into the kitchen. "Hi, Mom. Where's Dad?" I only asked because I saw his beat-up truck sitting out in front of my house so that I knew that he was here.

"Downstairs with Jed," she said.

"Men can find more things to do in a basement than anybody

I know," I said. "Rudy!" I yelled. "Wake up Mary and Rachel, we're going outside!" Damon smiled at me with that mischievous look he gets in his eyes when he knows I'm up to something and he wants in on it. "Now, Rudy, not in two hours."

Finally I heard the squeak from the spring in his chair and knew that he was up on his feet. Rachel broke the spring when she was two years old from jumping up and down on the chair. I was upset with her at the time, but I've since thought about giving her a reward for doing it. It's one of the ways I can tell if Rudy's still lounging or doing what I asked him to do. See, sometimes bad things turn out to be good things later—you just have to wait for it to happen.

I opened the basement door and yelled down. "Dad, it's snowing! Get your scrawny butt outside right now, or you're a good-for-nothing wuss. Come on, snowball fight now. I challenge you."

It was quiet at first. Then I heard him say, "Do I get to pick who I want on my team?"

"As long as I get Aunt Sissy, I don't care if you take all of New Kassel," I said and walked back up the steps. Tradition. Dad and I had a tradition that went back as far as I could remember. Every year we had one massive, all-encompassing, no-holding-back, test-of-skill-and-natural-instincts snowball fight. And he almost always won.

Not tonight. I felt lucky.

"Come on, Mom. You can come out on the porch and watch," I said.

She didn't hesitate one bit. She unlocked her wheels, went to get her heavy-duty poncho and headed out onto the porch.

By the time we all made it outside the snow was falling faster and heavier. At least three inches covered the ground. I let out a whoop of joy and pent-up energy. "Aunt Sissy, you're with me."

My dad took three large steps toward me, put his thumbs in his belt loop and stopped. He nodded.

I took three steps toward him, put my hands in my pockets and nodded. "I've got Sissy," I said.

"I take Damon."

Crap. I really wanted Damon, too. "I'll take Jed."

My father sort of smiled at that. "I want Mary."

"Fine. I'll take Rachel."

"Hey, doesn't anybody want me?" Rudy asked.

"I'll take Rudy," Dad said.

"Tillie's mine."

"I'll take her son, can't remember his name," Dad admitted, but still trying to seem tough.

"His name is Jeremy," I said.

"Okay, Jeremy."

"I'll take Courtney," I said, who was Damon's twelve-year-old daughter. "You can have Madison."

My dad nodded to me. I nodded back. "Okay, the chicken coop is your castle, the porch is ours. The object is to drive the enemy back to their castle."

My dad nodded to me again.

"The picnic table is the middle of the kingdom. You leave the backyard and you're disqualified. You can use anything in the yard. You get hit with a snowball more than ten times, you're out," I said.

I looked over at my kids. Rachel was rubbing sleep out of her eyes and scratching her head. Mary yawned, sending a billow of warm air out into the night. She might have yawned but her eyes sparkled with anticipation.

"Mom's referee," I said. Dad nodded that he understood the rules and that he probably wouldn't abide by them. He never did. My group lined up on the house side of the picnic table. Me, Aunt Sissy, in her cut-off jeans even in the snow and tennis shoes with no socks. Tillie, Damon's wife, was bundled so heavily she probably wouldn't be able to move much. She was about thirty-seven and five foot nine and she could kick serious butt if need be. I'd had her on my touch football team one year. Rachel, ready albeit groggy. Courtney, who was eighteen and taller than I was. I hate it when my cousins' children are taller than me. And Uncle Jed, who I'm not even sure was aware of where he was, much less that the object was to throw snowballs at the opposing army.

Dad's army lined up on the opposite side of the picnic table. Him, Rudy, Damon, Jeremy, who was fourteen and built like a football player, Madison, who was ten, tall and scrawny, and Mary, who just looked entirely too little to be on their team. They had youth and vitality on their team. Rudy was injured, though. So we had that going for us. My team was older, but we were . . . well, I'm not exactly sure.

Mom said her speech about being nice and playing fair, yada yada yada and GO!

Snowballs began whizzing and whirling around the backyard. I could never figure out how my father did it, but he could throw five snowballs for every one of mine. I picked up one of the kid's yellow snow saucers and used it as a shield.

"Oh, not fair!" I heard my father say.

I searched for Mary and found her over by the chicken coop doing nothing but making snowballs. They were using her as an ammunitions maker! She had a big pile of snowballs next to her in nothing flat, and all they had to do was go over there and pick up four or five and nail us! Gosh, I was infuriated. Mainly because I hadn't thought of it first. No wonder my father wanted Mary. He had this planned all along.

Tillie had shoved her way into Rudy's face and knocked him down on his back. She stood over him just pummeling him with snowball after snowball. Jeremy saw what was happening and went over and saved Rudy before Tillie managed to hit him with ten snowballs, so he was still in the battle.

Uncle Jed was already out. He was far too drunk to really know what was going on and he just stood there in the middle of the backyard with his arms up, saying. "Hey, that's not nice. Quit hittin' the old man." He talked about himself in the third person quite often. Especially when he was drunk.

Suddenly I felt the sting of a snowball in the neck. Oh, that stung! I turned around to find Damon up on top of the girl's swing set zinging snowballs down at unsuspecting victims. Like me.

Rachel was giggling way too much to be doing too much damage to anybody. We were losing ground fast. And then I noticed that Aunt Sissy had taken Tillie's guerrilla snow-fighting tactics and was rushing the enemy and knocking them on the ground. I did the same thing. Instead of being worried about getting hit with the snowballs, I just went after my victims and didn't stop until they were on the ground. In this case it was my father. He squirmed and tried to get away, but I just threw snowball after snowball in his face. Then as he tried to get away I shoved a big handful of snow down his shirt.

God, this was great. It was exhilarating and I could feel the tensions of the day just leaving my body. Maybe it was also because I was getting to pummel my father without getting in trouble, and I had a lot of pent-up anger against him at the moment. By the time the fight was over, it was Aunt Sissy, Tillie and me and we had backed the other team all the way to the chicken coop, what was left of them, that is. The only ones left at the end of the battle were Mary, who was still vigorously making snowballs, and Damon.

I had won.

"What in blazes is going on out here?" Mayor Castlereagh yelled from his yard. His floodlights came on with a blast of halogen brightness. A ladder went against my privacy fence and then his bald head appeared in the snowy night sky above the fence. He was not happy.

"People are trying to sleep around here!" he yelled.

"Evidently you're not trying hard enough," I said. We all walked back inside for hot cocoa and coffee, and left the mayor to stew in his own anger.

Thirteen

Morning came early and I bounded out of bed with abnormal energy. Part of it was because I knew that if I wanted to get this quilt going and find out who had sent me those newspaper articles, I had to do it fast. If I have a definite mission to accomplish I can make myself get up early. The excitement of finally pounding the living daylights out of my father at a snowball fight did a lot to give me that extra push to get out of bed as well.

I bought a large piece of white fabric at the local twenty-four-hour Wal-Mart and had the piece of material marked by ten o'clock. I traced the template over and over on the white fabric for the sections of the quilt that everybody was supposed to sign. I knew there was no way that I could get it all cut out and everything, so I was just going to have everybody sign one of the places and I'd cut them out later.

I came down the steps of my bedroom and found Uncle Jed sitting at my kitchen table. Uncle Isaac, the third child of my grandparents, sat across from him. About seventy-four years old, he was a retired steel worker, and a heavier version of my father. His hair was thinner and nearly white, but the same square jaw and prominent nose were evident. Looking at Uncle Isaac's hazel eyes was like looking at my father's, thus like looking at my own.

"Hey, Uncle Isaac, how are you?" I asked. I had barely had a chance to talk to him since he arrived.

"Fine, fine," he said. I got the distinct impression that I had interrupted something that I wasn't supposed to. I looked at Jed, who was staring at Isaac.

"Would you guys do me a favor and sign your name in one of these squares?" I asked. Well, they weren't exactly shaped liked squares but they got the picture. "I'm going to make a signature quilt to commemorate this reunion and I need everybody to sign it."

"Sure, sure," Uncle Isaac said. He had a habit of repeating the first word of every sentence. He didn't stutter, because it never happened at any other time and he didn't sound like he had trouble getting the word out. He just repeated it twice. Uncle Isaac was the very first one to put his signature on what would be the Keith Kin Quilt.

Uncle Jed took the pen and signed his name. The signatures were as different as night and day. Uncle Jed's was barely readable and shaky, Uncle Isaac's was by no means fancy but he exaggerated the first letter of his first and last names.

"Thank you very much," I said. "We are caroling tonight. You guys gonna be there?"

"Yeah, yeah," Uncle Isaac said. "Big as our family is, you're going to have an entire choir."

I giggled. "I doubt seriously if everybody shows up to carol. And it's been my experience that the men tend to skip out on this one, so you guys better be there."

They both smiled and agreed that they would be there and then they went back to staring at each other. It was obvious that they were waiting for me to leave the room so they could resume their conversation. Which made me not want to leave the room.

I went back up the steps to my office anyway. My mother would be so proud of me.

I found the other box that Aunt Sissy had brought to me. The one that had a bunch of junk in it. I put it up on my desk and began pulling stuff out of it. Aunt Sissy was correct. It looked like somebody had just dumped Grandma's junk drawer in this box. Except every now and then there would be an item that was a little too personal to be put in junk drawer. I found a grocery list from about 1974. She'd made a note to herself to bring cheese for Jalena, my mother, because she didn't like hot dogs. We must have been having a barbecue or something.

Buttons, scissors, shoe dye that must have been fifty years old. I found a box of cards that had not been used. It was just a box of assorted cards for all different occasions. I flipped through them and could tell almost immediately that they were ancient. These things must have been from around the 1930s or so. And in the very back of the box was a carefully folded piece of paper. I, of course, opened it.

In it was a handwritten letter, the handwriting an uncontrolled scrawl, but still readable. It was a letter to my great-grandmother, not my grandmother. I began to wonder how my grandmother had managed to come into possession of this letter, but once I saw the contents of the letter, I didn't care how she had acquired it. It said:

Della Ruth, *Feb '32*
I've got to know that you are happy. You made a decision thirty years ago that I don't think was all that fair. I've been patient. I've been silent. And I've loved you from a distance, while you've ignored me and pretended I was dead. I need to hear it with my ears and see your mouth speak the words. We were in it together. You should find it in your heart to grant me this much.
Bradley

My great-grandmother, and Nathaniel Keith's wife, would have been fifty-two years old when she received this letter. Who was Bradley? And what decision was he referring to of thirty years earlier? That would have been 1902. Della Ruth and Nathaniel Keith were married in 1898, when my great-grandmother was eighteen years old and my great-grandfather was twenty-two. Maybe Bradley had meant to say "about thirty years ago" and he was referring to Della Ruth choosing Nate Keith over him.

How did my grandmother end up with this letter? Or maybe she was not aware of the fact the letter had been put in the back of the box for safekeeping.

Then I noticed that the paper lining on the card box was a little lumpy. I pulled the paper up and stood with goosebumps dancing down my arms at what the brown paper revealed. There was another letter, but more important, two photographs. One was of my great grandmother, Della Ruth, with a young man. I flipped the photo over and it said; Me and Bradley F. The other photograph was a small square about one inch by one inch of just the young man's face. Again, it had the name Bradley inscribed on the back.

I didn't get it. Why would Della Ruth think it necessary to hide these photographs of this man? Did she make the wrong decision in men? Or was she forced to marry Nate Keith and really wanted to marry Bradley? I imagined my great-grandmother leaving this handsome young man standing at the altar, or something equally romantic.

I opened the other letter, which had deep creases in it, as if somebody had folded it and unfolded it many times. It read:

> Earth and sky, moon and sun.
> You and I have joined as one.
> All that's come before, and all to come after
> Will never touch our love and laughter.
> —Marry me, Della.

I felt like a really cheap Peeping Tom. I know I'm nosy as heck, but this was way too personal for me to have read. Then I thought, Maybe that's why Della Ruth put them there. So somebody, someday, would read it and know.

Hubert McCarthy's words came flooding back to me. *I always thought Della Ruth had an agenda of her own.* It was hard for me to believe, though, that my great-grandmother would have waited to kill Nate Keith until she was in her late sixties for a lover or a former lover. It seems like that was something she would have done at a much younger age.

I put the two letters and the two photographs in an envelope and slid it into my purse. I was going down to Pine Branch and Partut County. I absolutely had to know who Bradley F. was.

THE NEW KASSEL GAZETTE

THE NEWS YOU MIGHT MISS

by Eleanore Murdoch

People of New Kassel, I am here to ask you to reach down into the deep recesses of your heart, and give of yourself. There are four kittens at the rectory and they need homes. Wouldn't one of our elderly residents like a companion? Or how about a kitten for your children on Christmas morning? Father Bingham says he can only keep them until New Year's.

Rumor has it that Sylvia and Helen are not speaking to each other. Helen is still giving the tours at the Gaheimer House in place of Torie O'Shea, whose family is on vacation. Oh, and Chuck Velasco's pet iguana has escaped the confines of his cage. Chuck says there is a reward if anybody finds Teddy and returns it to him. Aren't iguanas coldblooded? Just curious.

And Sister Lucy says that the boys' choir, including the girls, all sang beautifully on Tuesday night. She thought she heard God himself applauding the children's efforts on "Joy to the World."

Until next time,

Eleanore

Fourteen

The inside of the library in Progress smelled like the inside of a grade school. I can't exactly say what that is, mind you, but it is its own distinct smell. The library is quite humble. It's very small and looked like somebody took a tin can, cut it in half, stuck it in the ground and painted it.

I didn't have time to order the census records that I wanted to be mailed to my library in New Kassel. It was much faster and easier for me to just drive the forty minutes down here to Progress and look it up myself. I was looking for all the families in Partut County that started with the letter F, in the year 1900. My grandmother was twenty then, so I could bet that Bradley was about that age as well. The 1890 census was burned and only remnants of it existed. One of the few things that remained was the records for the Civil War veterans. This is really frustrating because it always seems like 1890 was the year I needed to connect some ancestors with their parents or something.

Luckily, the 1900 census was in the form of what they call soundex. Meaning that it was listed with the first letter of the last name of the head of household, followed by three numbers, based on a code system that somebody came up with. So, all I had to do was just scroll through all the Fs for Partut County and find one that had somebody named Bradley. This could be a much bigger task as he could have been named John or Charles. Bradley is fairly uncommon first name.

I sat in a corner going through the census on the only microfilm reader in the blasted place. I had to look at every single page of this thing. I'd been at it about an hour, my neck was stiff and I had a horrible pain in my shoulderblade. A slow pace is the only way to do this, because I couldn't take a chance on blinking and missing a name.

Finally, I came on a Ferguson family living in the county in the township right next to Pine Branch. William Ferguson, age forty-three, and wife Rose, with a slew of children. Bradley age twenty-one, was one of them. There were twelve kids listed in increments of two years. This wasn't in the least unusual for the time and place, but it always amazed me every time I saw it. I have one ancestor who had twenty-three children by the same wife, and only two sets of twins. That means that woman was pregnant twenty-one times! If that had been me I would have made my husband sleep with the pigs. Or he would have met with a terrible accident.

I jotted down all of the information on this family. The problem was that there could be another Bradley F. in the census, so I had to go through the whole thing. Two hours crawled by and I found a Brad Franklin, but he was about forty and judging by the picture I had of Bradley, he was close to the same age as my great-grandmother, so this couldn't have been him.

I was finished. There had only been one Bradley with a last name that started with an F. I checked the 1910 census and the 1920 census for this same man. In 1910 he was still in Partut County, age thirty-one, living by himself, but his occupation was listed as the general store. Did he own the general store or did he work at one? I jotted that down, too. By 1920 the soundex showed him living in a large estate within Progress city limits and it still listed the general store as his occupation. If he owned a large estate he most likely owned the store. And that was as far as I could track him in the census, because the 1930 census was not available to the public yet.

The thing I noticed was that he had not married.

What was Della Ruth's father thinking? Nathaniel Keith was a drunk and a very poor farmer. He only farmed what the family needed, so he didn't even sell his crop. The only extra money that ever came into that household was from his son John Robert, who played his fiddle at weddings and things like that. And Della Ruth would quilt the wealthier women's quilt tops for them for either cash or for specific items like sugar or salt.

Della Ruth's father forbade her to marry Bradley Ferguson because he thought Nathaniel Keith would make a better husband? Unless Nathaniel Keith boasted of higher goals, I couldn't see how this could be. If she had married Bradley Ferguson she would have been one of the women paying a poor farmer's wife to quilt her tops. Then again, we wouldn't be here. None of us. Me, my father, my cousins, my grandfather, my children.

I rewound the census, relieved to be finished with that tedious job. I put it back in the box and went over to the librarian. She was a woman of about fifty-five years, tall and thin. Face powder caked in the crevices of her face and I noticed that her eyeliner was severely crooked.

"I need the census for 1880, please."

She handed me a book. Even though this was the first year for the soundex the historical society had gone through it and taken out all the families in Partut County and arranged them according to household. Sometimes it helps to know exactly where your ancestor lived in respect to a church, poorhouse, or another family. I found Nathaniel Keith's family in 1880, when he was three and half years old. I looked at the surrounding families to see who they were. Hubert McCarthy's story of the swimming accident had my interest piqued, too. Might as well get everything while I was down here.

The families in his township, who would have gone to the same church and same one-room school he went to, were about thirty in number. And of those thirty, about half of them had boys within three or four years of age. If you got any younger or any older than that, they probably wouldn't have played together.

Was I surprised to see that one of them was the Ferguson household? Sometime between 1880 and 1900 William Bradley moved from Pine Branch to a different township within Partut County. Bradley was a year old in 1880, and his older brother was three. I remembered what Mr. McCarthy said about the friends and neighbors being the one and the same with my family. So I wasn't the least bit surprised to find that the families living close to Nate Keith as a boy were the Claytons and the Elsters. Both married into the Keith family by way of cousins of Nate Keith's. As a matter of fact, there were probably only about five families in the whole township that I couldn't pin some sort of distant relation on, even if it was just by marriage.

I shut the book and jotted down some notes and then gave it back to the librarian.

"I was wondering if you could help me," I said. I came down here fairly often to use this library, but I didn't recognize this librarian with the crooked eyeliner and winning smile.

"I can certainly try," she said. Her accent sounded like she was from Arkansas or west Tennessee, which was only about two hours from Progress.

"I found a man in the 1900 census whose occupation was the general store. Could you tell me where I might find some information on the businesses in Progress around the turn of the century?" I asked.

"Well, I take it you don't want to spend hours going through the newspapers," she said. I shook my head. "Yes, I think there is a book . . . let me see."

I followed her over to a corner of the library. She fingered a few books and finally pulled out a history of the county. Then she walked across the room and pulled out a huge binder. I didn't follow her this time, I let her come back to me. "This is the historical society's newsletters in here," she said. "They spotlight individuals in the area, along with business, churches, that sort of thing. Try those two first and if you don't find what you need, let me know," she said.

"Thank you very much," I said and smiled. Librarians are your very best friend. And don't ever think otherwise.

I sat down at the table and thumbed through the history book. It looked fairly detailed so I flipped to the back to see if there was an index. So often the older histories, printed before the 1930s, don't have indexes. And you can't check these books out, because they are considered reference books. So unless a historical society or somebody with a lot of time on their hands comes along and does an index for it, you have to read the whole book in the library.

This one had an index. No listing for anybody with the last name Ferguson. I checked all the pages that had anything to do with the town of Progress or Pine Branch. It mentioned the great flood back in the forties, a flood even earlier, a warehouse district, the ferry that crosses the Mississippi and goes to Illinois and that was about it. The founding fathers of Progress were listed, one of which was an ancestor of mine. I'd found that out years ago.

I shoved the book aside and opened the binder of newsletters. It occurred to me that I had some of these newsletters at home. I used to belong to the historical society down here, about ten years ago. I think I stopped subscribing when money started getting a little tight and I thought I was finished researching. That would be the early nineties when Mary was born. I always knew, eventually, I'd get back into it, but I didn't know when.

Some of the newsletters were yellowed and well read. They spanned the time of about 1980 to the present. I slowly began going through each one of them. I'd been here at least four hours.

My family was going to wonder what happened to me. We had caroling tonight, and several of us were going in to St. Louis for dinner at Del Pietro's.

The librarian walked over to me and smiled. "Would you like a soda or something?" she asked.

I looked around the library. I was her only patron at the moment. I guess she could tell by the look on my face that I was confused. I didn't think you were allowed drinks and food in a public library.

"Nobody's here, just don't tell anyone," she said and winked. "I'm dying of thirst myself and you've been here forever."

"Sure," I said. "I'd love something to drink. Dr Pepper if you've got it, otherwise a glass of water."

She smiled and left to fulfill her errand. I went back to the newsletters. There were six newsletters for every year. Finally, I found an article of interest around 1995. "The Place to Shop in 1912 Was Ferguson's," the headlines read. It went on to say that a man named Bradley Ferguson had opened a general store in 1908. His parents had both moved here from Virginia when they were very young and Bradley's grandparents were from Scotland. The article stated that he put every penny he had into the store and that by 1912 Bradley had earned back what he'd put into it. The article went on to list some of the things that could be bought at the store and what some of the prices were.

"Thank you," I said to the librarian as she handed me a cold can of Dr Pepper. Reinforcements. I took a long, long drink and set the can down.

The article was a glowing review of Bradley's life. He was a kind man, letting poor people buy things on an account and pay it off a little at a time. He had other investments going that he started with the profits of his store. Around 1940 he married a woman half his age but never had any children. They spent much time abroad and it says that he died in Africa while he was there on vacation in 1950.

The article was written by Naomi Cordieu. I photocopied the article and returned the binder to the librarian. "I'm afraid I don't have time to go through much more," I said. "Do you know who Naomi Cordieu is?"

I figured that if Ms. Cordieu wrote for the historical society she was most likely a member. And if she was a member she probably frequented the library fairly often.

"Uh-huh, she's the corresponding secretary and co-archivist for the historical society," she said.

"Where can I find her?" I asked.

"Well, she's about eighty years old, somewhere around there. And I don't have her number, but she's listed. Or you can go by the historical society when they're open and they can get a message to her," she said.

"Well, thank you for everything," I said. "You were a big help."

"My pleasure," she said.

"Oh, one thing, though . . . I would be willing to pay you good money if you could look something up and have an answer for me by noon tomorrow," I said. I smiled a mischievous smile and hoped she was up for the challenge.

She raised an eyebrow but didn't say no.

"Could you check the newspapers for the 1880s, probably between 1880 and 1885, and see if there is anything on a swimming accident involving some boys out in Pine Branch? I don't have the time to do it and I need to know, like yesterday."

She shrugged her shoulders a little. "I don't have anything else to do. I'll only have about two hours left today, but I get in about eight in the morning. I'll have an hour before the library opens."

"Thank you," I said and wrote my name, phone number and address on a piece of paper. I turned to leave with my notebook full of notes, my photocopies and my half can of Dr Pepper. "And if you have time, anything on the subject of making the land in Pine Branch into lake resorts? The swimming accident is the most important. Only worry about the lake resort thing if you have time. That would have been about 1945."

The librarian giggled a little. "Anything else?"

"No, that should be it. What is your name?" I asked.

"Robin Keifer."

"Hey, I've got a cousin that married a Keifer," I said.

"Around here, almost everybody does. It's my husband's family and I think for the last hundred years everybody has had a family of ten boys. You just can't stomp that name out," she declared.

And so it is. You lose this in the big cities. In these little communities where people have been around for generations, everybody is everybody's cousin.

I thanked her again and walked out into the snow-covered world, sparkling with sunshine.

Fifteen

The Keith clan reserved the entire restaurant called Del Pietro's. Located on south Hampton in St. Louis, its sign is hot pink and the letters run vertically down its length. I sat upstairs at a large table with Rachel and Mary, my mother, the sheriff, Rudy, Aunt Charlotte, her husband, Curtis, Aunt Ruth and her husband, Wilbur.

Little groups of my family were gathered around all the tables in the restaurant. So far, this was the most people that I'd had at an event at one time for this reunion. There were probably forty to fifty people in this restaurant, all related to me. Even though that was pretty scary, it felt really cool.

Aunt Ruth had just arrived late yesterday evening and I hadn't gotten to talk to her much. She usually arrived as late as she could without being talked about, because she was basically a snob and liked to forget that most of her relatives were . . . well, related to her. Born in 1922, she was the oldest girl of the seven children. She and Wilbur had the perfect suburban family of two wonderful sons, who grew up to be a doctor and a lawyer. They had four grandchildren, played bridge every week, and still lived in the three-bedroom ranch house that they bought in 1953, eight years after Wilbur came back from World War II. Nothing bad ever happens in their house and nothing ugly exists within their one quarter of an acre of Americana. Even if they had to deny it and shove it under a really big rug.

Aunt Ruth was about as far on the opposite end of the spectrum from Aunt Sissy as one could be. It was no accident that they weren't seated at the same table. They got along okay, but never socialized. Aunt Ruth and Aunt Charlotte, although not close, were still better suited to each other. Aunt Charlotte was hard not to get along with because she was genuinely down the middle on so many things.

I really wanted to talk to the sheriff about what I had found out at the Progress library today, but thought it would look pretty funny if I just jerked him by the tie into the hall and talked to him for half an hour. My mother wouldn't appreciate it much either.

The conversation spilling around the table was about Uncle Curtis's latest investment adventure, in which Aunt Ruth assured him that he would lose the shirt off of his back.

"So, Aunt Ruth," I said. "What do you remember about Nate Keith?" It was as subtle as I could make it. The sheriff gave me a sharp glance over his glass of wine.

"The queen of segue," I heard the sheriff say toward me. He was at the head of the table with my mother to his left between us. He didn't have to say it very loud for me to hear.

Aunt Ruth, in her pink jacket and skirt, looked positively a seventy-six-year-old version of Jackie Kennedy. She smiled at me from directly across the table, but the smile never quite reached her eyes. "Still tracing the family tree?" she asked. "I thought you would have grown tired of that little hobby of yours years ago."

"Why should I?" I asked. "It continually amazes me."

"Oh, really?" she asked.

"I find out new things every week," I said.

"Like what?"

"Well, my great-greatuncle on my mother's side was a genuine bona fide horse thief," I said.

Aunt Ruth flushed a little and took a drink of her iced tea. "Not the sort of thing you would think that you would brag about," she said. "No offense, Jalena."

"None taken," my mother said.

"We are who we are," I said.

"Never could figure out why you wanted to know all that stuff about a dead person," she said. "For that very type of reason. Who knows what you could find."

Uncle Wilbur piped up and said, "Yeah, what if you find out you're descended from a . . . non-Caucasian person?" He could be politically correct even when he was dishing out racist slurs. Amazing.

"Uncle Wilbur!" I said. "I can't believe you just said that."

He absolutely had no clue as to why I was chiding him, so I just shut up. He was old and he would die thinking the way he thought, regardless of how many "all one people" speeches I tried to give him.

"Well?" he asked. "Just what would you do?"

"I guess I'd laugh a little, file it and move on," I said.

"Laugh?" he asked. Uncle Wilbur had absolutely no taste in clothes. Well, actually he did, it's just that most of it should be worn on a golf course by colorblind people. His jacket was almost always some sort of checked thing, and his pants a pinstripe, with brilliantly spit-shined black shoes.

"Yes, I'd laugh. It would be hilarious to imagine all of your faces when I told you the news," I said. My mother elbowed me slightly. It wasn't that she disagreed with me, she just knew that this argument was pointless.

"You know," I said. "Black people are probably just as shocked when they find out they have a white great-grandpa."

You could tell that idea had not occurred to him, because his forehead shifted about a foot backward and his eyes got real wide. "I never said anything about a black person."

"There aren't many non-Caucasian choices, Uncle Wilbur."

Aunt Ruth, who had remained dutifully quiet on the subject, finally said something. "Really, Torie. What's done is done. What does it matter to you what these people were?"

"You were pretty excited when I could prove that you were descended from King James the Sixth of Scotland. Remember?" I asked. "You invited me to your local historical society to explain to them just how the line of descent went. You have to take the bad with the good. We are what we are, and every single action that took place before us brought us to this very moment."

In light of my newfound discoveries, this particular philosophical statement had a lot of meaning. I wasn't just whistling Dixie.

"Nevertheless," she said. "Why did you want to know about Nate Keith? I thought you had everything you needed on him."

"Thought I knew everything about the man," I said. My girls were playing with the little butter dishes on the table and Rudy had struck up a football conversation with Uncle Curtis. Aunt Charlotte was all ears at the conversation on our end of the table, but said nothing. "Turns out—"

"Our food should be getting here pretty soon," Sheriff Brooke said.

I gave him the look of daggers. I'd been wanting to have this conversation with Aunt Ruth for a long time, because I had found out that Nate had been murdered and she was the first one to tell me the hunting accident story. Because she had chided me and hounded me every step of the way when I was heavily researching the family tree, until I found out about our royal lineage and suddenly she was even prepared to fund some of my research. Her two-faced, fake, variety-hour Donna Reed impersonation was just more than I could stand.

"I heard something about a swimming accident?" I ventured.

"When he was a small boy," she said, cautious. "How did you find out about that?"

"Believe it or not, very little is safe, Aunt Ruth. It was in the newspapers of the time," I said without really knowing if this were true. Like she was going to check.

"Do you routinely check the newspapers for information?" she asked and took a drink of her tea. I'd struck a nerve. If I discovered the swimming accident in the papers, what else had I discovered? A little murder on the front porch?

"When all the other resources dry up, yes. I'm not a fan of newspapers because you can scan through them for hours without finding anything on your family," I said. "But, when you do find something, you usually hit pay dirt."

"Really?" she asked.

"Yeah. So what about the swimming accident?" I asked.

The waiter came to our table with a big platter of food and an assistant waiter who helped him distribute the steaming dishes. I got the fettuccine Alfredo, of course. That is all I ever get at an Italian restaurant. Del Pietro's was the best I've ever had.

"Well, if you've found the newspaper articles," Aunt Ruth said smugly, "then you don't need my input. You know everything."

Darn. I wasn't planning on her taking that defense. "Well, the article was very brief and it just mentioned a bunch of boys swimming, Nate Keith being one of them, and that a boy drowned, I just thought maybe you would know a personal account of it. Nate being your grandfather and everything."

Still she said nothing. I was desperate now. What did I have to lose but to just throw out a name? "They mentioned a Ferguson boy . . ."

"Grandpa Nate swore that he didn't mean for anybody to get hurt when he made the dare. He mourned the death of that Ferguson boy every day," she declared.

The Ferguson boy? Bradley? "Ferguson," I said. "Um, you mean Bradley?"

"No, Bradley's older brother Wil," she said.

"Oh, yeah, that's right. Wil. And the others . . ." I snapped my fingers, pretending they were on the tip of my tongue.

"Patrick Elster and Zack Clayton," she said.

I knew it! "Weren't they related to us?"

"Yeah, you've got it all in charts," she said and went about eating her food.

"So it was a dare?" I asked. "The papers didn't mention that part."

"Is this what you've been after? You just wanted to know about the swimming accident?" she asked.

"Well, that and I heard that Grandpa Nate's barn was burned and his pigs poisoned . . ."

The color drained from Aunt Ruth's face like a Warner Bros. cartoon. "You didn't find that in any newspaper," she hissed.

"So is BJ playing hockey this year?" my mother asked Aunt Ruth. BJ was one of Ruth's grandsons. I had the feeling my mother had been trying to remember the name of one of Aunt Ruth's grandchildren for about the last two minutes to be able to jump in and stop this conversation. It was all right. I knew I was being bitchy and pushy. I was being as bitchy and pushy as Aunt Ruth had always been fake and two-faced.

"Yes, he is," Aunt Ruth answered my mother with much relief. "There's great hope for him that he will make the Olympic team. He's quite the little star. The apple of our eye." Never mind the fact that the kid couldn't read, had impregnated something like three different freshman girls, and stolen his mother's mink to buy an eightball of cocaine. All things that I had heard from BJ's mother.

I strained to see past Aunt Ruth at the table over by the window. My father, Uncle Melvin and loads of cousins. Another table had Uncle Isaac and Aunt Sissy and tons of cousins. I wondered if any of their conversations were as strained as the one at this table. Of course, I had to remind myself, that I ha

this direction.

I looked over at my mother who was holding the sheriff's hand and listening intently to Aunt Ruth go on and on about her wunderkind offspring. My mother seemed really happy with her life right now, my girls were healthy, I was pregnant and Rudy's nose was healing quite fast. The things that were important to me were good. I wasn't going to let an age-old irritation with Aunt Ruth sour my evening or my family reunion.

Damon stood and clanked his glass with his knife. "Announcement, everybody . . . If you are going caroling with us after dinner, you are to meet at the Santa Lucia Catholic Church. Okay? Everybody hear me?"

"Are you really going to let Uncle Isaac sing?" somebody said.

"Yeah, even Ike gets to sing," Damon said and sat back down.

I smiled to myself and ate the best fettuccine I'd ever eaten. I say that every time I come here.

Sixteen

"You know," my mother said. "You were pretty rude to your aunt Ruth." She was sitting in the passenger seat of Sheriff Brooke's yellow Festiva. The engine was running while she waited for the sheriff to come back to the car in the parking lot of the Santa Lucia church. He had pulled in here to check up on Father Bingham and make sure everything was all right before taking my mother home. Her circulation wasn't the greatest and being outside in the freezing cold for hours to sing probably wasn't the best thing for her.

"I know," I answered her. "I couldn't help myself."

"Help yourself? What is all this about?" she asked.

"You know that Aunt Ruth and I don't exactly get along," I said and hugged myself to shield against the cold. "She and I have had issues that go back years."

"I thought those had been settled," she said. A small crease had formed between her eyebrows.

I shrugged my shoulders. "She and I yelled at each other once because she told me I didn't have a right to know who my ancestors were. Only if my elders decided that it was all right for me to know. She's a fake. I hate fake people. I hate people who try to make the world believe that their crap don't stink."

"You don't have to get nasty," she said. "There's more to this."

I glanced across the parking lot and saw the sheriff standing on the steps of the rectory. "She and I have always been at odds. Remember how she used to bad-mouth Grandma, because Grandma's house had that linoleum in it with the rips? At Grandma's funeral that was all I could think about—was the look on her face when her daughter berated her for her floor."

"You're still peeved about that?" she asked.

"Well, it's everything. She was ashamed of her father because all he ever did was farm and play music. Forget the fact that he was one of the most kindhearted individuals in the world. He had a great sense of humor and she probably could have learned a lot from him, if she could have gotten past the fact that he didn't wear Topsiders and a suit. He wore flannel shirts and muddy work boots."

"So you decide to take out all of your anger on her tonight? I know there is more," Mom pushed further.

"I don't have time to go into it right now, Mom," I said. I took a deep breath and decided to just tell her. "Suffice it to say, I found out that Nate Keith—you know my great-grandfather—was murdered, and that all of my 'elders' knew about it and lied to me." My mother gave me a look like she was about to argue with me. "Mom, I've talked to the investigating officer. Everybody, including my father, knew it and lied."

My mother said nothing.

"Aren't you going to say something?" I asked.

"I don't know what to say. I thought your dad's grandfather was killed in a hunting accident?"

"Yeah, a hunting accident right on his own front porch. I don't think he was hunting. I think he was the hunted," I said. I could tell by the look on her face that she believed me. What doubt she had at first was now gone. My mother trusted me and trusted what I said to be true to the best of my knowledge. She was one of the few people who would put blind faith in me. She was also one of the few people that I was totally honest with.

"Remember the ancestor I told you about that killed his wife because he didn't like the way she cooked?" I said. My mother nodded. "That is so far removed that it doesn't really bother me. Most people have an ugly little thing or two on their family tree. It would be strange if you didn't have something like that hanging on your tree. It's part of finding out who you are and where you come from. But this one is different."

"Because it's so close to you," Mom said. It wasn't a question. She understood.

"Yeah, and because everybody I ever trusted lied to me about it."

"If they've all lied, there can be only one reason."

I looked at her. She gave me that wide-eyed-doe look. She wanted me to say what she was thinking, but I couldn't this time, because I wasn't sure what she was thinking. Most of the time I either know or I'm close enough that we can play this little game. This time, I truly had no idea. "What?"

"All of them wouldn't be ashamed of this. If they are all lying about it, it's because one of them did it."

"Gee thanks, Mom," I said. Sheriff Brooke was within fifteen feet of the car now. "I'll talk to you more about it later."

"You okay?" she asked.

"Yeah, I think so. This whole week has been really stressful and then I find out this. What else could happen?"

"Don't ever say those words," my mother said with a serious look. "I'm not superstitious, but one seems to invite trouble when one speaks those words."

"Gee thanks again, Mom," I said. "See you later or in the morning. Whichever."

Sheriff Brooke got in the car, but not without giving me one of those I'll-talk-to-you-later type of looks. I stepped away from the car and waved to them as they pulled out of the parking lot.

It's because one of them did it. It seemed no matter what I did, I kept coming back to that. One of my beloved, my trusted, killed Nate Keith. I breathed in deeply, relishing the snow smell in the air. It was going to snow again.

I was tired. My eyes burned in their sockets and my legs felt like they weighed thirty pounds apiece. This pregnancy seemed to just wear me out and make me tired. No morning sickness or anything like that. Just total exhaustion. Today had been a grueling day. Five or so hours at a library that was forty minutes away, dinner with fifty people at Del Pietro's and now I had to carol for two hours. It would most likely be midnight before I got to bed. It wasn't like I'd worked eight hours on my feet, but research time can be mentally taxing.

I still had to tell my mother that I was pregnant. I'd imagined just how I was going to tell her, hoping with all hope that her reaction would be like I'd imagined it. Happy, rejoiceful, supportive. My mother didn't take to well to change. It was part of the reason her relationship with the sheriff puzzled me. She was severely set in her ways, and sometimes a good thing could actually depress her.

One good thing that had come from imagining telling my mother about this baby was the fact that I was becoming more used to the idea of the baby. It wasn't just a blue stick at the doctor's office anymore. I could imagine pink pudgy toes and dimpled hands. When it's the size of an egg, it's so hard to imagine the living, breathing baby that will eventually be born.

I was going to have a baby. I was going to be a mom. Again.

"Hey, Torie!" Rudy yelled from across the parking lot. "Come on, we've got to get singing before it gets too late."

I walked over to my husband and the group of people standing around him. I smiled up at him and he instinctively kissed me. It was time to sing.

Seventeen

"Oh, Christmas tree, Oh, Christmas tree . . ." we all sang. My left hand held Rachel's and my right hand held a candle. She sang her little heart out. Snow had begun to fall and I couldn't believe our luck at this seemingly perfect moment.

The crowd of my family snuggled in together and in front of the Murdoch Inn. Eleanore and Oscar and the few guests that weren't my family members stood at the door to hear us. Other people on the street had come to their front doors to hear us, too. Uncle Curtis's deep baritone voice surrounded me like a warm glove from behind.

Aunt Charlotte often mentioned that Uncle Curtis was sort of homely but his voice is what had made her notice him. I don't think he was homely. He was just sort of plain looking, punctuated by absolutely no outstanding features at all and a semibald head. He couldn't even be bald all the way.

The next song was "Joy to the World." The song that can get stuck in my head and be there for a week. We all moved up along River Point Road with the river on our right. The water looked like black oil slithering south, swallowing up all the big fat snowflakes that fell into it.

Then I heard somebody say, "What is that?"

We all kept singing. I am fairly short and was surrounded by people so I couldn't really see what was going on. A few voices trailed off and people were beginning to walk over to the river. I'm not sure what to call that feeling you get, when you know something, and you have no real way of knowing it. But, I knew something was wrong. I made my way through the ten or so people in front of me dragging Rachel close behind me.

In the Mississippi, facedown, was a body. "All right, everybody back!" I heard Rudy yell. "Go on."

"Damon," I said. Damon, who stood about three people from me, walked over, staring at the body in the river the whole time. "Run up the road to my house. The sheriff is there taking my mother home. Tell him to get down here."

"Who is it?" I heard somebody ask. I think the voice was my cousin Wendy's, but I couldn't be sure. "Is he dead?" another voice asked.

"Okay," Rudy said. "This is nothing for children to see. Everybody go back to our house or to the Inn or a restaurant or something."

I was frozen, looking into the water at the body that floated there. "He could have floated for miles," Rudy said to me. He knew what I was thinking. He knew I was wondering if it was anybody that I knew. "Why don't you take Rachel and Mary home."

"No," I said. I looked around and saw Aunt Sissy standing by a fire hydrant. I walked over with Rachel and now Mary. "Could they stand back here with you, or would you take them up to Pierre's bakery for a goodie or something?"

"Of course," Aunt Sissy said. "I don't want to be here when they pull him out, anyway."

Aunt Sissy walked up the street. She'd make a left at the next street to get to Pierre's. Damon had run up River Point Road to my house, which was only two or three blocks away.

It might as well have been forty miles because the four minutes that it took to get the sheriff creeped by as we watched the snowflakes getting smaller. I thought I could actually hear them landing on the ground and the normal soothing lap of the Mississippi River seemed to echo in my ears. Finally the sheriff pulled up to where we stood by the wharf. He'd called the paramedics and everything from my house. It was another eternity before the EMTs got there. The whole time we all stood around trying not to say the obvious. One of us would say something like, "I haven't seen so and so in a few days." And then change the subject again real fast until one of us would say it again with a different name.

The one person that I'd seemed to forget about and hadn't noticed that he wasn't at the dinner this evening was Uncle Jedidiah. I thought it strange, though, that none of his offspring had asked where he was or mentioned where he was. The EMTs pulled the body out of the water and, unfortunately, I was right. It was Uncle Jedidiah Keith. The bottom fell out of my stomach and a cold sweat broke out along my back.

Oh my God. That was my uncle lying there in that freezing cold water! Tears rose to my eyes and froze on my cheeks as they fell. "Oh, Jesus," I said.

Rudy was instantly beside me with his arm around me. "It's all right," I heard his voice say.

"Oh my God," I muttered. "It's Uncle Jed . . ."

"I know," Rudy soothed. "I know." He held me close as I turned my head and sobbed heavily into his coat. I couldn't tell you what anybody else's reaction was. I couldn't even tell you who else was present. When I gained control of myself I took a good long look at the stretcher with my uncle's body and a white sheet draped over it. I doubted I'd ever forget this.

It had stopped snowing.

Eighteen

I sat at the kitchen table shoving a piece of banana cake with cream cheese frosting in my mouth as fast as I could. My eyes were swollen and my nose wasn't quite finished running from the crying fit I'd just had at the discovery of my uncle's body in the cold Mississippi River. My mother sat across from me, filling my glass of milk as fast as I drained it.

"I just can't believe it," I said with a slight hiccup.

"Just calm down," Mom said. "We don't know what happened yet."

"He's dead," I said. "That's what happened."

"Just wait until Colin gets back before you go and convince yourself that evil play is at hand. Okay?"

"Fine," I said. "You're right. But, I still can't believe it."

"What're the plans for the rest of the reunion?" she asked.

"As far as I'm concerned, it's over. We're all going to be at a funeral instead of a dinner at the KC hall. How can we go on and celebrate and stuff?"

"Well, you might want to ask his kids what they want to do. They may want to have the kind of wake where people party instead of moping."

I just looked at her.

"Well, you never know," she said, shrugging her shoulders.

Aunt Sissy had come back already and I'd put my girls to bed without telling them what had happened. Aunt Sissy didn't feel well so she went upstairs to my bedroom and lay down across the bed. Rudy had walked me home and then gone back with the sheriff.

"Why couldn't it have been Ruth?" I asked.

"Victory!" my mother snapped. "Don't you ever say something like that."

"I can't help it," I said. "Uncle Jed was a fun-loving drunk. He never did anything to anybody." All right, I felt bad over the statement I'd just made, but at the time I said it, I meant it. Actually, now I felt really, really bad. If something happened to her now I was going to just be convinced it was because I said it. My family wrote the book on how to feel guilty about everything. I can feel guilty about something that has nothing to do with anything.

My mother gave me her best I'm-ashamed-of-you look. Funny how that worked, because now I felt all ashamed of myself. "Sorry," I muttered. "I . . . I just feel so bad. I feel responsible because this happened in my town. I feel responsible because this happened at the family reunion that I was hosting. I feel guilty because I wonder if any of the stuff I was digging up on Nate Keith had anything to do with this . . . I just feel so many things. And none of it is good."

"That's perfectly natural," Mom said.

"It is? Is it natural to immediately feel guilty over everything?"

"Are you okay?" Mom asked.

"I think . . . well, actually no. I'm pregnant," I spit out.

"Tell me something I don't know," she said.

I stared at her with sheer astonishment. "What? What do you mean, tell you something you don't already know? What do you mean? Just . . . how . . . what do you mean by that?"

"You go almost twenty hours a day. The past two weeks you're nodding off at eight P.M. unless you have to go somewhere. You have a glow about you. You've been acting strange, aside from the fact that you've got fifty people who are related to you within a five-mile radius—and they are all relatives of your father's. If it were my family you wouldn't be so nuts. But you've been acting strange. The night Rudy smashed his nose, he was acting strange. You went to the doctor and yet you never told me what the results were. I just figured it out. Mothers know these things," she said with a big sigh.

"I hate you," I said.

"No you don't," she said and filled my glass up again. "You wish you could be just like me."

"You're insufferable."

"So anyway," she said smiling from ear to ear. "Congratulations. Where are you gonna put it?"

"God, I don't know. We could do a room addition. We've got the money from Rudy's bonus last year," I said.

I scraped the last bite of cake off my plate, making sure to get all the icing on the edge and savoring the richness of it. My mother always knew everything. That is so irritating. Plus she's so darn smug about it.

"Well, I'm getting married," she said.

The banana cake seemed to get hung right there at the part of my throat where pills and stuff always get stuck. I gulped down the milk and swallowed hard. I coughed a little and then just stared at my mother. She didn't say a word. I got up and walked to the living room and then came back to the kitchen. I started to speak and couldn't.

Married? Married. I assumed she meant she was marrying . . . God, life is just not fair.

I walked over to the back door and scratched my head. Then I came back to the table and sat down and looked at her again. She hadn't grown any horns or anything, so as much as I could tell, she was still my mother. I took my dirty dishes to the sink and set them in there a little too roughly.

I went back to the table and looked at my mother again. "Did somebody do a Vulcan mind meld on you?" I asked.

"That wasn't exactly the reaction I was expecting," she said.

"What about Sean Connery?" I asked.

"What about him?"

"I thought you were gonna marry him?"

"He's already married."

"That never stopped you from saying it before."

Flashing that get-real look at me, she crossed her arms and tilted her head, then fixed an expectant stare at me. Okay, she'd told me congratulations. She had been happy for me. I should do the same thing for her. I didn't want to, but I should. "Congratulations," I said.

"Thank you," she said. "This will work out good. The new baby can have my room."

"You're *moving*?" I asked, incredulous. "You don't have to move."

"Oh, Colin is going to move in here with you and Rudy, Rachel, Mary, and Junior," she stated.

No way in heck could I live with the sheriff in this house. I could barely live with the fact he lived in the same country. "No, I guess not."

There was a long, heavy silence between us. A tear ran down my cheek and I was surprised by this. I swiped at it quickly. "That's great, Mom. Congratulations again."

"Victory," she pleaded. "Don't cry."

"Don't cry? How can you tell me not to cry? I can cry if I want. My uncle just died. My mother is getting married. My mother is moving out of my house. And I'm pregnant, dammit. I can cry if I want to!" More tears fell and I continued to be surprised. If somebody had asked me what my reaction to my mother moving out would be, I would never have guessed that it would have been crying like a thirteen-year-old girl who's just been told her best friend is moving to Kansas.

"I'm going to miss you," I managed to say. "I . . . I can't talk now. I'm going to go lie down."

"I'm not moving a thousand miles away. We'll probably buy a house in Wisteria or here in New Kassel," she said.

I didn't care. I didn't care what words she spoke to try and make me feel better. My feelings were hurt. We were a team. We were best friends. I could give two hoops in the chicken coop if she moved in right next door. I was crushed.

I also realized somewhere in the back of my mind that I was being terribly childish and selfish. Try and rationalize that to an exhausted pregnant woman at midnight. What the heck had happened to my life? In one week it had just been torn upside down.

"I'm going to bed," I said. "I'm happy for you, Mom. Regardless of how many tears you see, I am happy for you."

With that I left her seated at the table and went upstairs to find Aunt Sissy sprawled sideways on my bed. I knew I couldn't sleep, but I was going to try before I found something new to cry about.

Nineteen

The room was dark and I could barely make out Aunt Sissy's form lying across my bed. She still wore her royal blue velvet jumper that she'd worn to the dinner. It was the only time other than weddings that I had seen her actually dress up. Black and white saddle oxfords were still on her feet, hanging off the side of my bed. I don't know anybody that can get by with wearing those after they turn eight. Aunt Sissy could. Actually I'm not sure that she could really get by with it either, she just did it and didn't care what people thought.

"Shut him up," she whispered. "Shut him up."

It didn't take me long to figure out that she was dreaming. I sat down on the bed next to her and she began to rock back and forth like a child does. "Aunt Sissy," I said.

"Ooooh, shut him up," she said. Small whimpers escaped her and she began to sob. She repeated that same phrase over and over in a trancelike rhythm.

"Sissy," I said, more firm. "Wake up." I shook her shoulder and repeated her name a few times. Finally, she startled awake and sat up, her eyes wide with fear. For a split second she came across like she was about ten years old.

"Shut who up, Aunt Sissy?"

Tear-filled eyes narrowed on me. She swiped at her face to remove the evidence that her dream left on the conscious world. "Nobody," she whispered.

"Were you dreaming about Uncle Jed?" I asked.

"No," she said and shook her head. "Poor Jed. Have we heard anything new?"

"Not yet," I answered. I figured out of all of my aunts and uncles, Sissy would be the one to be the most upfront with. What did I have to lose? "Were you the one that sent me the newspaper articles?"

She ran her fingers through her hair and looked confused for a minute. "No, I didn't." So far, I had collected about fifty-five signatures and hadn't had a chance to compare them with the note that came with the newspaper articles.

"What newspaper articles?" she asked.

I really didn't know how to broach the subject so I just shrugged my shoulders at her. "Never mind," I said. "It's nothing."

"You wouldn't have asked if it was nothing. Don't go acting like coy Wendy," she declared. "Go on, spit it out."

"I received newspaper articles on the death of Nate Keith," I declared. I watched her face closely to see what sort of reaction I was going to get. Disappointment was all I got, though. It was far too dark to read anything real subtle and there was no overwhelming reaction from her.

"I was wondering when it was going to come around and bite us in the ass," she said.

"Who? Bite who?"

"Us. The family. We've tried so long to keep it from everybody."

"Why?"

"A murder," she said. "An unsolved murder at that. Wasn't exactly the conversation you wanted to bring up when your boyfriend came to dinner. We all made a pact that nobody would know."

"How could you keep that from everybody? I can see, like your husband, he wasn't from Partut County. But what about Uncle Jed's wife and Uncle Isaac's? They were both from that area and adults when it happened. How could you keep that from them?"

"I don't know what Jed and Ike told their wives. If they told them, it never went to the next generation," she said.

"Why?"

"You wouldn't understand."

"Tell me what you know," I said. It wasn't a request. I stated it simply and plainly.

She sized me up long and hard. A deep long sigh came from within her. It seemed as though the sigh had been waiting fifty years to come out. "I really don't know very much," she said.

"You were there," I accused.

"It was hot," she said. "God, it was so hot, you could see the steam rising off of the chicken coop. Your dad and I had been down at the creek swimming with the neighbor kids. We were supposed to be eating dinner at Grandma and Grandpa's, which we did a lot. About four times a week Mom and Dad would take us all over there and help with the chores and cook dinner."

I didn't dare interrupt her, she seemed to be in a trance of remembering.

"Grandma had said to be back in time to milk the cows and get dinner going. So we came back around four or so. We noticed right away that something wasn't right," she said.

"Why?"

"Well, Jed had gotten married in the spring, and they lived in town. Jed was the only person that could calm Grandpa Nate down, and make him hear sense. If Jed was there, Grandma and Grandpa had been fighting. That's all there was to it."

"They fought a lot?"

"Enough. And when they did it was a doozy," she said. "So I headed into the house to put some clothes on and your dad went on to the barn to start milking the cows still in his swimming trunks. When I got inside, Mom took me aside and told me to go upstairs, that Della Ruth and Nate had been fighting something fierce and that Grandpa had threatened to kill Grandma."

Very interesting.

"I wasn't in the adventurous sort of mood, so I did what Mom said and went on upstairs. About ten minutes later I heard the gunshot."

Goosebumps danced down my spine and arms as I sat in the dark and listened to this fifty-year-old account of a tragedy.

"Well, my heart went in my throat," she said. "And it stayed there. I remember crouching down at the steps with my ear against the floor. Grandpa lay out there on the porch for hours. He was there at least three or four hours because it was dark before it stopped."

"Before what stopped?" I asked.

"Him. He moaned and cried and begged for help," she said, a sob tearing from her throat. Hands instinctively went to her face as she wiped at her eyes. I imagined that she was trying to wipe the vision of the memory away more than she was wiping at tears.

My goosebumps got goosebumps. "What?" I whispered. "You mean . . . nobody . . . you mean he just lay out there and nobody went to help him?"

"That's right. I heard Grandma tell Aunt Ruth that if she went near that door she'd put her in her own grave. Nobody was to touch him," she said. "And nobody did."

I couldn't believe what I'd just heard. She couldn't be for real. Could she? My entire family sat inside the house waiting for the man to die? Was that possible?

"I don't understand," I said and I didn't. "How could Della Ruth keep grown people from going outside? Aunt Ruth was in her twenties!"

"I only know what I was told," Aunt Sissy said. " 'Cause I never left my spot on the floor in the attic until he shut up. But I was told that Grandma sat at the front door with a shotgun across her lap and threatened anybody who went near the door with it. That's just what I was told," she said. "Like I said, I never left the floor."

Twenty

I awoke the next morning wondering if my family were the models for the folks out of *Deliverance*. Rudy came in very late and slept on the couch, while I slept the rest of the night curled up next to Aunt Sissy upstairs on our bed. I used to sleep curled next to her a lot as a kid, and she still smelled like White Shoulders perfume. When you're an only child and you go to stay at people's houses for a week without your mother, well, you find mothering arms.

I stumbled down the stairs to find Sheriff Brooke sitting at my kitchen table. A serious look pinched his features so that he looked like he was sitting on a sharp rock. I glanced down to see what I was wearing, and was relieved that it was the same purple and black velour outfit from last night.

"Good morning," I said.

"You look terrible," he answered.

"Same to you," I said as I got the orange juice out of the refrigerator. "Is Mom up?"

"I don't think so," he said. "Rudy let me in."

I looked in the living room at Rudy sprawled on the couch. The green and brown afghan that my mother made about ten years ago was barely covering him, and his mouth was open as he snored to high heaven. "That's the same position I saw him in last night."

"Well, I didn't say he woke up, he just unlocked the door and lay right back down on the couch," the sheriff said.

"Hmm," I said. I poured a big tall glass of orange juice and sat down at the table.

"You always have eyes this puffy in the morning?" he asked.

"You're just a bright bearer of glad tidings, aren't you?"

"Sorry," he said. "Just don't think I've ever seen you look this . . . haggard."

"Wow, you just keep going."

"I don't mean it bad . . . your mom told me you were, you know."

"Pregnant?" I asked.

"Yeah." He shrugged his shoulders. "She called me late, about two in the morning."

I got it now. Some people think that once you're pregnant that means you're frail and you're going to be sick and swoon and all that preconceived rhetoric. "I'm fine. I cried for about three hours last night. That goes a long way to making superpuffy eyes."

"Oh," he said. "Well, I don't want to make things worse . . ."

"Oh, but you have just by being in my house before seven-thirty in the morning," I said with a big fake plastered smile.

He tried his best to ignore the insult. "We found this in your Uncle Jedidiah's pocket," the sheriff said and held up a clear baggie.

I looked at him with venom. I wanted to be able to hurt him with just a look, but it never worked. I just came across looking like a hormone-driven housewife from hell. I took the baggie from him and looked at its contents. It was the piece of paper I had written *Roger McCarthy H's son* on, on that day when the sheriff had called me to tell me that he had found the investigating officer, Hubert McCarthy. The same piece of paper that I turned my back on and when I turned back around it was gone. Uncle Jed had taken it after all.

"Does this mean something?" I asked.

"You tell me," he said in a haughty tone.

"Get out of my house," I said.

Shock crossed his face. "I have the right—"

"You don't have the right to do anything!" I spat. Although he probably did have the right, I didn't think so at the moment and it was my house. "My uncle died last night and it's not even eight in the morning and I have a house full of grieving relatives. Sleeping grieving relatives, but grieving all the same. You just waltz in here to ask me about a stupid piece of paper . . . and you're marrying my mother and you can just go right back to your stuffy little office, with its icky brown paneling and stupid NFL decorations, and do this by the book. You come back at a decent hour!"

The look on his face was priceless. It was as if he'd never seen me before in his life. Which I didn't exactly understand because I know I've been a bitch before. This wasn't a new personality trait by any means.

He stood up and took the baggie from me. The look on his face was completely unreadable. His law enforcement training was switched on full power, suddenly. "They are doing an autopsy today, about three. I'll come by afterward."

"Good, you do that," I said.

I drank my orange juice as I heard the storm door shut after the front door. God, was my life ever going to be normal again? I wanted my life to be normal. I wanted Sylvia to yell at me. I wanted the mayor to threaten me. I was up to my neck with my family. I firmly believe that one can only take so much of one's family before one has to be fitted for a white jacket.

•

Two hours later the telephone rang.

"Hello, may I speak with Torie O'Shea," a female voice said.

"Speaking," I said.

"Hi, it's Robin Keifer," the voice said. Robin Keifer. Robin Keifer. Who? "From the library in Progress."

"Oh, gosh, I'm sorry. We sort of had a family incident last night and my mind just isn't here with my body."

"That's all right. You know what I always say. As long as nobody's dead," she said. I didn't bother to tell her that somebody was dead. I just gave a nervous laugh and she got on with why she called. "I had a chance to look that stuff up for you. I found the articles on the swimming accident, found a little on the resorts you asked about *and* Naomi Cordieu just happened to come in to the library about an hour after you left yesterday."

Okay, Naomi was who again? Jeez, nothing like a family crisis to just blow the heck out of your short-term memory. Ms. Keifer took my silence to be exactly what it was, lack of memory, and filled in for me. "The historical society. You asked about her."

Oh yeah, the lady that wrote the article on Bradley Ferguson. "Oh, okay," I said.

"I told her that you'd asked about her and told her what I was looking up for you and she got real interested in you. I told her that I couldn't give out your phone number, but she gave me hers and asked if I would give it to you. She said that she would very much like to speak with you."

Really. "Really?" I asked. "Why?"

"I'm not sure why, she just said that she could help you out with your questions," Robin said.

"All right. Well, give me her phone number," I said. She gave me the number, I wrote it down and then a silence hung in the air. I had promised her payment to look this stuff up and I didn't want her to think that now I was going to try and skip out on paying her, or that I didn't want the information. "Um, I'll be down before noon," I said. "To pick the stuff up and pay you."

"All right," she said. "See you then."

I hung up the phone, still feeling kind of oogie from the night of shock and tears and from lack of sleep. When would I ever get enough sleep? I looked at the phone number I'd written down and decided I would go ahead and call it. What could it hurt?

I dialed the number. A firm, resounding voice answered the phone. "Naomi."

"Hi, Naomi Cordieu? This is Torie O'Shea," I said.

"Oh, hello. I am so glad you called. I was hoping that you would. When can I meet with you?" she asked.

"Uh . . . well . . ." I sputtered.

"Are you John Robert's relation? You are, aren't you?"

I didn't know if I should answer her or not. This definitely was not what I was expecting. Even though, I couldn't really tell you what it was that I *was* expecting. "Uh, who are you exactly?"

"I am Bradley Ferguson's widow. I remarried a man named Arthur Cordieu after Bradley died in Africa."

"You are Bradley F.'s widow? Bradley Ferguson?"

"Yes."

I should have known that the glowing review of his life in the historical society paper was just slanted enough that she would be related in some way. I stood in the kitchen and scratched my head as Rudy came in and started rummaging around for something. He was making enough noise for ten people. I stuck my finger in my open ear and said, "I'm coming down to Progress to get some information."

"Yes, I know," she said.

"I'll come by and we can talk then," I said, straining to hear her and myself.

"Just tell me, are you John Robert's relation?"

"Yes," I said. "I am his granddaughter."

"I knew it," she said and sighed. She gave me directions to her house, which was right off the outer road. I had passed it a dozen times.

"I'll see you in about two hours," I said and hung up.

I stood there playing with my lower lip between my thumb and forefinger, staring at the kitchen floor.

"Have you seen the yellow pages?" Rudy asked.

“They are up there in that top cabinet,” I said. “Jeez, you know you could call information.”

“I’ll call information when it’s free,” he declared. He pulled a chair over and opened the top cabinet.

“Be careful of the deep fryer,” I said. “It likes to fall out and surprise people.”

“Are you okay?” he asked from the chair.

“Hmm? Yeah, I’m fine. I’m going down to Progress,” I said. “I’ll be back before three, because the sheriff is coming by. Take notes on any funeral arrangements or anything for Uncle Jed.”

“Okay,” he said.

Twenty-one

Before I left for Progress, I needed to go by and tell Sylvia that I would have to extend my vacation, probably to Monday or Tuesday, depending on funeral arrangements. I also wanted to check in and see if everything was all right. I mean, what if she liked Helen's substitution of me better than me?

I wore one of those big sloppy jean dresses with black tights under it, boots, and a red turtleneck. I pulled my station wagon off the main road and parallel parked it right in front of the Gaheimer House. Which, if Sylvia knew that I'd done it, she would have a fit and make me move.

I opened the door to the Gaheimer House and instantly smelled a tantalizing mixture of caramel and popcorn. Wilma was making her world-famous popcorn balls. Well, at least eastern Missouri famous. "Hello?" I yelled out.

I walked down the hall, passed my office on the right and went into the kitchen.

"Torie!" Wilma said and walked over with her arms wide to embrace me in a very padded hug. She wore a big green kimono-looking thing and I noticed that her hair was still down. The first time was an accident. I would venture to say that if she was still wearing it down it because she'd found a way to irritate her sister. "We have missed you so much."

"Well, thank you," I said. I wasn't so sure that Sylvia had missed me, but I knew that Wilma had.

"How have things been going?" I asked. "Helen doing okay?"

"Oh sure, sure. She and Sylvia have a fight every single day over something," she said.

"We do not," Sylvia said from the doorway. I turned around and was surprised to find myself happy to see Sylvia. My family definitely had to go.

"Hi, Sylvia," I said.

"Victory," she said and nodded. "What do you want?"

"Nothing. Just came by to see how things were going. My uncle died and I'm going to have to extend my vacation until the funeral is over. They haven't planned it yet, though, so I'm not sure when it will be."

"Jed, huh?" Sylvia asked.

"Yes, you heard."

"How could you not hear? Sirens going everywhere . . ."

"There was one siren," I corrected her.

"I think your father should host his own family reunions from now on," Sylvia said, pointing her finger at me. "Our town can't handle all of you Keiths at one time. Something bad always happens."

"Was he pushed?" Wilma asked. "We heard he was pushed. Murdered."

"No, Wilma," I said. Where had she heard that from? "Well, actually we don't know what happened just yet."

"So he could have been pushed," Wilma said.

"Could have, but unlikely," I answered. I had no particular evidence to back that statement up, I was just hoping with all my might that it was true.

"Wedding bells and pitter-patters," Wilma said back to me. God, she made my head hurt.

"What?" I asked. "What are you talking about, Wilma?"

"Wedding bells—"

"The sheriff and your mother," Sylvia chimed in. "We are just completely appalled."

"Well, I'm not going to argue with you on that one, Sylvia. How did you guys find out so quick?" I asked, not sure I really even wanted to know.

"And pitter-patter . . ." Wilma added.

I know my jaw must have hung open to my chest. How did they know about this? What was up with this town, anyway? I know that small towns are like living in fishbowls, but Jeez, this was ridiculous.

"Pitter-patter . . ." Wilma said, smiling from ear to ear. Sylvia stood with her arms crossed and one eyebrow raised.

"All right, yes, I'm pregnant," I said.

"Goody, goody," Wilma said and bounced up and down as much as a two-hundred-pound ninety-year-old could bounce.

"Oh, for Pete's sake, Victory!! Have you no shame?" Sylvia asked.

"Shame?" I asked.

"A woman your age . . ."

"My age? Sylvia, I'm only thirty something. Early thirty something. What is wrong with that?" Sylvia just rolled her eyes skyward, as if I would just never understand. I felt rather odd, standing there in the kitchen with Wilma beaming at me and Sylvia scowling at me. I felt odd because they knew things about my life suddenly that I couldn't for the life of me figure out how they knew. I could be really paranoid here and wonder if somebody had bugged my house or something.

"How do you guys know all of this stuff?" I asked.

"It's not hard to figure out. Rudy told Chuck the other night when they were playing pool that you guys might be building a room addition. Chuck mentioned it to Elmer who mentioned it to Eleanore and everybody knows that a room addition means a *room addition*. Not to mention, you've looked really tired lately," Sylvia explained.

"I do not look tired," I said. "Why does everybody keep telling me how tired I look? Did anybody ever think that maybe I look tired because I'm trying to juggle like fifty family members? No, everybody assumes it's something else!"

"And so far as your mother is concerned," Sylvia said. "Sheriff Brooke told Elmer that he was going to be taking a vacation in the summer. Elmer asked what kind of vacation because everybody knows that the sheriff doesn't take a vacation, and he said . . . the kind you take with the woman you love. Everybody knows what that means."

"Great Jehoshaphat," I declared. "Since the sheriff is your great-stepnephew or something like that, does this mean we are going to be related?"

"Absolutely not!" Sylvia stated.

"Remind me never to tell Elmer anything," I said and rubbed my head. I got what I wanted and that was for Sylvia to be yelling at me. God help me, I actually felt better.

THE NEW KASSEL GAZETTE

The News You Might Miss

by Eleanore Murdoch

'Tis the season and all that good stuff. Just twelve more shopping days to the big day! Remember, support your local shop owners and buy Christmas here instead of those big chain stores up in the city. New Kassel was voted by *Midwest Living* as the most charming small town in Missouri to spend a vacation. Pat yourselves on the back for coming across as wholesome and American while they were here writing their article.

Wedding Bells!! Jalena Keith and Sheriff Colin Brooke

are planning a summer wedding! It should be delightful. And Chuck Velasco has announced his engagement to Noble Quimbly's ex-wife, Susan. Not sure how delightful that one will be. No date is set as of yet.

Father Bingham wants everybody to know that he added an extra Mass on Christmas Day, so that nobody could have an excuse about sleeping in and not having time for the Lord.

And is it possible that one of our best-known faces is pregnant???

Until next time,

Eleanore

Twenty-two

I wasn't used to making two trips down to Progress in one week but today I needed the drive. The forty-five minutes it took to get there relaxed me and helped me cleanse myself of jumbled nerves and such. Images of my uncle floating in the freezing water. I could hardly think of that without tears instantly rising to my eyes, so I tried not to think about it. I thought of everything else. I did not want to think about Uncle Jed Keith.

The drive was beautiful. It looked as though I was driving in a crystal ball with all the snow and ice clinging to the trees and grass. I pulled into the parking lot of the library at exactly eleven-fifteen.

Robin Keifer waited for me behind the counter. She smiled that great smile of hers and patted a pile of papers to her right. "Just for you," she said. "I think you'll be pleased."

"I'm sure I will be," I said. "I can't thank you enough."

"It was my pleasure. I felt like I was doing something important. You know, to really help somebody," she said.

"Well, you certainly were." I got out my checkbook wrote her a check for the research she had done and handed it to her. She gave me the pile of photocopies. All I could think about was when would I have the time to read them?

"If you ever need anything else," she said. "You let me know. I do this sort of thing every now and then. All of us librarians do. As a matter of fact, I looked up a bunch of stuff on the Keith murder a couple of weeks ago for somebody."

I stopped, frozen by her words. "The Keith murder," I repeated.

"Yeah, back in the late forties, a man was killed on his front porch. This research was easy, though, because the man knew the exact date that it happened."

"What man? Who did you look this stuff up for?"

A puzzled look crossed her face. "I really don't know. He came in, requested it and came back a few hours later to get it. I couldn't charge him anything, though, because it was done on library time."

"And you didn't get a name?" I asked.

"I might have gotten a name on that day, but I don't remember it. He was middle-aged. Forty-five to fifty-five. Somewhere around there. That's all I can tell you," she said.

"Okay, well, you've got my number. Call me if you remember anything else," I said.

"I will," she said and smiled again.

So whoever sent me those copies of the newspaper articles didn't just happen upon them. They sent them to me on purpose. They wanted me to know. I let that thought brew in my brain for a while as I got in the car. I drove back out to the outer road off of the highway and found the yellow two-story colonial-style home that belonged to Naomi Cordieu. I had passed this house on my way to Progress or out to Pine Branch to visit my grandparents a thousand times. I wondered if she had lived in it all those years.

I walked up on the front porch, noting that her porch furniture was clean and that she had two quilts draped over the swing and the chair. A colorful bird house was about two feet from the porch in the yard, painted to look like a miniature of its owner's house. The door opened before I could knock.

"Torie O'Shea," the woman said. "Come in, come in."

I walked into her house and was immediately bowled over by

the heavy scent of a real Christmas tree. It stood right next to the door in front of the picture window and it was decorated with mauve and pink ribbons, bows and clear glass ornaments.

"I'm Naomi," she said. "Have a seat, I'll be right back."

A blue Victorian love seat, with clawed feet and curvy scrolls on the arms, was the nearest thing I could find, so I sat on it. I worried about whether I was supposed to sit on it, because it didn't look like sittable furniture, if you know what I mean.

Naomi came back in rolling an actual real live tea cart and she poured me a cup of tea from ancient bone china with pink roses on it. "One lump or two?" she asked.

I'd never been asked that before. "Probably three, if you don't mind. I like my tea sweet." She smiled and obliged me with three lumps of sugar. I tasted it and realized that if I were alone, I would have probably taken four lumps. I'm just not a lady, I suppose.

She sat down and I finally got a good look at her. She had been flitting around so much that I could barely get a look at her. She was a big-boned woman, about five seven, with blue hair and a hump on her back. She was at least eighty, probably older. Her sharp brown eyes were clear and I was surprised when I realized that she did not wear glasses.

She crossed her hands and smiled at me. "John Robert in the flesh."

"Excuse me, but I'm really confused."

"Well, you look like him. I only saw him once, but I've got pictures. You can have them if you like."

"Wait, you have pictures of my grandfather?" I asked.

"Yes, ma'am," she said.

"Why?" I asked.

"What I'm about to tell you, you may not like, you may not take to—shoot, you may not even believe—but I swear to you that it's all the truth," she said.

"What do you know about the drowning?" I asked.

"Oh, I'll tell you about the drowning, if you want me to," she said. "But you're going to be much more interested in the other things I have to tell you."

For the first time in my life, I wasn't so sure that I actually wanted to know something. It was a first. I could feel the earth actually slow on its axis. I almost told her to never mind, that I really must get going, but then the nosiness in me rallied and I found myself perched on her love seat waiting in anticipation. I know, I know, curiosity killed the cat.

"Bradley Ferguson was the father of John Robert Keith, your grandfather," she stated triumphantly. She'd been waiting forever to speak these words to somebody and her moment had finally come. You could see it written all over her face. The smile crossed her face with pure joy and sparkles flew from her eyes.

Oh, brother.

"I'm sorry," I said. The teacup and saucer that I held began clanking together. "What did you just say?"

"Bradley Ferguson was the real father of John Robert Keith, not that good-for-nothing, cow-licking, woman-beating, horse-thieving Nathaniel Ulysses Keith!" she said.

"You have no proof of this," I said.

"Oh yes, I do," she said and smiled even bigger.

Okay, for the sake of argument, let's say she did have proof. "Why? Why would you just suddenly tell me? Why not one of John Robert's children?"

"You think they're gonna listen to me? Oh, Felicity might, but there is no talking any sense to the likes of Ruth, or Isaac for that matter. Besides, I don't really think any of them give two hoots," she said.

"Why would I give two hoots?"

"You're a genealogist," she said. "A historian. It's in your blood, you hunt down the truth with your very fiber. Just like me. Just like all of us."

What was that? The genealogist pride song or something? My

breathing came in little ragged spurts now and I thought I might actually swoon. I'd never swooned before.

"What did you find?" Naomi asked me. "You found something or you wouldn't have been down here researching the swimming accident and the life of Bradley Ferguson. What did you find?"

"I found . . . I found two pictures of him, tucked and hidden in a box of cards that had belonged to my great-grandmother. And . . . two letters," I said with dawning realization. "And a poem. A proposal, actually."

"Oh," she said and placed her hand on her chest. "Della Ruth was the love of his life. The great tragedy of his life."

"Why didn't my great-grandmother just marry him? Why did she marry Nate Keith in the first place?" I asked.

"She couldn't marry Bradley. He went off to college at seventeen and Della Ruth was but fourteen years old. They were neighbors, friends, but neither one knew that there would be much more. When he came home from college, Della Ruth was married to Nate already and had given birth to Granville and Lea," she said.

"You mean that they were lovers? They had an affair?"

"Yes, and John Robert was the fruit of that affair," she said. "When Bradley found out that Della Ruth was pregnant with his child, he begged her to marry him. He begged her to leave Nate and come with him, that they'd go off around the world together."

I just stared at Naomi. "Forgive me," I said. "You are Bradley's widow?"

"Yes," she said. "Never a finer man in the world."

"So, aren't you being awfully generous about your husband's great love of his life and all that?" I asked.

"I used to be insanely jealous of Della Ruth. Insanely. One day I realized that if Bradley felt about Della half of what I felt for him . . . I don't know. I suddenly felt sorry for them and I quit being jealous. Plus, I knew that Bradley loved me. He really did. And time had numbed him a little toward Della. And I shared a bunch of memories with him that she would never have."

"Oh," I said. There were tons of things I should ask, but I'll be darned if I could think of any of them.

"Some say that Nate found out about John Robert not being his," Naomi said.

"What do you know about his murder?" I asked.

"A blessed event, if you ask me," Naomi said. "Imagine him getting all fired up about John Robert not being his, when half the county knew that he had at least three illegitimate children of his own. One was born just two years before he died. But to protect that person's privacy, I'm not going to tell you who it is."

That irritated me slightly. How dare she tell me that she knew who that baby, my relative, was, then not tell me. "So how did he find out?"

"Bradley told me that he wanted to leave John Robert something in his will. So he went out to talk to Della Ruth about it, she told him not to, because if he died anytime soon, she'd have to explain to Nate why all this money had been left to John Robert. Nate Keith was dead three days later."

"Did Bradley leave John Robert anything in his will?"

"No. He went by Della Ruth's wishes."

"Do you think that Bradley killed him?" I asked.

"If he'd a been smart, Bradley would have killed him when he first found out that Della was pregnant with John Robert, but I don't think Bradley had it in him," Naomi said. "But then again, maybe he did."

"Yes, but then he wouldn't have been free to marry you later," I said.

"This is true. We never had any children," she said. "That's part of the reason I was so excited to see you. You are his living descendant. You are all that is left of him."

"Oh well, that's not quite true. John Robert had seven children, and tons of grandkids and great-grandkids. There's plenty left of him," I said. Without realizing it, I'd just admitted believing her story.

"True," she said. "You look like them. The Fergusons."

"I know I look like my father."

"Who looked like his father." She got up and picked up a box that was sitting on a round corner table with a large lace doily on it. She handed me the box and then sat back down with a moan. "Oh, arthritis in my hip."

I opened the box and it was full of pictures. Right off the bat I recognized a photograph of my grandfather. I looked to Naomi for an explanation.

"Della Ruth wouldn't have anything to do with Bradley after John Robert was born," she said. "She wouldn't talk to him, see him, nothing. If she saw him on the street, she ignored him. For one thing, if Nate Keith had found out . . . she'd have been dead. But the one thing she did do was send Bradley photographs. She entered a drawing and won one of those cheap cameras. Every year at Christmas she sent Bradley an envelope with three or four pictures of John Robert from the previous year. That's all of them in there," she said and pointed to the photographs now nestled in my lap.

"So . . . Bradley goes out to talk to Della Ruth and three days later Nate Keith is dead. You really believe that Nate found out?" I asked.

"Yes," she said.

"Do you think John Robert knew the true identity of his father?"

"I think so, but I could never be sure," Naomi said. "He came to see me a few years after Bradley died. Said he just wanted to see how I was getting along without my husband. I tell you, it took everything I had not to say something. I think he suspected, though."

"And how did Bradley die?" I asked.

"On a safari in Africa. He was hunting a lion. The gun misfired," she said and hung her head in a moment of silence.

"Who do you think killed Nate Keith?" I asked.

"I always suspected Della Ruth myself."

I know the look on my face must have been pure shock. Of all the scenarios I had imagined, Della Ruth was never the one that I truly suspected. Even though Hubert McCarthy had alluded to it.

"God would have opened the gates of heaven personally for her," Naomi said. "Nate Keith was a horrid man."

"And the swimming accident?" I asked. I hadn't even been able to read the particulars on it yet. "He all but killed Bradley's brother. Everybody knew that. The barn burning? The poisoned pigs?"

"Think the barn burned at the hands of some local farmers, because Nate dumped lime in their water supply. The poisoned pigs, I believe, was the father of a girl Nate got pregnant. Can't prove any of that, but I believe that's what happened."

My head hurt.

I fumbled through the pictures, quickly, just to get a peek at them. One picture caught my interest and I wasn't sure why right away. I stared at it and stared at it.

"What is it?" Naomi asked.

"Not sure," I said. "In this picture here, I think I recognize the man with my grandfather, but I can't figure out who it is."

"Let me see," she said. I handed it to her and she squinted a little and then reached into the pocket of her dress and pulled out reading glasses. I smiled at the fact that she was a little vain over her glasses. "Oh, that's Hubert McCarthy. He and John Robert were best friends."

That time, I nearly dropped the china teacup and saucer.

Twenty-three

I drove home in sort of a stupor. Was it really possible that Bradley Ferguson was the father of John Robert, my grandfather? If so, that meant that he was my great-grandfather instead of Nate Keith. Which meant that about three years of genealogical research of the Keith line of my family tree just blew out the window! That thought made my head hurt.

I also had to struggle with the choice of telling everybody or not. Some people in my family wouldn't be too thrilled to learn this. Others wouldn't care, really. Nate Keith was just a name on a chart to most of them, so what difference would it make if I slipped in the name Bradley Ferguson? I wasn't entirely convinced that Bradley was the father of my grandfather. I couldn't explain how Naomi got all those pictures of him, though. Or how she knew so much.

I pulled into my driveway and gathered the papers that the librarian had found for me. I walked inside and found my cousin Joanie seated on the couch next to Aunt Sissy. Joanie was Uncle Jed's middle child and was the glue that kept her siblings together. Her large brown eyes were red and swollen. It was obvious she had been crying.

"Hi, Joanie," I said and walked over and gave her a hug. "I am so sorry about your father."

"It's okay," she said. Sweet and mild mannered were Joanie's strong points. She was always about fifteen pounds overweight, a young-looking forty-four, with the most adorable dimples in the world. Her sweetness was genuine. "He was seventy-eight, and with the way he drank and stuff, I'm surprised he wasn't dead years ago. I consider myself lucky I had him this long."

"It's still tough, though," I said. I felt the back of my throat constrict and quickly thought of something else. "How is everybody else?"

"They're fine. My daughter Allison is the youngest of his grandkids, and she's the most shook up."

"Aunt Sissy," I said, "have you seen Rudy?"

"He's out back playing with the kids in the snow."

"And the sheriff? Has he been by here?"

"Not yet," she said.

I glanced at my watch. It was two o'clock. The autopsy was at three and he'd be by afterward. I probably had two hours before he showed up. "I'm going to be up in my office for a while. I've got tons of stuff to catch up on."

Aunt Sissy nodded.

"Joanie, have you made any plans yet?" I asked before leaving the living room.

"I think the funeral will be Monday," she said. "And if it's all right with you, I think we would like to have the big dinner at the KC hall, after the funeral on Monday. I know it was supposed to be on Sunday, but everybody is taking the extra day off from work for the funeral anyway."

"That would be fine," I said. "I'll call Elmer and make the arrangements for Monday instead."

I was a little surprised that they had decided to do this. Maybe my mother was right, and they wanted to celebrate instead of being mopey. Some of the family members that couldn't attend every event all week would come and go, but they almost always try to attend the big dinner at the very end of the festivities. This year, they would almost all likely be here for other reasons as well.

I went upstairs to my office and sat down at my desk. I pulled out the big piece of material that I had traced the pattern on for the Indian Hatchet quilt design. Then I reached into my top desk drawer and found the note that came with the original newspaper articles. I scanned each relative's signature on the material and compared it to the writing on the note. The thought had occurred to me that somebody not related to me could have sent this note with the articles. I preferred not to believe that, though, and went on.

I traced my finger over Uncle Jed's signature and remembered asking him to sign it. He and Uncle Isaac had been having what appeared to be a not so happy conversation. Now I wondered what that could have been about. I just couldn't believe that the wonderful old coot that was my Uncle Jedidiah Keith was dead. Not possible.

About halfway through the signatures, I stopped. The *w* in the letter had a distinct little loop on it. The same little loop that was in the *w* for Dwight. The slant was the same. And the *th* was connected so that the *t* was crossed with the beginning loop of the *h*. It was my father. The handwriting matched my father's. Dwight Robert Keith.

Okay, not only did he lie to me about how Nate Keith had died, *knowingly*, but also sat at my kitchen table and pretended to have never seen those newspaper articles before in his life! And all along, he was the one that sent them to me. I just wanted to scream. I wanted to scream and pull his hair out of his head.

How dare he? How could he? *Why* would he? Why would he and then pretend it wasn't him?

He wanted me to know about it and, obviously, do something about it. He just didn't want me to know that he put enough faith in me to actually do it. God, he was infuriating.

I rubbed my eyes and let out a huge sigh. I would deal with him later. Then I took the stuff that I had received from Robin earlier and began to read those articles.

The first article reported the drowning of a Pine Branch boy, William Ferguson, out in Pine Branch creek. Half a mile up the creek just south of where the creek came out of the river, there was a strong undertow and crossing of currents. So actually they were swimming in the river just before it became a creek, I realized.

I stopped a moment and thought about this. I remember being warned about that spot in the river when I was a little girl and went down to my grandparents' house to visit in the summer. I remember specifically my grandfather telling me that when he was a young boy he could remember the time that somebody lost some cargo in the river and it would disappear under the surface and reappear a few minutes later, only to be sucked back down. "Never, ever go there," he'd warned me.

The article went on to say that the boys were daring each other to swim across the area, knowing that the undertow was there. Nathaniel Keith and William Ferguson were "always real competitive," neighbors reported. Bradley Ferguson reported that Nate Keith kept calling his brother a girl and so William swam across that area of the river three extra times, I suppose to prove he wasn't a girl. On the last time, he became too tired and hesitated just long enough for the undertow to grab him. William Ferguson surfaced five minutes later, a very dead boy. The year was 1884.

I was depressed. It seemed that everything Nate Keith touched, he ruined. Frankly, I was tired of thinking about Nate Keith. If I woke up tomorrow and had no idea who he was, I would be happy.

The article on the lakefront development really didn't help me much except to give the particulars of how big the lake would be, whose property it would incorporate, and how much revenue it would make in the long run for the county. The only name I caught was Paddington Elster. The Elsters were related to us. I believe Paddy was a first cousin to Nate Keith. The article mentioned that he was one of the strong supporters for the Pine Branch people to sell to the lake developers. He was tired of farming and wanted to make some money on the land that had taken his youth from him. I really didn't think that the resort and lake development was the reason Nate Keith was killed.

So, what did all of this mean?

Would I ever know what all of this meant?

I put the stuff in my top drawer of my desk and shut it. I had about an hour until the sheriff would be here. I decided to find my children and take them to get an ice cream.

Twenty-four

Rachel, Mary and I arrived back at the house at about four forty-five, and the sheriff's squad car was parked in front. Rachel had bombarded me with questions about death all the way to the ice-cream place and back, while Mary just kept adding to her Christmas list. I think she had about 115 things on it.

Inside the house I was surprised to see that the only people there were Rudy, the sheriff and my mother. Not a single other family member. Wow. I was a little apprehensive, because the last words the sheriff and I had had were not real friendly to each other. He was in formal dress and seemed all business-like.

Rudy came over and gave me a kiss. The coats came off the kids and onto the floor.

"Hey," I said. "Pick up your coats." I repeat that every single day. Do they just not hear the things that you repeat more than once?

Mary picked up her coat and headed for her room to play. Rachel grabbed a cookie out of the cookie jar, grabbed her coat, and went to the living room to watch TV. My mother, who was peeling potatoes, smiled at me. I was pregnant. I guess she was going to smile like this for the next eight months.

"Torie," the sheriff said.

"Hello, Sheriff. How did the autopsy go?" I asked.

"Well, we won't have the results to some tests for a while, but it looks like a straight drowning," he said. "Now, whether or not he was pushed or he just fell, I don't think we'll ever know."

That didn't make me feel any better. "A sign of a struggle?"

"No. He didn't have any bruises, nothing under his nails except about a week's worth of grime," he said.

"Hmm."

"Isn't that what you wanted to hear?" he asked. "Did you want me to tell you there was foul play?"

"No, rather I wanted to hear you say for sure that there wasn't," I said.

"There's just no way I can say that. If he was as drunk the night he fell in the water as he was the rest of the time he was here, it wouldn't have taken much for somebody to just shove him off the pier." The sheriff rubbed the brim on his hat. "If he was as drunk that night as he was the rest of the time he was here, he could have just as easily *slipped* off the pier as well. Unless there is a witness, I don't think we'll ever know."

Which translated into: my conscience would never be clear. I felt tears sting my eyes and I wiped at them. I took a deep breath and let it out slow. "Are you cooking?" I asked my mother in an attempt to change the subject.

"I'm starting on the potato salad for Monday. I'm going to have to make a ton of it," she said.

"Can I talk to you for a minute?" the sheriff asked. "Outside or in your office?"

"Outside," I said. "I need the air."

I still had my coat on from taking the kids out earlier, so I just walked out the back door of my kitchen into the backyard. There were four snowmen in the backyard, perched in front of the chicken coop as if in protection. One was wearing my good scarf.

"What's up?" I asked him with my arms crossed.

"Okay, you gonna tell me about this piece of paper, now?" he asked.

"The day you called, I jotted those two names down on a piece of paper. I turned my back for something and when I turned back around the piece of paper was gone. There were a few people in the kitchen and even more throughout the house, so I wasn't sure who took it. Or why they would have taken it."

"That's it?"

"Yeah, actually I'd forgotten about it until you showed it to me this morning. I guess now I know, Uncle Jed took it." I looked down at my feet. "Do you think he went to see him?"

"See the McCarthys?" he asked. I nodded my head. "I don't know. Guess we could give them a visit and see."

"I feel so bad, Colin. I am just distraught," I said.

"What have you learned that's new about your great-grandfather?"

I looked at him speculatively. He tilted his head and gave me that look that my high school principal used to give me. The one that said, Tell me now and I'll let you live.

"Basically, I've learned that somebody shot him on his front porch—"

"You knew that before," he cut in.

"Yeah, well now I know that my great-grandmother held her grandchildren and her two sons and daughter-in-law at gunpoint to keep them from going out to help him. They were made to stay in the house while he died. It took almost four hours," I said.

He was speechless. Judging by the look on his face, I don't think he quite believed me. Not that I blamed him. This was a hard thing for me to swallow. I knew, though, that Aunt Sissy would not have lied about her account of that day.

"I know that my dad was in the barn when it happened and I'm not sure where Uncle Jed was. Everybody else was trapped in the house. I intend to ask my father about this tomorrow or tonight if I can. He's the one that sent me the newspaper articles," I said.

"Really," the sheriff said. "Why do you suppose he did that? Why didn't he just come out and tell you?"

"I think part of it is that he didn't want to be the one to break the silence with his brothers and sisters, yet he wanted me to know," I said. "I'm not sure exactly. It's one of the things I plan on discussing with him."

The air was brisk and cold against my face. The smell of wood being burned was heavy in the air. Strange how good and comforting that smell is. I hugged myself to ward off the cold, which never worked. Why do we do that?

"So are you saying that there are no suspects other than your family?" he asked.

"I'm saying that either Della Ruth took advantage of the fact somebody had shot her jerk of a husband for her, and wanted to make sure he died, or she knew it was going to happen."

"You mean she hired somebody?"

"Or she cashed in a favor."

He pondered over that one for a minute.

"Could she have pulled the trigger herself?" he asked.

"She was present and accounted for in the kitchen when he was shot," I said. I watched him as he thought in silence again. "If somebody else did do it, and she was unaware that it was going to happen, she did nothing to save him."

"Gunshot wound in the forties?" the sheriff said. "Nothing would have saved him."

He was most likely correct on that one. "Then she wanted him to know that nobody gave a damn."

"So who would have been in a place where they could have seen who did it?" the sheriff asked.

"Nobody knows where Jed was, and we'll never know now. Which makes his death all the more curious. My dad was in the barn, he could have seen. If somebody was in the living room . . . I don't know. I'd have to ask each one of them, and I know some of them aren't going to answer me."

"Aside from your family, who else is there?"

"Bradley Ferguson," I said.

"Who?"

"A man who was in love with Della Ruth, and also just happened to be the little brother to the boy who died in a swimming accident that was, for all intents and purposes, Nate Keith's fault. I suppose any of the Fergusons would be suspect. Paddington Elster, he wanted to sell the land to the lakefront developers. And the most disturbing piece of evidence yet . . . a photo of our Hubert McCarthy with his arm draped around my grandfather, John Robert. They were best friends."

"Are you telling me the investigating officer of the crime was best friends with John Robert?" the sheriff asked.

"Yup."

"Interesting."

"Yeah. The thing that is the most discouraging is I don't think we are ever going to know. The murder is just too old and most of the people involved are dead. Unless one of my family members decides to speak, it's going to be unsolved for all eternity." I know it was a little melodramatic, but after everything that had happened this week, I felt a little melodramatic.

"Let's go see Hubert McCarthy," the sheriff said.

"Why are you being so nice to me?" I asked. "Oh, yeah, you're marrying my mother. That's why you agreed to find Hubert in the first place. You wanted to soften me up for when I heard the news."

The sheriff shrugged his shoulders a bit. He at least had the decency to look embarrassed. "Maybe," he said, without making eye contact. "I can also see that this is really bothering you. If I were you, I'd take advantage of my niceness while you can."

Between him and my father, I didn't know which one I wanted to haul off and punch the most.

Twenty-five

After dinner, I gave the girls a bath, read them a few books and then settled them in front of the TV with their father to watch *Rudolf the Red-Nosed Reindeer* and *Frosty the Snowman*. The sheriff and I went to see Hubert McCarthy. His son Roger was just as congenial this time as he was the first time that we visited.

The only lights on in the congested and dark living room of the McCarthys' were the Christmas lights and light from their television. The McCarthys were watching the same seasonal Christmas shows that my children were at home watching.

"Mr. McCarthy, the main reason we are here to see you is that Torie has made a discovery that we are a little perplexed about," the sheriff said with complete authority.

"What's that?" Hubert said from his wheelchair.

"I found a photograph of you with my grandfather," I said.

"So?" he asked.

"With your arms around each other. You two look like best friends," I stated and waited for him to either deny or confirm.

Hubert McCarthy was quiet a moment. Roger looked at his father and then back to us and then back to his father. Roger seemed just as anxious to hear his father's reply as I was. Finally, Hubert clicked his dentures together and spoke.

"We were best friends," he said. "I did not let that interfere with my investigation."

"How could it not?" Sheriff Brooke asked. "Did John Robert Keith just stand back while you drilled each one of his children over and over? No father would have stood for that, and no investigating officer would have let up."

"We were best friends and I repeat, it did not interfere with my investigation," Hubert McCarthy said.

"I apologize if we sound like we're accusing you of something," I said to him. "You must know how this came as a shock to us."

"I understand," Hubert said. "After you left the last time, I sent my son up to the attic to find my old files. I have the one on Nate Keith, if you want it."

I was a little taken aback by his generosity in light of the fact we'd come here to accuse him of having a conflict of interest on this case. I wondered at his motive for this. Maybe he really wanted us to get to the bottom of it after all these years.

"We can take it and look at it," the sheriff said. "We'll bring it back."

Hubert McCarthy motioned to his son to go and get the file from some other room. The room was silent except for the music coming from the television set. Everybody in cartoon land was happy-go-lucky and singing a wonderfully cheery song. Roger came back in less than two minutes and before he could choose which one of us to give the file to, the sheriff held out his hand. Roger handed it to him and Sheriff Brooke nodded his head to him in acknowledgment.

"What did you think of Nate Keith?" I asked. Somehow I just didn't feel comfortable with the fact this man was my grandfather's best friend, and then the investigating officer of his best friend's father's murder. Maybe Hubert knew who killed Nate and just looked the other way. Maybe he'd just pretended to have not solved it all these years.

"Nobody liked Nate Keith, the good-for-nothing. My grandma used to say that sometimes evil came to the earth and walked around in the disguise of men. That was Nate. He beat his boys in the head with his fists until their ears bled. John was a musician. Last thing he needed damaged was his ears," Hubert said. "Evil or not he was killed by evil and whoever did it should have been sent to jail."

"How do you know it wasn't self-defense?" I said.

"Coulda been," he said and shrugged. "Considered that a few times."

"Well, Mr. McCarthy, we're going to go now. I know you should be in bed. I'll return your file to you as soon as we've read it. If you can think of anything, give us a call," the sheriff said.

"You can keep the file. It's not state property. Was my own private files," Hubert said. Then he turned his attention to me. "You been finding out about your family?"

"Yes," I answered him. "After this, I think I may just stick to names on a chart and the heck with the 'other pertinent information' section."

"You talk to your father," Hubert instructed.

I nodded to him and the sheriff and I left. He had driven the official car, by the way. As soon as we were in the car I asked to see the file.

"Let me look at it first," he said.

"Why?" I asked.

"He might have pictures in it," the sheriff said. "You don't want to see pictures of your great-grandfather lying there with his guts spilled on the front porch."

"Thanks for sparing me," I said, trying to erase the visual he'd just given me. Little did he know my imagination was far more vivid than any photograph I would see. It was a nice gesture, though.

"What do you think?" he asked me. We were all the way to Loughborough in nothing flat.

"About what?"

"About his statement. Do you really believe he could have been the investigating officer without the conflict of interest?"

"I think you'd be more likely to answer that than I would. What do you think?" I asked.

"I don't see how he could. If he really drilled them, and kept going back and going back, like a good detective would have . . . you know what that would have done to his friendship," the sheriff said. "Because, if I were a father and was worried about one of my sons being carted off to jail because of killing an—"

"An evil man that deserved it," I finished for him.

"I didn't say that."

"That's what you were going to say. Are you telling me, Sheriff, that there is a type of murder that you wouldn't pursue?"

He rubbed his eyes and thought about it for a moment. "No," he said. "What I'm saying is, if I were a father and it were one of my children . . . I don't know what I've would have done. Protect them, most likely. Especially if it was a self-defense. If it were just coldblooded murder, child or not, I'd turn him in."

I stared at him for a moment. It took a lot for him to say that, because he was basically saying that there was a circumstance when he would break the law. And being a sheriff, that was saying a heck of a lot.

"It's obvious the man was a monster," he said.

"Well, the thing I noticed," I said, "was that Hubert never once said that he and my grandfather were still friends later, after the murder. He said over and over they *were* best friends. Maybe that's exactly what happened. Maybe he did do his job, and my grandfather told him to take a hike. In all my years at my grandparents' house when I was a child, I never heard Hubert McCarthy's name mentioned. I never saw his face. And I met a lot of the old-time friends of my grandparents. And I hung on every word the adults talked about. I don't think their friendship made it through the investigation."

"Either that or . . ."

The sheriff hesitated a little too much. He wanted me to answer for him, but he was not my mother and I couldn't play those little mind games with him. "Or what?"

"You ever think maybe Hubert McCarthy killed Nate Keith?"

I was silent for a long while. A couple of blocks at least. We passed the Nationals grocery store on our right and then the sheriff got on to southbound Highway 55.

"Not really," I said. "I had thought that maybe he knew who it was and just pretended to investigate the murder. But for him to actually be the killer. No, I never thought of that. What reason would he have had?"

"Who knows? Maybe he just happened to be out there that day and maybe Nate started in abusing John, your grandfather, and maybe Hubert just snapped," the sheriff said. "Tired of seeing his best friend treated like that, and then realized he could cover it up by doing the preliminaries to an investigation and calling it unsolved."

"Well, it's a nice thought," I said.

"Why?" he asked me.

"Because he's like the first real suspect that isn't blood related to me. I think." If Naomi was right, Bradley would have definitely been related.

"I understand," the sheriff said. "You're really down."

"Part of it is hormones," I said. "But, yeah. I'm down. My uncle is dead, my father has lied to me, and my great-grandfather was either a monster or a murderer."

The sheriff just looked at me oddly, because he didn't know what I knew about Bradley Ferguson. About all the things Naomi Cordieu had told me. "Can you check something else for me?" I asked. The sheriff didn't answer so I went on. "Check on Bradley Ferguson. He would have died in Africa on a safari around 1950. He's buried down in Pine Branch."

"Why?" Sheriff Brooke said.

"Just check to see if there was an autopsy or anything out of the ordinary about his death. Supposedly the gun misfired. He was hunting lions."

The sheriff nodded to me. I sighed heavily. I was miserable. There didn't seem a way to make me feel better. Well, there *was* one way.

Twenty-six

I knocked on the door to my father's two-bedroom flat in south St. Louis. I stood there with my knees knocking partly from the cold and partly from the fear of confronting the man who'd dished out the majority of my groundings and punishments as a child. They were just normal childhood punishments, but he ruled with an iron fist when I was younger and the thoughs of me confronting him over something this big . . . Well, I was suddenly ten years old standing on his porch.

I'd gone home and tucked the kids into bed and kissed my husband, who said something about missing me of late. He really is an angel, when you think of the things he puts up with. When I get involved in something, I throw myself into it. There doesn't have to be a murder for me to get lost in what I've just discovered. And he just rides the tide, making his own dinner or whatever, until I've satisfied myself with whatever it is.

After I apologized to him profusely, with lots of promises of staying home all week next week, I hopped in my car and drove back up here to the city.

My father answered the door and gave me a look of surprise which soon turned to satisfaction. He'd been expecting me. Maybe not tonight, but he'd been expecting me, eventually.

"Hi, Dad," I said. "Can I talk to you?"

"Yeah, sure," he said. "Come in."

He motioned me into his flat and offered me a seat in the front room. The front room was the music room, with all of his instruments and recording equipment. Some of his old violins and stuff that he collected he had mounted on the wall, along with a big 11 × 14-inch photograph of my two daughters that I'd had made one year as his Christmas present. My mother got one, too.

The house was smoky—that was no surprise—and stuffy warm. He had the old radiator heat and there was no regulating it. Let's just say he was never cold in the winter. The coffee table was covered with coffee rings, and two ashtrays that were heaping full.

"Want something to drink?" he asked.

"Water is fine," I said.

He went to get me a glass of water and I saw that he had his photo album out, and it was turned to a page with a few pictures of Uncle Jed on it. When he came back in, I noticed his eyes were a little puffy. He handed me the glass.

"I'm gonna bury a brother tomorrow," he said.

"I know. It's awful and I feel so bad."

"It sucks. That's all there is to it. How can you have the Keith clan without Jed?"

"Dad, can we change the subject?" I said. "I don't want to break down. The state I'm in I don't know if I could stop."

"Sure," he said and sat down on the couch. I sat down in a chair directly across the room from him.

Where to start? "Um, I hope you didn't hear it through the grapevine. I'm pregnant."

"Oh, no kidding," he said and smiled. "That's great, kid. Congratulations."

"Thanks," I said. There was no way I could bring up this subject without just stubbing my toe on it and saying it.

But he knew it. He knew why I was there. He was just waiting for me to say something. He picked up one of his acoustic guitars and started strumming some old Jerry Reed song.

"You sent me those newspaper articles. Why?"

He raised one eyebrow as if surprised that I finally had the guts to say what it was that was on my mind. "What makes you so sure?"

"The handwriting is a pretty good match, and the librarian that you asked to photocopy the stuff for you said a male between forty-five and fifty-five You're fifty-eight," I said. "Why?"

"I thought you should know. Everybody should know."

"Then why didn't you just tell everybody?"

The plucking of guitar strings abruptly stopped and he sat forward on his couch. He wore a gray work sweatshirt that made his skin look a little gray, too. His red hat was lying on the back of the couch. He looked tired and, I hate to say it, old. Not ancient. Just weathered.

"You don't understand," he said.

"Who killed Nate Keith?" I asked him.

He said nothing.

"Look, you gave me this information for a reason. You either wanted me to pursue it and find out who it was quietly or you wanted me to bring everything to light for you. Now answer me."

He still said nothing.

"I've talked to Sissy. She said you were in the barn. She also said that Della Ruth wouldn't let anybody out on the porch until Nate was dead. I've spoken to Hubert McCarthy," I said. With that, both of my father's eyebrows went up. "And Naomi Cordieu. I've found more things out that I'm not real sure I wanted to know. Now answer me. Who killed Nate Keith?"

"I don't know," he said finally.

I stood up abruptly and paced across his living room floor. "How can you not know?"

"I was in the barn getting Daisy ready to milk. I heard a commotion. Some yelling and stuff. I knew that Grandma and Grandpa were fighting. Jed was there. Then I heard the gunshot and I froze." He seemed rather aloof about his whole retelling. Not terrorized like Aunt Sissy had been. I think it was because he'd pushed it away for so long that he'd forgotten it had really happened. "It took me a while but I finally managed to get my legs to walk over to the door and I saw Grandpa lying on the porch. I heard more commotion and footsteps, running."

"You didn't go check on him?" I asked.

"No. I was afraid the killer was still there and I didn't want to be shot, too. And I was eight years old. I was too afraid to go to the porch. I didn't want to see what I knew I'd see," he said.

"This is amazing," I said, still pacing across his front room. My boots clicked on his hardwood floor.

"What do you mean, amazing?"

"I just can't believe that this has been in my family's past all of this time and nobody even so much as gave a hint! My father witnessed a murder—his own grandfather—and I knew nothing about it," I said. "It just scares me. What are people hiding every day? The lady at the grocery store, the librarian, the mayor? How could you keep this from me?"

He went back to plucking his guitar.

"How long did you stay in the barn?" I asked, my blood pressure rising with every question.

"About half an hour."

"It took him four hours to die. Where were you for the remaining three and a half hours?" I asked.

"Jed had been in the smokehouse. I think he hid out in there for a while like I did, because he didn't want to get shot himself. When it was evident that the killer had left, he came and got me. He knew I was out there," Dad said. "The two of us walked to town."

"You walked all the way to town? Nine miles. Why didn't you

go to a neighbor's house and borrow a car? Or a horse? Where was Jed's car?" I asked.

"Dana had dropped him off and gone back to town to shop," Dad said. "Not that many of our neighbors had cars. This was 1948 in dirt-poor rural Missouri. Besides, Jed told me he didn't want to involve any of the neighbors. Said we wouldn't appreciate any of our neighbors mixing us up in something ugly like this, and he wasn't going to do it to them."

"Wasn't anybody concerned about saving the man's life?" I asked, my voice raised just a little too loud.

My father stopped playing his guitar once again and looked me straight in the eyes. "No," he said simply. "Couldn't of anyway. Gunshot. Gut wound. He was as good as dead as soon as he was shot."

"So you walked to town," I said, frustrated.

"Yeah, and we went straight to Hubert McCarthy, who drove us back out to the house," he said.

"How do you know Jed didn't do it?" I asked.

"Because he said he didn't do it," Dad answered.

"Yes, but how do you really know? He could have lied to you."

"He was my brother. If he said he didn't do it, I believed him," Dad said.

"So tell me, Dad. How do I find out who did do it? Who saw it?" I asked.

"I'm not sure if she saw the whole thing or not, but when I peeked out of the barn doors at the house, your aunt Ruth was looking out the window in the house. She might have seen who it was," he said.

"Great," I said. "Aunt Ruth. The one person who wouldn't tell me even if she wanted to just for spite." There was a lesson here about burning one's bridges. I'd think about it more when my head wasn't hurting so bad and I wasn't on a personal quest.

"And there was nobody else outside? Hubert said something about one of Granville's daughters or something?"

"Dolly. I think she was in the chicken coop."

"How old was she?" I asked.

"About sixteen," he said. Old enough to hold a shotgun, I thought.

"And her story?" I asked.

"I don't know," he said. "She died that winter of typhoid. She never spoke of it, and none of us ever asked her."

"So, you sent me the articles because you didn't want to be the one to break the silence."

He said nothing.

"You lied to me when I asked you about them. Thanks for dumping this into my lap, Dad. Thanks for letting your daughter have the responsibility of deciding whether or not to tell the family."

"I didn't dump anything," he said.

"Yes you did. You knew I wouldn't be able to leave it alone. You knew," I said. I walked toward his front door.

"What are you going to do?" he asked, standing.

"I don't know," I said. "I'm going to try to find out who did it by every means possible, except involving Aunt Ruth. If I can't do it any other way, then I'll have to ask her."

"No, I mean about telling everybody?"

"I don't know, Dad. It's a lot more complicated than that. I'm not even sure Nate Keith was the father of John Robert. Do I want all the family to know that, too? I'm not sure. It's a huge responsibility telling people ugly things—a responsibility you so cleverly avoided."

Twenty-seven

The next day I went to Velasco's Pizza for lunch.

I needed to be away from my family. All of my family. Except Mary and Rachel, whom I had brought along. I couldn't handle another cousin, aunt, uncle or anything. My children and I were enjoying a pepperoni and mushroom pizza, thin crust with extra cheese and a big pitcher of soda.

"So anyway," Rachel said. "So, like Buffy comes out and stakes this vampire, like she usually does, but she's wearing this really cool black dress."

"What was the vampire wearing?" I asked.

"Huh?" she asked. Her large dark eyes rolled heavenward. "Who cares what the vamps are wearing, unless it's Drusilla. You should have seen this dress, Mom. I want one just like it."

My soon-to-be nine-year-old was acting entirely too old for my own good. I wasn't upset about her choice of TV material. When I was her age, I couldn't wait to watch *Nightstalker*. It's a universal thing, I guess. I was a little perturbed by the fact that she was more concerned over what the slayer was wearing than the fact that she was slaying at all. It made her come across as fourteen and unconcerned with the world, unless it was fashion-based. At her age, she was supposed to still be human and caring about living things. Or undead things, as the case may be.

"Mom," Mary interrupted, "do you think Santa will bring me a Tigger sleeping bag or Mulan?"

"Why do you need a sleeping bag, Mary?" I asked. "It's not like we go camping that often."

" 'Cause they're cool," she said. My five-year-old just said cool. This lunch was depressing me. "Besides, I don't hafta go camping to sleep in it. I can sleep in it in my bedroom. On the floor."

"You have a bed," I answered.

"So," she said and gave me this look that said I was totally stupid.

"You'll just have to put it on your list," I said. "With all the other two hundred items."

She smiled, her green eyes dancing at the thought of adding another object to her list. It didn't bother me too much, because so far on Christmas mornings, she's been thrilled with what she gets and forgets what she asked for in the first place.

"Hi, Sheriff!" Rachel said and waved across the room. I turned around and saw the sheriff walking over toward my table with a file folder in his hand. He stopped at my table and ruffled each girl's hair, which infuriated Rachel to death. That was all right. She needed some infuriation.

"What's up?" I asked him.

"Got a minute?" he asked.

"Yeah." I told Rachel to scoot down so that he could sit next to her and across from me.

"I've read through the file," he said. "Most of it is just his personal notes jotted here and there. There are a few snapshots of the house, the porch and all that in relation to the barn, the smokehouse and the chicken coop. There's a photograph of the porch with . . ." The sheriff glanced over at the kids. "Not a person, but a puddle," lowering his voice.

"Gotcha," I said.

"A puddle of what?" Rachel asked.

"Nothing, Rachel," I said.

"He's got everybody down on the date that he interviewed them, and why he thought they were suspect. Let me just tell you that Nate Keith was just awful. And his actions had long-reaching repercussions. One man killed himself after he found out that his youngest son really belonged to Nate. He might have been a monster, but the women seemed to be very . . . attracted to him."

"Great," I said.

"And that's pretty much it," he said and handed it to me. "Nothing you can't see and I didn't take anything out of it."

"A puddle of what?" Rachel asked again, more demanding this time.

"The way I see it, half the county had a reason for killing him," I said, ignoring her.

"Kill *who* Mom?"

"Yeah, but only one of them actually did it," he said.

"Yes, and about a hundred people benefited from it."

"Can't argue with that," he said.

"Want some pizza?" I asked.

"No, I can't stay. Jalena and I are going to go see about renting the KC hall for our reception," he said.

He could have gone his whole life without telling me that. I smiled and pretended that he didn't really say anything. He got up and said goodbye to all of us and he was out the door.

"Do I have to call him Grandpa?" Rachel asked.

The thought of the forty-something sheriff being called Grandpa was rather humorous. It was actually very funny. "Will it bother you to call him Grandpa?" I asked.

She shrugged her shoulders and said, "No, guess not."

"Then, yes, you should call him Grandpa. It will make his whole life," I said.

"What puddle was he talking about?" she asked.

Twenty-eight

Harlan Clayton hung himself in August of 1942. He fed his pigs, hosed his barn, ate his dinner and went out to the garage to die. He left sixteen children and a wife. Nate Keith had stolen what self-respect the man had when Nate announced to the world that Harlan's youngest son, Charlie, was actually his. Mrs. Harlan Clayton had not denied it.

Gee, that was a nice new reason to hate my great-grandfather. There was a new one every day. I only hoped that I found out who killed him soon, so that I could congratulate them.

I looked at the photographs in the file and was amazed at how much the place had changed from the late forties to the early seventies when I was a kid. It had changed even more in the past few years. It was now abandoned.

In a few photographs there was a large puddle of blood right in front of the door on the porch. There had always been a rug there when I was a child. I'd played right there with my Sweet April Play Land. There were two windows from which the porch was visible, one in the living room and one in the bedroom. And there was another window on the east side of the living room, looking out on the yard and the dirt road and the barn.

The last page of notes in Hubert McCarthy's file was a piece of paper with the words *Nobody saw anything. Nobody saw a soul. Nobody knows anything.*

The words were repeated over and over, as if McCarthy had been doodling his last few days on the case—the doodling of a frustrated man or the doodling of a man trying to convince himself that nobody saw anything.

I called the hotel that my cousin Damon was staying at and asked him if he'd like to take a ride down to Pine Branch. I wanted to go down to the old house, but I didn't want to go alone, and Damon was the only one I felt I could tell any of this to, if he asked. He agreed and I picked him up a half-hour later.

"So, what's this all about?" he asked.

"What? Why do you ask?"

"You've been acting strange this year, Torie. I mean, you've always been a little stranger than most of us," Damon said. "We just assumed it was from your mother's side of the family."

"Ha ha ha," I said to him. "I'm pregnant."

"I heard," he said. "Congratulations."

I looked over at him as he looked straight ahead, eyes on the road. He wore a navy blue parka, with a red and black flannel scarf. The rich colors complemented his swarthy complexion and black hair.

"Who'd you hear it from?" I asked. "No, don't answer that. I don't care at this point."

"Aside from being pregnant, something is going on. We're all shook up over Uncle Jed, but you should have seen your face that night. You looked like a ghost. And now you invite me on an impromptu trip to the old place," he said.

"Can you keep a secret?" I asked as I turned off the highway and down the outer road. We were nine or ten miles from Pine Branch. We went down the outer road and finally I turned onto a two-lane blacktop. We were in the country. Houses dotted the landscape every half mile or so and once in a while we'd come upon a farm with all the outbuildings and such. For the most part all we saw were snow-covered trees and fields with cows looking bored.

"A secret, eh? One that deals with the family?" he asked.

I sighed heavily. "It seems that we, the heirs of one Nathaniel Ulysses Keith, have inherited not a fortune or a legacy but a secret. An ugly little secret. Nice inheritance, huh?"

"What is it?" he asked, eyes sparkling with interest.

"Nate Keith was murdered."

"The man you were asking me about the night we were ice skating," he said.

"One and the same. And the only, thank God," I said. "Shot on Grandma and Grandpa's front porch, only then it was his front porch," I said.

"No way. Get outta here," he said.

"While the whole family was held at gunpoint by Great-Grandma Keith to stay put in the house, until he was finished dying."

"Holy Jesus," he said and gave a whistle. It took him a minute to really hear what I was saying. The whole family included his mother. The dawning realization hit with force as he turned to me, eyes wide. "You mean my mother . . ."

"Yes. Aunt Charlotte was in the house with the rest of them, except my father, who was in the barn, and Uncle Jed, who was in the smokehouse. They had a cousin, Dolly, who was in the chicken coop. Everybody else was inside," I said.

The blacktop road had now turned into gravel and I had to raise my voice a little to be heard over the pinging of the rocks on the underside of my car. "Did she ever mention it to you? She ever mention anything at all?"

"No," he said with a glassy look in his eyes. "Wow. Did Great-Grandma Keith do it? Did she kill him?"

"I don't think so, but she was certainly an accomplice."

"Wow," he said again. "How'd you find all this out?"

"Don't ask," I said. "It makes my head hurt just thinking about it."

"Why? Why was he murdered?"

"He was a horrible person. Poisoned farmers' crops, slept around and had several illegitimate children, ruined people's investment chances, beat his boys until their ears bled—"

"Then why do you care?" he asked. "Why do you care who killed him."

"I can't explain it. I'm nosy, Damon. Really nosy. I have an insatiable curiosity and . . . and . . . Aren't you the least bit interested?" I asked.

"Yeah," he said. "As long as I knew it wasn't going to be *my* mother that killed him. Yes, I want to know. How could you not want to know?"

"Exactly."

We were silent a moment as we passed the Pine Branch Methodist Church. It was the postcard-perfect white clapboard church and steeple with a well-kept cemetery in back. As soon as you rounded the corner and went down a hill, we'd be at our grandparents' old house. We both instinctively got quiet so as to brace ourselves for what we were about to see.

We came down over the hill and I slowed down a bit and drove the remaining quarter of a mile at a snail's pace. "There it is," Damon said.

"Yup," I answered.

"I don't think you can get in the driveway," he said. He was right. In the summer the place must have been completely overgrown. Tall grass and twigs from trees long dead were in the middle of the driveway, covered in snow. The two walnut trees by the pond were dead. And the pond was nearly dried up.

"Okay, we'll walk in," I said. I pulled off to the side of the road and put the hazard lights on, so that if anybody came upon the car they wouldn't hit it. I went to the trunk and handed a baseball bat to Damon and dug around for the jack for me. Then I put my heavy-duty gloves on, pulled my scarf around my head and shut the trunk.

Damon just looked at me.

"What?"

"You think we're gonna need weapons? What's here besides old ghosts?"

"You never know," I said. "There could be hobos living in there or there could be a bobcat. Just carry the darn bat and hush."

"Okay, okay."

We walked onto the property by the pond, bypassing the driveway all together. The barn door was falling off, hanging loosely by one hinge. It was no longer red, it was brown and it had taken on a slight list to the right. The chicken coop was gone. I couldn't even find a remnant of it, except some wire almost totally covered with snow.

Damon and I stayed together as we walked the property. We both checked out all the buildings, conveniently ignoring the house. "Look at that," Damon said and pointed about a hundred yards west. "Is that the outhouse?"

"Yeah. It's in pretty good shape."

"And the smokehouse looks exactly like it did."

"It didn't look none too good when we were kids," I said. "You're right, it doesn't look much different." The green shingled siding was torn in places and falling off, but it was like that when I was a kid. The roof had old bird nests sticking out of the corners of it, and in the spring a generous congregation of wasps must live there, judging by the size of the nests that hung from the overhang of the roof.

There was nothing left to look at, so we turned to the house. We walked around the front, neither one saying anything. The swing lay on the ground and you couldn't even tell what color it was anymore. A flash of a memory as a child came to me. The swing was white with red trim. My grandmother sitting in it in spring with flowers from the flower garden she'd planted blooming behind her. Pansies were her favorite.

The house that used to be white with red trim and red shutters was now a washed-out gray. Rust-colored streaks stained the metal roof, making it look as though the house was melting. And indeed, rust-colored icicles hung off the roof, which covered the front porch. The porch that Nate Keith was murdered on.

"Hello?" Damon called out. "Anybody here?"

His voice echoed off the hills around us. There were no houses to be seen from where we stood. We were all alone.

"I don't see any tracks or anything," he said. "What looked like a dog's tracks over there by the smokehouse, nothing else, though."

The wind whipped around and whistled through the naked oak trees in the front yard. I closed my eyes, took a deep breath and remembered. Green. The place was always green. Even in the winter it seemed as though the green was hiding and if you looked at it just right it was there, peeking out at you. Barking dogs and butterflies. Mimosa trees and strawberries. And the starlings that my grandfather was always and forever trying to figure out how to annihilate.

And the front porch, which now sagged in the middle, with fallen shutters strewn across it. The front porch where we kids ate hot dogs and baked beans. The front porch where my grandfather sat and smoked his pipe. The front porch where my grandmother sat and crocheted. The front porch where my great-grandfather's blood had been spilled.

I came out of my reverie and looked to Damon to see if he'd noticed that I'd slipped away for a minute. If he had, he said nothing.

"Look at this place," he said in a hushed tone. "I can't believe it."

"You are aware that we're trespassing," I said.

"Yeah, who owns it now?"

"Same guy that owns the farm over there on the southwest

ridge. He just bought it for the land. He didn't really want or need the house," I said. The place came with about 150 acres and it connected to his property. It was a good investment for him.

"This place was the center of our lives for so many years," Damon said.

"I couldn't have said it better."

I walked toward the porch and Damon held out a hand. "Where are you going?"

"I'm going up on the porch to have a look."

"Be careful, it looks pretty rotted."

"Well, it's only about a three-foot fall if it gives way," I said. I walked up the two concrete steps and stopped. The rug that used to be in front of the doorway was gone. Believe it or not, I was a little disappointed to see that there was no bloodstain. It was probably cleaned up and painted over many times. How many times had I sat right there? Right there on that very spot. How many times had my sitting there triggered a memory in my aunts' and uncles' minds that they quickly dismissed?

From where I stood I looked toward the barn. My father would have had a good view of the porch, but a limited view of the sides of the house. From the chicken coop Dolly couldn't have seen anything. From the smokehouse, Uncle Jed would not have been able to see the porch but he would have gotten a good look at whoever ran away, if he had looked quickly enough after the gunshot.

I stepped across the spot where the blood had been and jiggled the door handle.

"What are you doing?" Damon asked from the yard. "Torie?"

"I'm going inside."

"What? Oh no you're not."

I turned around to face Damon. "I want to be able to see who could have seen what from where."

"Can't you just try and remember what it was like from when you were a kid?" he asked.

I weighed his suggestion. I pressed my face to the glass on the door and peered inside. It was dark . . . What was that? "Damon?"

"Yeah?"

I moved over to the full-size window on the porch and looked inside just as a face looked back out at me. I screamed bloody murder and dropped my tire jack. Damon was on the porch next to me in seconds, grabbing my hand and dragging me off the porch.

"What?" he yelled at me as we ran away from the house. "What was it?"

"Face," I said. "Th . . . there's somebody living in it. Homeless."

We ran all the way to the car without looking back or stopping. I slipped in the snow once, but Damon grabbed me and kept me from falling. My adrenaline was coming out the top of my head and once we reached the car I had to bend over and put my head between my knees.

"Jesus," Damon said, out of breath and scared. "God."

"I second that."

"Let's not stand out here. Get in the car."

I did as he said and fumbled for my keys, which I finally found and put in the ignition. My heart pounded so hard I could feel my eyes jolting. The ends of my fingers were numb.

"Drive," he instructed.

I did as he said, turning around in the middle of the dirt road.

"Just like when we were kids," he said as we drove away. "Remember all the scrapes we used to get into? Just like when we were kids."

Twenty-nine

"I want to stop at the church," I said.

"Why?" Damon asked.

"I want to stop at the cemetery."

"Why?"

"When was the last time you were at the cemetery, Damon?"

"Why?"

"When was the last time you paid respects to Grandma and Grandpa?"

Damon was silent a moment as I pulled into the church parking lot. He looked back over his shoulder all nervouslike. He looked at the cemetery and back at me.

"Look, that homeless person isn't going to follow us all the way here. He knows he's trespassing. I wouldn't put it past him to protect his haven and hurt us if we'd stuck around . . . but he ain't gonna follow us here."

Damon was still silent.

"Okay, even if he did, he can't run that fast," I assured Damon. "Am I having any luck at persuading you?"

"All right," he said. "If you insist. But make it fast. I mean like ten minutes, Torie. Ten minutes." He held up five fingers.

"You mean ten," I said and held up all ten of mine.

"Whatever."

We got out of the car and I couldn't help but smile to myself at Damon's sudden chicken demeanor. When we were kids we were pretty even, only he'd had just a little more dangerous edge to him. Marriage and kids, college and a successful job must have dulled him a little.

We walked through the gravel and came to the wire fence, rusted from years of exposure. A chain was looped on the inside of the fence to hold it closed. It wasn't meant to keep people out. I unfastened it, noticing the rust it left on my gloves. My mother bought me these gloves. She would have a fit. I found myself wondering what miracles I could use to get them clean, when I looked up at the simple, beautiful church next to the cemetery. My grandfather helped build this church. His children played on its porch. There are pictures of my dad and his siblings sitting at various stages on the steps.

Our shoes crunched the snow as we made our way past the church and into the cemetery. The cool thing about this cemetery is that almost all of my family is buried here. There are only about ten people in the whole cemetery that aren't related to me. My grandparents, their parents, their brothers and sisters and so on were all here. And now, Uncle Jed would be added to it. The next generation.

Well, that thought depressed me no end.

We made our way to our grandparents' graves and stood silent as winter itself. I don't know what Damon was thinking, but I was thinking how much I missed them and how much I wished that one of them had broken the silence about this whole blasted mess. There was a plastic nosegay of flowers stuck in the ground. I picked it up and brushed the snow off it and put it back. Then I used my coat sleeve to wipe the snow off the front of the gray and white marble tombstone, exposing their names.

It was silly, I know, here out in the middle of nowhere. Like anybody was going to come here anytime soon and walk to this grave and look to see if it was readable. I just couldn't help myself.

I looked around the snow-covered cemetery with the barren tree branches bending every so often with the slight wind. "You know, almost everybody here is related," I announced.

"Really?"

"Yeah . . . Over there is the Duncans, they're not related. The Elsters over there are, sort of, by marriage. And that part over there by that big cedar tree, that's the Claytons," I said and stopped abruptly.

"What?" Damon asked. "What is it?"

"The Claytons. Harlan Clayton." I walked over toward the cedar tree and stopped and searched the tombstones for Harlan Clayton.

"What are we doing?" Damon asked, his breath leaving him in big billowy gasps.

"I'm being morbid," I said.

"Well, be morbid quickly because your ten minutes is about up," he demanded.

"There," I said and pointed to a sandy-colored stone. I walked over and stood in front of it. It read:

HARLAN CLAYTON
BORROWED FROM GOD ON 21 JUNE 1880
RETURNED ON 4 AUG 1942
WE LOVE YOU, DADDY

"What am I looking at?" Damon asked.

"A victim," I said.

"Huh?"

"That's one of Nathaniel Keith's victims. For some unknown reason, Nate Keith had a way with the ladies. He either had an exceptional libido or he forced the women to have affairs with him. Which wouldn't surprise me. He seemed like the type of person that gathered information on people to use later," I said.

"You mean, he blackmailed the women into sleeping with him?" Damon asked.

"I can't prove that. It's just a theory I have. This theory is based solely on my own inability to believe that women could find him attractive and want him in any way. We don't know what life was like in 1948 in the clearing farthest away from anything. Maybe the women around here were just bored and craved the excitement. Either way, Mrs. Clayton was one of those women."

"And?" Damon asked.

"According to the investigating officer's notes, Harlan Clayton hung himself when he found out that not only had his beloved wife had an affair with Nathaniel Keith, but their youngest son was actually Nate's and not his. Of course, it didn't help that Nate Keith announced it to all the neighbors at a meeting one night when he was drunk."

"Oh Jeez," Damon said.

"Yup," I said. "Well, we should get going."

We turned around and had walked about three feet away from Harlan Clayton's grave when I suddenly remembered something. I turned around and walked back.

"What?" Damon asked. "What is it?"

"The date he died," I said.

"What about it?"

"It was August fourth."

"And that means what, Torie?" he asked.

"The same day, six years later, that somebody put a chunk of metal into Nate Keith," I said. "Six years to the day."

"Does that mean something?" he asked.

"Either it means something or it's one heck of a coincidence."

Thirty

Damon and I said our goodbyes and I dropped him off at his hotel. We'd see each other tomorrow at the wake. I couldn't believe how many trips I would have made to Pine Branch before this reunion was over. Normally, I go down two or three times a year. I'd already done that just this week.

I entered my house and it was terribly quiet. More quiet than it needed to be. Like it was deliberately quiet. "Hello?" I asked.

Nobody answered.

I walked into the kitchen and I was immediately bombarded with, "Surprise!" There was my mother, her mother, the sheriff, Rudy, Rachel, Mary and my father.

"What is this all about?" I asked.

"Go out on the back porch and see," my mother said.

"Okay." I was a little hesitant because I couldn't for the life of me figure out what was going on. I headed in the direction of the door.

"It's not a surprise about the baby," Mary said and smiled.

"It's not?" I asked. Which meant it was. "Okay."

I opened the back door on the porch and there was a baby bed with a gorgeous blue and pink quilt with appliquéd rocking horses, a matching dresser and chest that looked like antiques, and a hand-carved wooden cradle. I was speechless. My hand went to my mouth and I just stood there for at least a minute.

"The baby bed is from us!" Mary announced, unable to hold her excitement any longer.

"What do you mean?" I asked and turned around.

"Colin and I got you the chest and dresser from his antique shop," Mom explained. "Rudy and the girls got you the baby bed. Oh, and the quilt is from Mom, your grandma. And your father made the cradle," she said.

"You made the cradle?" I asked. "You just found out yesterday."

"I started making it when you had Mary, but I didn't get it finished in time. Remember, you had her almost four weeks early. So I put it in my basement and forgot about it. I worked on it all night to get it sanded and stained," he said.

"Wow," I said and turned back to the porch. "I don't know what to say." Tears welled up in my eyes and before I could stop them they spilled over and down my cheeks.

"Oh Jeez, she's crying," Rudy said.

"She's pregnated," Mary said. "She's s'posed to cry."

"Who told you that?" my dad asked.

"I don't know," Mary said.

"You did a good job on that cradle," my grandmother said.

"You didn't do too bad a job on that quilt for an old blind lady," my father answered.

They all went about their own conversations while I stood there and cried. I couldn't believe they had all gone to this much trouble so early in the pregnancy. I know part of it was because I'd been feeling so tired and stressed out from this whole family reunion and Uncle Jed. They wanted to make me feel better. It was also because they were excited about the baby and happy to have a new addition. And so was I.

I felt Rudy's hand on my shoulder and he turned me around to face him. His eyes were still purply underneath, but the bruises were starting to turn greenish. They were healing and he did look better, even though every time I looked at him I grimaced. "We love you," he said.

"Sometimes I forget that," I said, with tears still running down my face.

"We all do," he said. "We all think from time to time that nobody really loves us or pays attention to us."

I took a deep breath and let it out slowly. Behind all the bruises were still those brown eyes that I loved so much. They still spoke to me without saying a word. "Are we going to leave the furniture out here on the porch?" I asked.

"No," Rudy said. "We're going to put it in the basement until your mother's wedding."

I came back into the kitchen and my grandmother walked over and pinched my cheek as hard as she could. "Still frisky, eh?"

"Yeah, Gert. Still frisky," I answered, rubbing my cheek. Gosh, that smarted.

Her face wrinkled up as she smiled from ear to ear. Her eyes seemed to disappear behind her wide cheekbones and heavy brow. "Spice of life, kiddo. It's the spice of life," she said. Then she patted my stomach. "It's gonna be a boy."

"Rudy will be happy to hear that," I said.

My father came over to me and messed up my hair. God! Pinched cheeks and ruffled hair. Nobody ever takes me seriously. "I think that you should invite Aunt Ruth out to lunch tomorrow. Before the wake," he said.

"Why?"

"Just her. Nobody else. She might talk to you, if you ask nicely," he said. "And . . . beg, plead, bribe . . ."

"Yeah, yeah, yeah," I said.

"No, seriously," he said. "I told her that you know. I told her that I told you."

So, he took responsibility for telling me, even though he didn't actually tell me. I think he'd just admitted to me that he should have done it in the first place, so he was doing it now. "Okay," I said. "I will."

"Sheriff," I said. He dropped my mother's hand and looked at me. He didn't say anything. He just sort of stood at attention, waiting for whatever it was I wanted. "Thank you very much for the furniture," I said. "That was a very nice gesture."

I couldn't believe I'd actually just said that. Even though he deserved it. It irked me that he deserved it. That he'd actually done something that was nice to me. It's harder to hold a grudge this way, darn it.

"You're welcome," he said and smiled.

"Real quick, before I forget," I said.

"What?"

"Harlan Clayton, the one that hung himself," I said.

"Yeah?"

"He hung himself on August fourth," I said. "Now it could just be a coincidence that Nate Keith was shot on the exact same date, six years later. Then again, it might not be. Clayton had sixteen children. I'm thinking maybe one of them might have killed Nate Keith on the anniversary of their father's suicide."

"It's a possibility," he said.

"I'm going to check it out later," I said. "The whole McCarthy connection makes me uncomfortable, too. Have you checked on Bradley Ferguson."

"Yeah," he said. "Your hunches may have been right. I don't see how the gun could have misfired."

"Why?"

"If it had misfired while he was shooting game the fatal wounds would have been to his face and neck area. You know, because he's holding the gun up to aim. It wasn't, though. The undertaker made extensive notes that the wounds were in the gut area. Other than that, I haven't found anything else on it," he said.

"Wow," I said. Sounded familiar. It was interesting information, but just what did it mean?

"Are you ever going to stop? I mean, is there ever going to come a point when you just say, 'oh, who cares?' and quit looking?" he asked.

"When I've covered every angle. Then if it can't come out in the wash, then it can't come out. After all, it is a fifty-year-old stain."

Thirty-one

On one of the bookshelves in my office at the Gaheimer House was a publication that I needed. Even though there was a tour going on, in which Helen was doing a fine and respectable job—except I think I talk a lot louder—I snuck into the office. I walked down the hall just as she took the tour up the steps.

I scanned the bookshelves in my office. Land records, census index, mortality schedule and so forth. There on the second shelf was the book I was looking for: *Partut County Marriages 1880–1940*. I had compiled this book myself, from hours and hours in the courthouse. I compiled one for 1800–1880 as well which the Partut County Historical Society also published.

There was the marriage record for Harlan Clayton and his wife, Elizabeth. I checked the index for all the Claytons. There were quite a few. I went to every one, then flipped back to the index and got the page number for the next. I didn't know exactly what I was looking for. I was just hoping that something would pop out at me and scream "Hey, I'm peculiar! Take note."

That's exactly what I got. It was as if as soon as I saw it, that was exactly what I was looking for. In 1937 one Sarah Clayton married one Hubert McCarthy. Hubert married one of the children of Harlan Clayton, who later hung himself on August 4. Then, six years later, Nate Keith is murdered on the same day and who is the investigating officer? Hubert McCarthy. And who does he happen to be best friends with? The victim's son. And what case is the only one he never solved? This one.

Was it just me or did this just not jibe? Well, actually, it jibed too well. This was just too perfect. I sat on the edge of my desk and sighed a big sigh. I looked at my watch. I had scheduled lunch with Aunt Ruth in thirty minutes at Fräulein Krista's.

Just how was I going to confront Mr. McCarthy about this? I couldn't just call him up and say, Hey, I think your wife did it. Or could I? If his wife had done it, and if I had proof, would I turn it over? The woman was dead, right? She'd been seeking revenge for her father's death even though that by no means made it right. What would happen? Hubert McCarthy might be made to answer for his coverup, so to speak, and it would go in the solved file.

This just didn't feel like I thought it would.

Besides, I didn't know that she did it. And might never know. I took the book with me as I turned the lights off in my office and headed over to Fräulein Krista's.

Aunt Ruth, early as always, was already seated. I watched her from a distance as she absently rubbed the rim on her water glass. What must it be like to live a complete and total fabrication? She lived in a make-believe perfect world. Either because she couldn't face reality or she'd faced it and decided that she didn't want the rest of the world to know what her life really was.

I walked over and sat down opposite her. "Hello, Aunt Ruth. It is good of you to come," I said.

"Torie," she said. "Your father explained to me what has happened."

I wasn't exactly sure what he'd told her, so I had to ask. "What did he say?"

She pushed her glasses up a little farther, but they just slipped back down. Her lipstick was an orange cakelike substance that I couldn't help but stare at. "He's told you the truth about Nathaniel

Keith," she said. "I'll have you know, he had no right to do it."

"Well, I am his daughter. Maybe he wanted me to know. I haven't told anybody else," I said, and then remembered that I had told Damon. He was the most trustworthy cousin I had, though, so I dismissed it.

"And now you can't rest until you know the truth," she said in a haughty tone.

"I don't mean for it to come across in a bad way, Aunt Ruth. It's not like I'm going to shout it from the rooftops. I just have to know. Would you please tell me what you know? Or what you saw?" I asked. I was amazed at how I had managed to keep my voice calm and actually sound sincere when asking her politely for information.

"I don't see what it will hurt, now," she said. "Except of course I should just say no because you have always been such a wretched little girl."

"I know you're not real fond of me, Aunt Ruth. I know that I was a brat as a child, but I've done nothing to you as an adult, nothing that didn't stem from the fact that you and I are on opposite sides of the fence. Is that a crime, Aunt Ruth?" I asked. "Is it a crime to be different and to think differently?"

She said nothing.

"Please, just tell me what you saw that day," I said. "I will never ask you for another thing and I will walk a wide path around you."

"I told your father I would tell you. Only because he is my baby brother and I love him," she declared. Whatever the reason, I didn't really care. And I hated catering to her. "I forgive him for telling you," she said. "Although, of all people, why he had to tell you, I'll never know."

Because he knew if he told me, I'd do something about it.

"It was a blistering hot day," she began. "I was engaged at the time, but wasn't married yet, so I would still go with Mom and Dad for family outings and such."

Just then the waitress came up to take our order. Aargh! Just as she was getting comfortable. "I'll have the hot turkey on sourdough," I said, hurriedly. "Extra pickles, Dr Pepper and bring me a big order of those seasoned fries."

Aunt Ruth stopped and looked at the menu, stroking her chin, then finally ordered her lunch. "I want the quiche, with a salad and tea. No lemon," she said.

I waited patiently as she commented on the outfit that the waitress wore and the lack of speed with which she took our order. Nothing like this occurs in her home town . . . and, okay, she was ready to get back to the subject of Nate Keith.

"So I went with Mom and Dad to Grandma and Grandpa's house. Your daddy and Aunt Sissy went to the creek to swim. The day seemed like any other day. Uncle Granville was there talking about his sick horse and how he and Aunt Lizzie were finally going to take a real vacation to California, just as soon as he sold off those extra fifty acres that he didn't need anymore," she said.

The waitress was at the table with our drinks but Aunt Ruth kept right on talking. "I noticed that Grandma wasn't acting right," she stated.

"Wait," I said. "Della Ruth was acting strange—how?"

"Nervous," she said. "I asked her about it and she said she had a bad feeling. Bad feeling that something was going to happen. Well, we all just figured that was just her acting spooky."

"Acting spooky? What do you mean by that?"

"She'd do that, every now and then. Say she had a bad feeling and a day or two would go by and if somebody in the next county died, she'd say, See? Told ya. I think she just wanted attention," Aunt Ruth said and stirred her tea.

"Except this time, she was right," I said.

Aunt Ruth ignored that statement and went on where she'd left off. "Then she and Grandpa started fighting. I've never been able to figure out just what they were arguing about. Grandpa would say something like, 'I don't believe you. You're a lying bitch.' Which he said a lot. I mean, this wasn't new behavior."

"But you don't know what the subject matter was?" I asked.

"No. Before you knew it, though, he was throwing things at her and so forth. Jed showed up and took him outside to calm down," she said.

I can't tell you how afraid I was that she was going to tell me that Uncle Jed had shot him. Please, don't let that be it.

"Sissy and your daddy came back and Mom sent Sissy upstairs. Your daddy went outside," she said. She took a drink of her tea and began to twist the fake strand of pearls around her neck. "I heard some commotion going on and I went into the living room and looked out the window."

"Which window?"

"The one on the side of the house, not the one that looked out onto the porch," she said. "I heard Grandpa say something along the lines of 'Go on back to where you came from,' that whoever it was wasn't wanted around here and so forth. I think he said a few profanities and insulted the person and then I heard 'Move, I said!' in this hateful voice and then the gunshot."

I sat there for a moment taking everything she said and storing it in my mental filing cabinet. I didn't want to rush her, yet I didn't want her to think I wasn't interested, either. I'd considered taking notes on the napkins, except they were cloth.

"Who was it?" I asked. *Please don't let it be Uncle Jed.*

"I don't know."

"Aargh! That's not possible," I said. My voice actually cracked from the stress. I shoved my hands through my short hair and then took a deep breath. "You saw them."

"I saw somebody. I can't say who."

"You can't or you won't."

"I can't because I didn't get a good enough look to exactly say," she said back to me.

"What was he wearing? Was it farmer's clothes or a wealthy man's clothes?"

She watched her glass intently for half a minute and then she looked me square in the eyes. "It was a dress. *She* was wearing a dress."

She. It was a she. Sarah Clayton McCarthy?

"That's all I know," she said.

"Wait a minute," I said. "Account for all the women that were there."

"I was in the house, Mom was in the kitchen with Grandma, Sissy was upstairs . . ."

"Aunt Charlotte?" I asked.

"Downstairs in the cellar."

"You're sure?"

"Yes," she answered.

"Is there a way out of the cellar other than coming in through the house? Is there an exterior exit?" I asked.

"Yes," she said. "But it was padlocked. She would have had to have the key in the basement with her to get out . . ."

"And . . . your cousin," I said, snapping my fingers. "Dolly, that's it. She was in the chicken coop? Did anybody see her come out of the chicken coop?"

"Dolly couldn't have done it," Aunt Ruth said.

"Why not?"

"She was about sixteen years old. A frail and puny thing. A shotgun would have left a bruise on her, if it didn't knock her a hundred feet."

"Not if you shoot it from the hip. It wouldn't bruise then," I challenged. "Besides, I shot my first twelve gauge at fourteen."

"You don't understand. Jed found her shivering in the chicken coop, back underneath some of the nests. Shaking and everything. It wasn't her. She weighed about ninety pounds. You would have to know her to understand," Aunt Ruth said.

"Okay . . . What about Uncle Jed's wife? Aunt Dana. She dropped him off, what if she came back?" I asked.

"Why?" Aunt Ruth said. "There is positively no reason for Dana to have killed her husband's grandfather. She can't defend herself since she's dead, by the way."

Regardless of what Aunt Ruth said, Dolly could have done it. Aunt Charlotte could have somehow got out of the cellar and done it. Aunt Dana could have come back, even though I don't know of a reason. Or it could have been Sarah Clayton McCarthy.

Or it could have been Della Ruth's sister who lived three miles down the road or one of the women that Nathaniel Keith had gotten pregnant. It didn't have to be somebody who was on the property. I don't think this helped at all. It seemed like it made it worse. I was unaware of all the people that it could have been until Aunt Ruth said it was a woman. It narrowed it down but it also opened it up.

"So now you know," Aunt Ruth said. "Are you satisfied?"

"Well, it certainly makes a difference," I said. "I appreciate you sharing this information with me."

The waitress came and gave us our food and then set the check down on the end of the table. Aunt Ruth looked at it and then gave me a sharp glance. That meant I was picking up the tab. Which was fine, I had intended to all along. She just didn't have to be so blasted annoying about it.

"Do you think you can drop the subject now?" she asked. "I don't want to hear a word of this mentioned at Jed's wake later today. Not one word."

Oh yes, ma'am! I couldn't very well say anything. She'd told me what I wanted to know. I would owe her for the rest of my blooming life! I bit into my turkey on sourdough and watched her eat her quiche across from me.

"Just one more thing," I said.

Aunt Ruth rolled her eyes heavenward and clenched her jaw. "What?"

"Why did Della Ruth sit at the door with a shotgun and threaten everybody if they opened the door or went outside? What was that all about?"

"Who told you that?" she asked with narrowed eyes.

"Did it happen?"

"Yes," she said. "Grandma was trying to *protect* us."

"Protect," I repeated.

"Yes. That's all she needed was for us to go outside and get shot, too. Who's to say if the killer was still there or not?" Aunt Ruth countered.

"So, you think she was keeping you all inside so that none of you would get shot?" I asked. "Then why did she make you wait until Nate Keith was dead? Why not an hour before or an hour after? How come it was just until he was dead?"

Aunt Ruth shrugged. "Guess she was just being safe," she said. "Now, can we drop this? For good?"

"I will never speak of it to you again," I said. I now knew that it was definitely a woman. "Oh, except one thing. Did you tell Mr. McCarthy that it was a woman?"

She thought on that for a moment with a mouth full of quiche and then nodded her head. "Yes, I did."

I would be seeing, or talking, to Hubert McCarthy tomorrow.

Thirty-two

I hate that dead body–formaldehyde smell. I hate funeral homes. I stood in the foyer of the Progress funeral home with its fancy chandeliers and real wood moldings and doors. And that smell. It was the same funeral home that both of my grandparents were laid out at the day before their funeral at the Pine Branch Methodist Church. I waved to my cousins as I made my way through the winding hallways and passed several other rooms with "occupants." Rachel was on one hand, Mary on the other and Rudy bringing up the rear.

Finally, I made it to Uncle Jed's room. My father was standing next to the casket with his hands clasped behind his back. He didn't own a suit, so he was dressed in his best black shirt and jeans with his dress shoes, and I'd bet you ten to one, white socks. I waved to Aunt Sissy who stood next to her very pregnant daughter.

"Girls, get your coats off," I said. "Set them on the end of the pew."

"Is this a church?" Rachel asked.

"No," I answered.

"Then why is it called a pew?"

"I don't have any idea," I said. "I guess they try to make it look like a church."

"Why?"

"Because they used to have funerals and stuff at churches."

"Why don't they now?"

"I don't know," I said. Which I truly didn't. "Sometimes they do."

"Mom," Mary said. "What is that?" She pointed to the casket at the end of the carpet runner.

"That's Uncle Jed," I said. "I told you he died."

A horrible mixture of fear and disgust played across her face. Then a tad of curiosity and a long silence as she weighed what I said against what she was seeing at the end of the room. "Do they just let dead people lay around here?"

"Yes," I said. "They lie here until the family has had enough of a chance to say goodbye and then the family takes the body and the casket to the cemetery and they bury it."

"Why?"

"Can I tell you later?" I asked. I really didn't want to go into the fact that the body would start to smell and turn colors and all that gross stuff, when Uncle Jed's children and grandchildren were within earshot.

"No, tell me now," she demanded

"I'll tell you later," I said.

"Mom," Rachel said. "Do we have to go up there?"

"Not if you don't want to."

"Good," she said with relief.

"Does he smell?" Mary asked.

"Rudy, why don't you take the girls down the hall and get a soda," I suggested. Rudy, who had been studying the lint on the carpet looked up with a knowing smile. It was as if he was saying, Glad you got those questions and not me. He nodded and took the girls' hands and they disappeared.

I took a deep breath and walked down the carpet runner to the casket. Gladioluses sprayed forth from nearly every bouquet of flowers that surrounded the casket. My mother-in-law always said that she would never plant gladiolus in her flower garden because they were the funeral flower. She won't go to a cemetery after the person is buried, either. I laced my arm in my father's arm, and he gave me a nervous smile.

"You okay?" I asked.

"No. Dumb question," he said. "Why does everybody ask that question?"

"Because they don't know what else to say." I laid my head on his shoulder for a second and then took another deep breath and walked over to say my goodbyes. God, I hated this kind of stuff.

The person lying in the casket was not the person I'd known three or four days ago. It was just a shell. He didn't look like himself. Dead bodies hardly ever do. For some unknown reason the undertakers apply tons of makeup and fix their hair and make them look, well, like mannequins. Real people don't look like that. I remember the one thing I noticed about my grandfather when he was laid out, was that they'd covered the tobacco stains on his chin with makeup. For months, I was convinced that he had been replaced with a body from the FBI bank of unknown cadavers.

Jedidiah Keith was also in a suit. Uncle Jed had never been in a suit in his life. Why should he start in death? He should have been laid out in his flannel shirt. Why do we do this? Where did all this ritual begin? Just who was the brilliant person who said we had to drain all the bodies of fluids, sew their mouths shut, pop their eyeballs out, pump them full of a toxic substance, put this shell of a human being on display for everybody to see, and then stick them six feet under the ground? Am I the only one who thinks that this is morbid?

"Well, Uncle Jed. I know you're not in there anymore, but I'm going to say this anyway," I said softly. "I don't want you to take this the wrong way, wherever you are, or if you can hear me. I really hope that you were just drunk and fell into the river on your own accord. I need for that to be true. I apologize from the bottom of my heart if you are dead because of me or because of anything I might have said or done."

That really sounded horrible.

He, of course, said nothing back to me. No thunder or lightning or skies parting. No apparitions, not even so much as a cockroach went across the floor to give me some sort of sign that he heard, understood or forgave me. I reached into my coat pocket and pulled out a pint of whiskey.

"This is for you," I said. I laid it in the casket next to him. "It's even the good stuff. Crown Royal. The quickshop was out of Jack Daniel's."

I fought back tears as I said, "Goodbye."

My father came over and took my hand and sat me down in the front pew. He crossed his leg and, sure enough, white socks. Why do men do that? "Whiskey?" he asked me with a smile.

"I know it's not him. All that was him is long gone. It left the moment he died," I said. I swiped furiously at the tears on my cheeks. "I just . . . I don't know. Call it a peace offering. In case he could see me."

My father looked at me strangely. Which he does a lot, but this time he had a specific meaning behind it. He didn't understand, exactly.

"To me, that is just a hunk of flesh. But in case he can see me somewhere, I wanted to give him the whiskey," I explained.

"I see," he said. "You know, he could never afford the good stuff."

"I know," I said. We sat there a moment in silence. Father and daughter. More alike than I ever wanted to admit. I was amazed my mother hadn't gone crazy from having such a close copy of her ex-husband as her daughter. It was weird. The things I liked about my father, I prided myself on, too. The things I didn't like about my father, I tried to pretend didn't exist in me. We were both stubborn and predictable in an unpredictable sort of way. All of my obsessive traits . . . from my father. My mother has never been obsessive over anything a day in her life. My father? He gets on something and he doesn't stop until he's mastered it.

If only I could figure out what side of the family the nosiness comes from.

"I should go rescue, Rudy," I said.

"How did your lunch go with Ruth?" he asked as I was about to get up.

"Good. If she wasn't lying, she told me quite a bit of useful information."

"I'm glad."

"Of course, I had to write it in blood that I would never bring the subject up to her again," I said.

He smiled. "I thought as much."

"Hey, have you ever heard of a woman named Naomi Cordieu?" I asked.

"No," he said. "Though there are some Cordieus from around here."

"She seemed to be under the impression—you absolutely cannot breathe a word of this—that your father might not have been the son of Nate Keith."

"What?" he asked.

"Was that ever the subject of an argument at your grandparents' house?" I asked. "That you can remember."

He gave me the raised eyebrow.

"Naomi has a box of pictures of your father . . . said that they were given to her late husband from Della Ruth."

The other eyebrow went up. After all, how could you explain that unless Della Ruth was a close personal friend of either Naomi or Bradley Ferguson? Even then, why only pictures of John Robert? Why not all the other kids?

"Are you sure?" he asked.

"Yes," I said. "She gave them to me. I have them at home."

"I can't answer that," Dad said. "I really don't know."

"Okay," I said. "Just curious."

We sat there a few more minutes and finally I stood up. I looked at Uncle Jed's body lying on the white satin lining of the casket from the pew.

"I truly believe he was drunk and slipped on the ice," Dad said.

"Really? You're not just saying that?" I asked, desperately wanting to believe him.

"Yes," he said. "I really believe that."

Thirty-three

Hubert McCarthy sat in his wheelchair looking pitifully pale, darn it. I couldn't be ruthless if he was looking all pitiful and puny. His son was at the grocery store and Hubert had yelled at me to come on in.

He also had a look of expectation. Either he expected me or he couldn't wait to find out what it was that I had to say. "Please, sit," he said.

"No, thank you," I said. I didn't want to sit. I didn't want to let my guard down for a second. I wanted to remain in charge of the situation.

He pointed to the magazine rack by his television. "There's a present in there," he said. "For you." Since his Christmas tree was tiny and on top of his television, the magazine rack doubled as a present holder.

Great. Just what I needed. A present. Maybe he did this on purpose, to throw me off. So that I wouldn't say what it was I came here to say. Actually, I wasn't exactly sure what it was I was going to say. I'd rehearsed it a thousand times on the drive up here to south St. Louis. Nothing sounded right. It always sounded like I was accusing his dead wife of murder. Okay, so in a roundabout way I was accusing his dead wife of murder. But all he had to do was convince me of it otherwise, and I'd drop it.

"Mr. McCarthy, I'm sure you're aware that your wife was the daughter of Harlan Clayton," I said.

"I'm aware of that."

"Harlan Clayton hung himself."

"Yes."

"Because of Nate Keith."

"As I live and breathe," he said. I wasn't too convinced that he was doing too good a job at breathing, myself.

"Were you aware, I don't know how you couldn't be, that Nate Keith was murdered on the anniversary of Harlan Clayton's suicide?" I asked.

He narrowed his filmy eyes at me and then he smiled. Crooked yellow teeth peeked out behind thin gray lips. "You're good," he said. "You think you got it figured out?"

"No, not exactly. I wouldn't be here asking questions if I did. I know that the murderer was a woman," I said.

"Really?" he asked. "I see you got somebody to break the silence."

"Mr. McCarthy, the individual that gave me that piece of information also said that they told you that same thing," I said. He said nothing. He just went about his business of trying to breathe. "Which means either they didn't tell you and lied to me about it, or they did and you kept it out of your report for fear that your wife or one of her sisters would be suspect number one. Considering the August fourth date and all."

"What do you want me to say?" he asked.

"Did you know? Did you keep it out of your report?" I asked.

"My wife did not kill Nathaniel Keith," he said.

"How do you know?" I asked.

"Because she was my wife. I know."

"Everybody thinks that their loved one—father, best friend, wife—couldn't have done something horrible based on the simple fact that they are their father, best friend or wife. Somewhere along the line, somebody gets disappointed," I said.

"My wife did not do it!" he said. It took every ounce of energy he had to raise his voice to a convincing yell. His chest rose and fell heavily, trying to make up for the exertion he just exhibited. "Nathaniel Keith caused her and her family enough pain, without his death dragging their reputations through the mud, too."

"I understand what you're saying," I said. "But, if one of them did do it . . ."

"My wife did not kill Nathaniel Keith."

"Did you know the killer was a woman?"

He just looked at me. If he said yes, he was admitting to leaving information out of his report of the investigation.

"Did you know?" I asked.

"No," he said. "Yes, Ruth did tell me that she saw somebody in a dress. That doesn't mean a woman pulled the trigger. It doesn't mean that she was alone. It doesn't mean that a woman did it. Ruth could have seen her cousin, Dolly, walking around in the yard. So, yes, I knew that Ruth said it was a woman. No, I didn't know that it was a woman. Can you say without a doubt that it was a woman?"

Well, gee. When he put it that way, I guess not. I lowered my eyes and looked away. I sat down on the edge of his couch and rested my head in my hands. "My head hurts," I said. "I'm almost to the point of not caring. I've never been to the point of not caring."

"I'm impressed that you persuaded the family to open up. Especially Ruth," he said. "You've done good."

"Oh, who cares," I said and slouched back on his couch. I couldn't believe I was actually sulking in this man's house. I couldn't help myself, though.

"You've got them to admit and acknowledge that this did happen," he said. "After I closed my case, they never spoke of it again. You did good."

"Yeah, well, I feel like crap. I feel like a failure. I feel like . . ." Just what did I feel like? "Did you know that my uncle Jed died?"

"No," Hubert said. "I'm sorry."

"Did he try and contact you in the last week?"

"No," he said. "Why? Was his death suspicious?"

"No," I said. "Not that we know of. We think he slipped on the ice and fell into the river when he was drunk."

"He's been drunk since he was twenty," he said. "How did his liver keep going?"

"I don't know. I'd written your name down on a piece of paper and it turned up missing. When they fished him out of the river, he had the piece of paper in his pocket. Do you think that he contacted somebody, other than you, who might have wished him harm over this whole thing?"

Hubert McCarthy thought a moment and then he answered. "No. I think he was just afraid of somebody finding out about the whole mess. So he swiped the piece of paper. I think it was as innocent as that."

"Still trying to cover up after all these years," I said.

"Yes."

Like he could be doing right now, and how would I ever know the difference? I was frustrated and depressed. I had a funeral to attend tomorrow and tons of presents still to buy and wrap for Christmas. I was truly getting tired of thinking about this whole mess.

"The important thing is, you got them to face it," he said. "Now, reach in there and get your present."

"Mr. McCarthy, I can't accept—"

"Oh, just hush up and reach in there and get it."

I sorted through the three or four presents in the magazine rack. I found the one that said simply *Torie*. It was wrapped in the same paper as the other presents. Cheap red paper with snowmen holding presents on it. It was the kind you'd find in the four rolls for a dollar bin at Walgreen's.

I opened the present and found my grandfather staring back at me, holding his beloved fiddle in his left hand. The photograph was in a nice wooden frame. He must have been about twenty at the time, young and handsome. You never knew people's stories just by looking at them. He looked wholesome, happy and pure, not like someone from a horribly dysfunctional family. His hair was parted in the middle and his hazel eyes smiled, even though his mouth was not overly curved. It was a studio picture, professional.

"It was a promotional picture he had made. Advertising his fiddle playing," he said. "Never could figure out how hands that worked so hard could caress a fiddle like they did."

I'd only heard my grandfather play a few times and he had been old and arthritic. Even then, though, there was a special sound to what he did. I think it was the sound of love. He loved what he was doing.

"Thank you," I said. "Thank you very much. I will treasure it, always."

"He was my very best friend," Hubert said.

"I don't remember you at his funeral," I said.

"I was there," he answered. "You were young. Thinking of other stuff. I was in the back of the church."

"Well, I should be going. Thank you again," I said.

"You're welcome. I had a whole bunch of pictures of him. A few of him and me," he said.

"Oh, yeah?" I asked.

"They came up missing," he said. "I haven't moved in thirty years, and yet . . . I haven't seen those pictures in fifteen years. Don't know how long they been gone."

"Oh, that's a shame," I said. "Maybe they will turn up."

Thirty-four

"Okay, Sheriff, I know this seems strange . . ."

"No, it's not," Sheriff Brooke said. "You've done this to me before. Just hauled me off to some unknown destination because you have a hunch on something."

I looked at him sharply to see if he was being facetious or what. "You're driving," I said. He looked over at me from behind the wheel of his squad car, in his perfectly laundered tan and brown uniform. I wish somebody would come up with a different color for sheriffs to wear.

"So?" he said.

"So I'm not hauling you anywhere. I'm the passenger here."

"You have to be the most annoyingly argumentative person that I know," he said. "Did you go to school to learn that?"

"No," I said. "Comes quite naturally. Father's side of the family." He rolled his eyes as we made headway down the highway at seventy miles per hour. "Be happy you're not marrying my father."

"I am happy that I'm not marrying your father. Very happy," he assured me. "So, you want to start from the top on all of this?"

"Okay. Did I tell you about the old lady, Naomi Cordieu, that worked for the historical society?" I asked and pulled my left foot up under my right leg to get comfortable. I wore my red Converses today, jeans and my big blue sweatshirt that said WEST VIRGINA MOUNTAINEERS. My grandmother bought it for me last year for Christmas. She might have moved from there forty years ago, but she's never forgotten her favorite football team.

"I think, vaguely," he said.

"She just happened to come into the library and found out that I was asking questions about Bradley Ferguson and the drowning of his brother and all sorts of things. I mean, the ironic part is I would have eventually gotten around to contacting her even if she hadn't left word for me to do so. Are you following me?" I asked.

"Yes."

"She is the widow of Bradley Ferguson."

"And Bradley Ferguson is the one you had me check on. The hunting accident in Africa. Right?" he asked.

"Yes. Bradley Ferguson was in love with, and I'm fairly sure had an affair with, my great-grandmother, Della Ruth. He was also the little brother to Wil, who drowned in the accident for which Nate Keith was largely responsible."

"Okay . . ."

"So, when I first visited this Naomi Cordieu lady, she told me that her widow, Bradley Ferguson, was madly in love with Della Ruth before he met Naomi, and they had an affair," I said.

"So, why are we going to see her?"

"Because . . . here's where it gets sticky. She also told me that Bradley was the father of my grandfather, John Robert," I said. The sheriff's eyebrows went up a bit and he gave a little whistle. "I know, I know. Well, at first, I'm thinking . . . who am I to say that it wasn't true? I mean, I found evidence of this affair, so who's to say she didn't get pregnant?"

"Yeah, well, I can see that. Go ahead," he said.

"What really convinced me that maybe she might be telling the truth was this story that she told me about how Della Ruth would send Bradley photographs of 'his son' John Robert once a year. She had a shoe box full of these pictures and she gave them to me."

"Where did she get the pictures?" he asked.

"Exactly. I believed her, because . . . how else would she get all these pictures of my grandfather?"

"So why do you doubt her now?"

"I went to see Hubert McCarthy last night," I said. "He gave me a photograph of my grandfather—"

"Why did you go see Hubert McCarthy?" he asked, a sudden sharpness to his voice.

"Uh . . . well, Aunt Ruth—"

"Torie, blast it!" he said and hit the steering wheel a good one. "You just can't go off on your own like that. I would have taken you if you'd have asked."

"Aunt Ruth had told me that it was a woman," I said, ignoring his outburst. "She saw somebody in a dress in the front yard before the shot. Hubert's wife was none other than Harlan Clayton's daughter."

"The one who killed himself," the sheriff said.

"Yup, and Nate Keith was killed—"

"On the anniversary of Harlan's suicide."

"Exactly, so I'm thinking . . . Hubert's wife did it and he covered up big time. Well, he says his wife didn't do it, and he admitted to leaving out the bit of testimony from Aunt Ruth saying it was a woman."

"You still don't know that it wasn't Hubert's wife," the sheriff said. He sounded like he was ready to scold me.

"No, I know . . . but as I'm leaving he gives me this picture of my grandfather, right? I say nothing. He mentions the fact that he had tons of pictures of John Robert, but he doesn't know where they all went to," I said. "Disappeared on him one day."

A smile slowly started in the corner of Sheriff Brooke's mouth and worked its way across his face until he had a full-grown grin.

"So, you're thinking Naomi stole these pictures of John Robert."

"Yes. My only problem with this is why? Why would she steal these pictures? If she did steal the pictures, it makes perfect sense," I said. "That's why I wanted you to come along."

"I can't misrepresent myself," he said. "I can't say I'm working a case if I'm not."

"You don't have to do that, boy scout. Just look official."

"Oh, so I'm like a trophy sidekick," he said.

"No, no, look official and make it seem like you're just checking into a theft reported by Hubert McCarthy."

"What?" he asked. "I can't . . ."

I gave him the best pleading look that I could possibly come up with. The one that works on Rudy. Nothing works on my father.

"As long as I don't really say that, I guess it will be all right," the sheriff said.

"Good. Now, don't let her spinster-superhostess act get the best of you," I said. Although it did me. "I'm not real comfortable with believing Bradley Ferguson's misfired gun was actually a misfired gun."

"I'll try not to," he said. "I was a little surprised by that myself. When I checked into his death, I expected it to be straightforward. I didn't expect the little inconsistency of a gut wound instead of a facial wound."

"Oh, turn here," I said and pointed to the outer road.

"Here? Right here?"

"Yeah, it's the yellow house there on the outer road."

I'll give the sheriff credit that he kept his comments to himself as we stood on Naomi Cordieu's picture-perfect country front porch. The door opened and Naomi looked at the sheriff oddly, then looked at me. Recognition registered on her face and then she looked back at the sheriff as if in worry.

"Hi, Naomi," I said. "Can we come in for a minute?"

"Well, I wasn't expecting company," she said.

"Oh, don't be worried, this is my stepfather," I said. "We were out . . . Christmas shopping."

She opened the door and let us in. The sheriff gave me a look that would have melted the polar icecaps. I was not a polar icecap, however, and I quickly looked away and followed Naomi into her house. Actually, I was smiling on the inside that I'd found a way to use the sheriff's upcoming nuptials to my benefit.

"Have a seat," she said and pointed to the same couch that I'd sat on during my first visit. Naomi was dressed in a royal blue dress with large, loud yellow flowers all over it. "So, you're Torie's stepfather. She never told me that she had such a handsome individual in her family. How fortunate," she said.

"Oh, I'm just the most fortunate girl in the world," I said through clenched teeth. The sheriff's chest puffed a little and a smug smile cut the corners of his mouth.

"So, what brings you all here today?" Naomi asked.

The sheriff looked at me, waiting for me to speak. I, however, had no intention of speaking—for once in my life—and just smiled at him.

"Well," the sheriff began and took a deep breath. I knew he really wanted to strangle me right now. But, hey, it's not like I haven't wanted to strangle him a time or two. "Torie and I were visiting an acquaintance of ours, Hubert McCarthy."

"Oh, really?" Naomi asked. Outwardly I saw no difference in her. But there was a new edge to her voice.

"Yes, do you know him?" the sheriff asked.

"Well, of course. Not well, but everybody from these parts knows Hubert and his family. Why?"

"This is going to sound kind of strange—"

"Would you like some tea?" she asked abruptly.

The sheriff looked to me for guidance.

"Uh, yes. She has wonderful tea," I said to the sheriff.

"I'll be right back," she said and went off to get her tea cart.

"Stepfather!" the sheriff semi-yelled as soon as Naomi was out of hearing range.

"You are . . . or will be. Just not yet. It's just one minor—"

"Lie."

"Time discrepancy," I said.

He growled at me. I smiled. Naomi came back in wheeling her tea cart about five minutes later and seemed not to notice the frown on the sheriff's face. "One lump or two?" she asked the sheriff.

"Uh . . . two," he said.

"So go on with your story," Naomi said as she poured our tea and doled out our sugar lumps.

"Mr. McCarthy mentioned a large quantity of photographs that he once owned of John Robert Keith, and that they were missing. That they'd been missing for a while."

"Really," Naomi said.

"And then, Torie here says that you gave her a box of photographs of John Robert and we were just wondering if there was any way they could be Mr. McCarthy's," he said.

Nicely done, Sheriff.

"Torie, I already told you how I came by my photographs," she said.

"I know, but I was wondering if there was some way that Bradley Ferguson could have actually got them from Hubert," I said. I followed the sheriff's lead of not outwardly blaming her but giving her a way out. All she had to do was take it. "I know that you said that Della Ruth sent them to him, but that was before you were married to him. Is there any way that he actually got them from Hubert? Hubert and my grandfather were best friends. It seems likely that Hubert would have pictures of him."

"Bradley wouldn't have lied to me," she said. "I don't think."

We could be here all day, I thought. She could never say what we wanted her to say. And even if she did, I wasn't real sure what to do about it. "Do you have a bathroom that I can use?" I asked Naomi.

"Yes," she said. "Down the hall to the right."

I followed her instructions. The hallway intersected twice with cross hallways. I found her bathroom, all decorated in pink and roses. I used it as quickly as possible as I didn't want to miss anything that was going on out there in her living room. I washed my hands, turned off the light and walked out into the hall.

I thought I'd gone down the correct hall, but I hadn't. I figured I would still end up at the other end of the house, just one room over. Sure enough, I found myself in the kitchen, which was next to the living room. Her kitchen was bright blue gingham and sunflowers. This lady liked flowers.

On the kitchen counter was an open bottle of prescription pills. Okay, I knew this was none of my business . . . but when has that stopped me? At least I felt guilty about it. I walked over and picked up the bottle. Sleeping pills. I read the label. December 5 was the fill date, thirty tablets. December fifth. That was like nine or ten days ago. Then why were there only three pills left in the bottle?

There was a residue on the counter. *Like somebody had ground up the pills quickly*. Oh my God. The tea.

I walked quickly back to the living room and tried to get the sheriff to look at me. But he was intent on the story that Naomi was telling him about one of her many trips around the world. I sat down next to him and noticed that he'd finished his tea. Naomi poured him another cup.

"You haven't touched your tea," Naomi said to me. That's right, I hadn't. And I wasn't about to now.

"Yeah, I thought you said her tea was so good," the sheriff said. A thin layer of sweat had broken out on his skin. I had to get him out of there. Depending on the drug it could take as long as an hour to work or ten minutes. I guess it depended on just how many pills she'd ground up and put in the darn teapot!

Or there could be another explanation, I told myself. I took a deep breath and gave her the benefit of the doubt. I decided that I could have jumped to conclusions and she hadn't drugged the tea. Then I noticed the sheriff shaking his head, as if to clear it. I looked at Naomi, who was looking at me. I was not drugged. What would she do with one drugged and not the other?

"You really should have some tea," she said.

"Why don't you have some?" I asked.

"Torie," the sheriff said. "I don't feel too good. Maybe we should . . . do this some—some other time."

"Sure, Colin," I agreed. "That sounds good to me."

I stood up and held my hand out to him, which he leaned forward to take but only managed to look at before falling back on the couch moaning. "Sheriff, let's go."

He rocked his head back and forth, with his eyes rolling back in his head. He tried to reach up and either touch his head or his eyes, but his hand never quite made it to his head and flopped back down on the couch. My God. Naomi had drugged him just as sure as it was December! I had immediately suspected her of the worst, and now that it was happening, I could barely believe she'd actually done it.

"Naomi," I said. "Call 911."

Naomi just looked at me. What did she think? Did she think I couldn't physically overtake her and call the number myself? Her confidence worried me. Did she know judo or something? Did she have a gun somewhere?

I leaned down and whispered in the sheriff's ear. "You've been drugged, Sheriff. Don't fight me." I have no idea if he comprehended what I said or not. I pretended to be crying on his shoulder. Maybe Naomi would feel really secure and make her move, whatever it was. While I was on his shoulder, I reached down and took his gun from his holster. It was awkward at first, because I had to unsnap it and everything.

As I pulled it out, the sheriff mumbled something and made a vague effort at trying to stop me. I stood up with the gun pointed at Naomi Cordieu, the little old lady from hell.

"All right, Naomi," I said, holding the gun on her. I held it like they do in *Charlie's Angels*, with my left palm under the butt of the gun, but I had no idea what I was doing. I'd never shot a handgun in my life. Only hunting guns for target practice and skeet shooting. I assumed the safety was on, but I was clueless as to how to turn it off or even where it was. Did I just shoot or did I have to cock something?

Naomi looked startled. "What are you doing?" she asked.

"Don't play the innocent bingo lady, Naomi. You drugged the tea. I saw the bottle in the kitchen," I said.

Her face changed quickly, to surprise and then slight fear. She wasn't sure just what I was going to do. I must admit I didn't either. The gun was heavy in my hand, and grew heavier with each second. "Do you have anything that will make him throw up?"

"What do you mean?"

"Do you have any ipecac or anything like that?" I asked.

"No," she said.

I was afraid to leave the sheriff, but at the same time, I had to do something. I walked across the room to where her phone sat on a table, the gun on her the whole time. I picked up the phone and dialed 911. I explained that there was a drug overdose at this address, and then they were on their way.

I walked back over to the sheriff. I slapped him on the face. "Sheriff, you need to throw up," I said. His breathing was labored and slow. "Sheriff, come on. Stick your finger down your throat or something. You have got to throw up. It's sleeping pills, just throw up."

A sob escaped me. Crap. I couldn't stand here and cry. "Why, Naomi? Why?" I asked through tears.

I walked into her kitchen backward, with my eyes on her as much as possible, wiping my face occasionally with my left hand.

I opened her drawers until I found the silverware drawer. I pulled a spoon out and walked back in, with the gun still held on her. I didn't really think that was necessary. She wasn't going to do anything.

"How did you get Hubert's pictures?" I asked. I set the gun down on the couch next to the sheriff, and inches from my knee. I pulled the sheriff's head back, opened his mouth and stuck the spoon back into his mouth, to tickle his gag reflex. He coughed a little and his head came forward, but he didn't throw up. He was a little more alert, though, so I tried it again. This time he lurched forward, spewing vomit all over Naomi's wonderful mauve rug and her delicate little tea cart.

I picked the gun up and went back to holding it on her. I heard the sirens in the distance and breathed a sigh of relief. I wasn't sure how I was going to explain this to the paramedics, but it didn't matter. They would get here in time to save the sheriff. I hoped.

"How did you get Hubert's pictures?" I asked, louder and more forceful.

"I broke into his house years and years ago to find what he had on the case. All I could find were photographs and personal things. I just took what I could find," she said. "I was interrupted."

"So, you killed Nate Keith," I said. "Why?"

"He wasn't supposed to die," she said. "I had no intention of killing Nate Keith. It was Della Ruth that I was after."

All this time, I'd tried to figure out the motives and such for killing Nate Keith and it never occurred to me that he just happened to be in the wrong place at the wrong time. That the victim was supposed to be somebody else. He was so mean and good for nothing, I assumed the killer got the intended person.

"Della Ruth," I declared, amazed. "You . . . you were jealous."

"Bradley never got over her. Never."

"It had been decades since they'd been together, Naomi. Jesus."

"Della Ruth had finally decided to leave Nate Keith. After all those years. Sixty-something years old and she finally decides she's had enough. Idiot woman."

"So Bradley was right there. He was going to be there for her, wasn't he?" I asked.

"I don't really know. I couldn't take a chance on it. I couldn't lose him to her. I'd just gotten used to having what remnants she'd left of him. She wasn't going to get those, too," she said. "Turns out, after Nate was killed, Della Ruth told Bradley to go on about his business, that it had been too many years. I didn't need to kill her after all."

"So that is why Della Ruth sat there with the gun. She really was protecting everybody," I said to nobody in particular.

"I don't know what Della Ruth did in the house. I didn't mean for the gun to go off and kill Nate. I was saving it for Della Ruth. Once I did it, I got scared and then I noticed that the place was crawling with people. Somebody in the barn and out with the chickens. I had to get out of there fast."

"Did Bradley know?" I asked.

Naomi glared at me.

"Did Bradley know that you killed Nate Keith? Did he know that you went there to kill Della?" I asked. "I bet you were in a panic when you realized that you'd killed the only person that had ever stood in the way of Della Ruth and Bradley being together in the first place. How fortunate for you that Della Ruth just wasn't interested anymore."

"You'll never prove this to anybody," she said. "You can't. I'll deny every word."

"No, but they can get you for attempted murder of me and the sheriff," I said. I didn't know if they could or not. She was ancient, after all.

"Why invite me here and why tell me all of this horse manure about Bradley being John Robert's father? It is horse manure, isn't it?"

"Della Ruth was already pregnant and didn't know it when she and Bradley had their affair. John was Nate Keith's. But Bradley didn't care. He proposed anyway and told her she could come and live with him with all of her children. She wouldn't. Because she was pregnant. I think if she hadn't been pregnant, she might have done it."

"Why did you invite me here?" I asked.

"If you were snooping around about Bradley and Nate Keith and everything, I wanted to know how much you knew and if you were actually looking for information on his murder. You would have gotten around to me anyway. I thought I'd look like less of a suspect if I contacted you first," she explained.

The sirens were loud now, right outside the house. The sheriff was moaning and rocking back and forth on the couch. "Why did you give me those pictures? It was the only thing that linked you to suspicious behavior?"

She shrugged her shoulders a little. She shook slightly, I assumed from fear. "I wanted to destroy whatever you thought John Robert and his parents were. I wanted you to believe that he was conceived in an affair. I wanted you to think badly of Della Ruth." The pictures, in her mind, would "prove" her little story of Della Ruth sending them to John Robert's supposedly real father.

The door burst open and in came the paramedics and the local police. Immediately, their guns came out of the holsters and shouts of "Freeze!" and "Put the gun down!" came from all directions.

I immediately threw the gun on the floor. "It's the sheriff's gun. This woman drugged our tea," I said. To which they all looked at me as though I was nuts.

Thirty-five

The next day the sheriff was still in the hospital, recuperating. He would be fine, although probably a little ticked at me. I made him throw up early enough and the paramedics got to him soon enough, so he was okay. Not to mention that the doctors said that the amount he drank probably wouldn't have killed him, but he'd have been out for a long time. I'm not sure what Naomi was thinking. Maybe she was going to hack us up or something, while we were unconscious. Who knows? Maybe she just panicked.

I missed my Uncle Jedidiah's funeral because I was in a police station filling out reports. That was okay, though, I'd said my good-byes already. He would be sorely missed.

Right now his entire family was at the Knights of Columbus Hall in beautiful downtown New Kassel, eating to our hearts' content. This was definitely the type of party that I wanted when the time came for me. Laughing, food, music and young children—the next generation.

Dad and his brother, Melvin, had brought their guitars and equipment and were set up in the front, by the roasted pig, and a cousin filled in on the drums and another cousin filled in on bass and everybody took turns singing and it was just like every get-together I could ever remember at my grandparents' house. Music and food. Food and music. If you took away the music from this family, you might as well take away the food.

"So, your mother is getting married," Aunt Sissy said.

I was heavily in a daze watching my father, as I'd watched him at least a thousand times before. "Yes," I said. "She and the sheriff are supposed to get married in August."

"And when is your baby due?" she asked.

"August," I said. "Ought to be an interesting summer, considering my grandmother and I are making a trip to West Virginia in July," I said.

"Oh Jeez," she said. "Are you happy for your mother?"

"Yes," I said. "Anytime a person finds love, be happy for them."

"Thought you and the sheriff were sworn enemies," Aunt Sissy said.

"No. I think we're building respect for each other," I said. "You can't make a guy puke all over a little old lady's house and not bond. You know?"

"Yeah," she said. "That'll do it."

"He makes my mom happy," I said.

Aunt Ruth came over and joined us. "What are you girls talking about? How handsome my brothers look up there playing music?" she asked. I wanted to hit her. She always hated the fact that they played music. That they were "musicians." They were the white trash of the family, she always said. If, however, they had chosen classical music, that would have been different.

"Actually, Aunt Ruth, I know that you told me never to speak of this again, but I have to tell you this," I said.

"Torie. I don't want to hear anything on the subject!"

"No. I wanted you to know that you were right. Della Ruth was protecting everybody and herself that day when she sat there with the gun," I said.

"Torie," Aunt Ruth pleaded.

"No, now listen. *She* was the intended victim. Naomi Cordieu went there to kill Della Ruth, not Nate Keith," I said.

"Why?" Aunt Sissy asked.

"A man. Naomi's husband, or he might have just been a fiancé then, I'm not sure, was in love with Della Ruth. He had been since they were kids," I said. "It seems that Della Ruth was actually considering leaving Nate Keith. Naomi couldn't take the chance on Bradley running off to be with Della Ruth, so she went there to kill her. She killed Nate instead and when she realized what she had done, she ran off."

"And Bradley," Aunt Sissy said. "Did he ever know what happened? The truth of it? I knew him. And Naomi. All of us were from the same small town. You know everybody's business in a small town."

"Yes," I said. "I think Bradley either knew it or found out later or maybe she confessed it to him. Strangely enough he died very mysteriously in Africa just two years later. My personal opinion is that Naomi killed him, too. Although I can never prove that."

Aunt Sissy rubbed my back affectionately and smiled, a tear catching in the corner of her eye.

"Well," Aunt Ruth said. And that was all she said.

I looked across the room and saw Rudy dancing with our two daughters. He had Mary up on his shoulders and Rachel standing on his feet as he danced around, all of them laughing and smiling.

"How lucky I am," I said.

Aunt Sissy smiled wide. "Yes, you are lucky."

Somehow, my life had come back to being normal. Everybody would leave for their cities and homes tonight. I'd solved the burning question of who killed Nate Keith. My father and I had reached a certain level of understanding, I think. My mother was happy and getting married, even though I hadn't really faced the thought of life without her in my house. I was in denial, I admit. I was healthy and pregnant and happy about it. The sheriff owed me big time! And tomorrow, Sylvia would get to yell at me about how she was going to have to alter all those dresses for my soon-to-be-rounded figure. Well, more rounded than it already was.

I was content. For now.

Read on for an excerpt from
Rett MacPherson's latest book

A MISTY
MOURNING

Available in hardcover from
St. Martin's Minotaur

Let me say for the record that "Ninety-Nine Bottles of Beer on the Wall" is no fun with somebody who can't remember which bottle you're on.

Three fast-food stops, sixteen bathroom breaks, four unfinished conversations, one irritating rendition of "Ninety-Nine Bottles of Beer" and twelve hours after I left Rudy standing in the driveway in New Kassel, my grandmother and I pulled up in front of the Panther Run Boarding House in central West Virginia. I'll be honest and say that I hadn't thought I was going to make it. Gert had this annoying habit of not finishing her sentences until about seven sentences later once she'd thought of how it was supposed to end, and it was up to me to figure out which sentence went with which ending. Flying would have been much faster, but I have a huge fear of flying, and I'm just certain that in some twisted act of revenge, God will crash the plane while I'm on the toilet. When I do fly, I don't use the toilet. So, not an option in my current state.

Gert and I both looked up at the boarding house, nestled into a mountain side as if somehow it was molded into the mountain. To the left and right of the house were brilliant green pastures that narrowed as the mountains closed in upon the postcard valley. A two-lane road ran in front of the boarding house, and the Gauley

River ran in front of that. On the other side of the river were gently sloped mountains plunging into the river.

I loved these mountains. I loved the entire Appalachian range from Georgia to Maine. They were comfortable mountains, like a well-used baseball glove. Soft, smooth, gentle slopes seemed to wedge themselves snugly into the land around them.

The boarding house, on the other hand, was not nearly so pleasing to the eye. It was a large two-story building with what looked like an attic in the center above the second story. There was dingy white lattice work, about three feet high, all the way around the porch of both floors. The floor of the porch was a slate blue, as was the trim on all the windows. The building itself was supposed to be white, but the paint was so old that it gave the building an overall grey look. In the center of the building, below the pointed roof, was a white lattice-work star.

The front steps were cracked and leaned to one side and the screens on the windows and doors were so rusty that you couldn't see through them. The fact that it was early evening and the sun was almost behind the mountain that sat directly behind the boarding house added to the overall dingy grey appearance of the building.

"Gee," I said. "Does this look anything like what you remember?"

My grandmother smiled faintly. "Yeah," she said. "Needs some work, but it's the same place."

My grandmother had actually worked at this boarding house when it was owned by "the company." Meaning, the Panther Run Coal Company, during the late twenties and early thirties. She was a small girl at the time, but I remember her vivid tales of having to get up at three in the morning to fix the coal miners their breakfasts and pack their pail lunches. Then she had to go on to school after that! If somebody woke my girls up at three in the morning for anything, you'd have certified zombies on your hands.

Gert and I got out of the car and stretched. My back was killing me. It felt like it had a horse sitting on it. It must have been a dead horse, because the pain hadn't let up for about a month now.

I opened the trunk of the car to get the suitcases out just as a high-pitched scream erupted from somewhere within the building. Gert gave a little jump, as did I. The noise got louder and louder until it burst through the front door of the boarding house. A teenage girl ran out of the building to the edge of the porch and jumped over the lattice work into the yard. About ten seconds later came an older man, probably about seventy, who thrust through the door, down the steps, and around the boarding house after her.

Gert gave me a quizzical look. I shrugged.

Just as we made it to the steps with our suitcases, the teenager jumped up into the air and over the lattice work on the opposite end of the porch. Unfortunately, her thonged foot had become hooked on the lattice railing and she went splat on her stomach onto the porch floor.

The seventy-year-old man came around the boarding house now, huffing and puffing. He stopped at the steps, bent over at the knees catching his breath, right in front of us. His glasses came tumbling out his shirt pocket and fell onto the steps.

"Oh, let me get that," I said and stepped up to help him.

The teenage girl had now came to her feet. She stood up, tears running down her face. "You can't have it," she said to the older man.

"I'm your grandpa, and you'll do as I say. Now give me that ring!" he demanded.

"No!" she shouted, stomped her foot and reached for her nose. "If I'm your granddaughter without my nose ring, then I'm your granddaughter with my nose ring. I won't take it out! You can't have it."

"The devil's work," the man said. "What will your great-grandma say when she sees it?"

By this point, Gert and I were standing on the steps. I'd given the man his glasses case, which he took as if I were invisible, and I couldn't help but stare at the poor teenage girl. By the amount of tears she had shed, it was obvious that her heart was broken. She wore those wonders of all retro wonders, faded bell-bottom jeans, a tie-dyed shirt, a hemp bracelet and choker, and a big silver nose ring. Her hair was nearly to her butt, bright strawberry red, with little braids pulled back from her temples.

"Granny has already seen it," she hissed at her grandfather. "What do you care? She'll be dead soon anyway. Isn't that what you said?"

"Excuse me," I interrupted. Both the man and his granddaughter actually looked at me for the first time. "This is the Panther Run Boarding House, correct?"

"Yes," the man said. "Who might you be?"

"Oh, I'm Torie O'Shea, and this is my grandmother Gertrude Crookshank—" I didn't get to finish my sentence. The man let out a whoop and a holler, and went over to my grandmother and squeezed the daylights out of her with a big bear hug.

"Lordy, Gertie Crookshank!" he said. He then turned to me. "Of course, she was Gertie Seaborne when I ran with her."

My grandmother steadied herself with her cane and studied the man closely. "Well, Lafayette Hart, you old geezer."

"You look as pretty as the day Sam Crookshank ran off into the mountains with you," he said.

"Ran off into the mountains?" I asked. Sam Crookshank was my grandfather, Gert's ex-husband. "Gert, what is he talking about?"

"That Sam," the man went on. "Now he knew what he wanted in a woman. And none of them simpering misses stoked his far, if you know what I mean."

"Far?" I asked.

"Fire," my grandmother said.

"Oh, fire. Of course."

"Gertie Seaborne sure stoked it a plenty," Lafayette said and winked at my grandmother.

"That's nice," I said. It was no surprise to me that the teenage girl had taken this opportune moment to run in the boarding house and away from her grandfather. I was wanting to do the same thing.

"Can we go inside?" I asked. "I have a headache."

"Why of course," he said. "Let me get them bags for you. You shouldn't be carrying them heavy bags in your condition."

I really had a headache. The dead horse had moved to my head.

•

An hour later Gert and I were seated at an elongated table in the dining room with six other people, including Clarissa Hart, the one-hundred-and-one-year-old woman who had invited me to this place.

The food was served in clear cut-glass serving dishes, which sat in the middle of the table on top of ivory-colored doilies. Either that or the doilies were dirty, I wasn't sure which. On my right was my grandmother, on my left was the teenage fugitive from earlier. The problematic nose ring was still defiantly in place. I'd since learned that her name was Danette Faragher and that she was the daughter of Lafayette's daughter Faith, who was not yet in attendance. It seemed as though Danette had arrived with her grandfather.

To the left of Danette was Lafayette himself. On that end of the table was Maribelle Lewis, Lafayette's sister and Clarissa's only daughter. To her left was Maribelle's husband, Prescott Lewis, and to his left was an unknown boarder. At least, unknown to me. Finally, to the boarder's left and my grandmother's right, was Clarissa Hart, seated in her wheelchair at the head of the table.

I'm used to Sylvia, my boss at the historical society, looking so young and spry. Of course, she isn't one hundred and one, but she's only shy of it by about six or seven years. Clarissa Hart looked all of her one hundred and one years. She was hunched over in her wheelchair, with an oxygen tube loosely placed at the bottom of her nose, the hose wrapping around her to the tank hanging off the back of her wheelchair. Her hair was snow white, her eyes blue under droopy eyelids, and her skin was pink and splotched. Her mouth puckered from years of wearing false teeth, but what amazed me the most was the sheer amount of wrinkles that the woman had. It seemed if you could straighten out the wrinkles on her face, she'd have had enough skin for two people.

But that was on the outside. On the inside she was sharp as a tack.

"I'm so glad that you could make it, Torie, and bring Gertie back to see us," Clarissa said and aimlessly laid a hand on my grandmother's arm.

"It's my pleasure," I said.

"I'll just bet," Prescott Lewis said to me from across the table. He never looked up at me when he said it, so I let it go. He was a large man, late sixties, with a full head of grey/black hair.

"After dinner, come to my room. I have a lot to discuss with you," Clarissa said.

"Of course," I said.

"When is your baby due?" Maribelle asked me.

"The middle of August," I said.

Maribelle smiled, revealing a gold tooth amidst a mouth full of stained teeth. She was in her mid-sixties, short, plump, and she had dyed hair that I'm sure was supposed to be some sort of reddish-brown but looked nearly burgundy. Like it was a bottle of wine that had stained her head.

"I remember when I was carrying," she said. "Was the best years of my life."

"Really?" I asked, thinking that the woman was nuts.

"Women are their prettiest when carrying," she said.

I'd have to argue with her when my skin was stretched so far across my stomach that my belly button was turned inside out and purple. But I'll bet she never looked at her belly button when she was pregnant. My nose was starting to swell, too, which had happened with every pregnancy I'd ever had. Oh, yeah. I was a regular Marilyn Monroe.

"There are things I must tell you," Clarissa said, bringing the conversation around to her end of the table again.

"Yeah, like where to spend her inheritance," Prescott piped in.

"Whose?" I asked. Nobody answered me. "Whose inheritance?"

My grandmother just shook her head because she didn't know what he was talking about either.

"How long has it been since you been home, Gertie?" Lafayette asked.

"Since 1986," she answered.

"I had four sons," Maribelle said, as if we were listening to her.

"Only one is worth two hoops in hell," Lafayette said.

"Pass the bread," Danette said to me.

"Tell me, Torie, how long have you been tracing your family tree?" Clarissa asked.

"Oh, since the early eighties," I said, happy to return the conversation to something I thought was harmless.

"Do you have lots of information on your ancestors?" she asked.

"Some lines of the family are easier than others. I have some lines traced back to the medieval times, some farther, if you count the royal lines. Others end in the mid 1850s with an ancestor of mine in the poorhouse and pregnant, with no clue as to who the father was. Just depends," I said. "One common thing, though. Except for the French side of the family, my father's mother, almost every line I have came from or through Virginia at some time or other."

"Only people worth anything," Prescott said. The entire meal, he still hadn't looked up from his plate.

"Pass me the pinto beans," the boarder said.

"Torie, this is one of my boarders, Norville Gross," Clarissa said. When she spoke, she stopped and took long deep breaths in between every third word or so. But she never forgot where she was going with her sentence. Wish I could say as much for Gert. If she blinked she got distracted.

"Hello," I said. Mr. Gross just nodded his head and tore into his pinto beans.

"I chose you," Clarissa said. "Out of all of Gertie's grandchildren and children, I chose you."

"Why? For what?"

"We'll talk more later. Come to my room as soon as you're finished," she said. With that she pushed a button on her electric wheelchair, backed away from the table and went down the hall. A clanking noise came from down the hallway, and I jumped at the sound of it.

"It's Granny's elevator," Danette said. "She had it installed before I was born."

"It's one of those old kinds with the wrought iron gate that closes," Lafayette said.

"Oh," I answered.

"Granny likes you," Danette said. "I can tell. She doesn't like too many people."

"Give you the store, she oughta like you," Prescott said.

Okay, I couldn't let this go anymore. "What is he talking about?" I asked.

"Pay him no never mind," Lafayette said.

"Well, obviously he thinks I'm guilty of something, or I've done something," I said. "What do you mean, give me the store? What store?"

"The boarding house," Prescott said and finally looked up at me. His eyes were black and fierce little things, set back into his head, with a big Neanderthal brow above them.

"The boarding house," I said. "You're joking, right?"

Nobody said anything. Everybody ate their food with new interest, except Prescott, who stared directly at me, and Norville, who seemed oblivious to the conversation at all.

"Why else would she have asked you here?" Prescott asked.

"I'm sure that's not what she asked me here for. I'm the family historian. She wants to tell me something," I said.

"Yeah, well, you're not *our* family," he said.

•

I did as Clarissa Hart said after dinner and went directly to her room on the second floor of the boarding house. In truth, I hated to leave Gert in the company of Prescott Lewis, but she seemed happy to stay and visit with Lafayette and Maribelle, whom she had known as a child.

I hadn't had much of a chance to look around the boarding house. We had thrown our suitcases in our room and headed to the dining room for dinner. Now, I didn't want to keep Clarissa waiting because it was heading for nine o'clock, and I knew that she would go to sleep early.

I couldn't help but notice all of the photographs hanging on the wall of the stairway, though. Old photographs hung along the wall in an almost pictorial diary of sorts, although I did not know the cast. There were little photographs, big photographs, some in plain metal frames and others in large, fancy, wooden ones. The people in the frames watched me all the way up the stairs until I reached the landing, where the photographs ended and the second floor began.

Clarissa's room was at the very end of the hall on the right. I entered the room and she was already in her bed, which was a hospital bed. She still had the oxygen tube on her face, and she lay on piles of pillows, which made her seem small and weightless.

"I'm so glad you came," she said and held a hand out that beckoned to me.

I walked over beside her bed and felt just a little awkward, because until today, I'd never met the woman. We'd exchanged letters a few times in the past. I'd written to her asking if she had any information or pictures on my great-grandparents. She had obliged with some copies of old photographs and a few old letters. Now, she acted as if she'd known me all my life.

"Do you know I was already old when you were born?" she asked. Her accent was as strong as her son Lafayette's.

I did the math in my head, and she had been in her late sixties when I was born. Not exactly ancient, but I understood what she meant.

"I didn't think I was gonna live much longer *then*," she said. "Look at me. Who coulda known?"

"You know, I read about a woman in Texas who was something like a hundred and fifteen," I said and smiled.

"Oh, don't you say that," she said. "Fourteen more years like this?"

I just shrugged. "Why was it so important for me to come to West Virginia?"

"You know that I was best friends with your great-grandmother, Bridie McClanahan? Before she met Mr. Seaborne and got married," she said.

"Yes, of course," I said.

Clarissa took a moment to breathe deeply. "You don't look much like her," she said.

"No," I said. "I look like my father. Except he has black hair."

"Nowadays you can dye your hair any color you want," she said. "Look at Danette. Caribbean Sunset. That's the name of the color she put on it."

"Caribbean Sunset," I said and flashed back to Danette's bright strawberry hair. I would have almost thought it was natural.

"Bridie did me a favor," Clarissa said. "Long, long time ago. And now it's time to return the favor. A debt repaid."

"What sort of favor?" I asked. I must admit that even though I asked the question, I was a little worried about what the answer might be. I waited patiently as she reached up and straightened her oxygen tube.

"I picked you because you care," she said, ignoring my question. "You know about the hills and the people who came here from the highlands. You know about the coal mines and the history. Most people don't know what went on twenty years before their time, and don't care. Just plain ol' don't care. Not you. You're one of the smart ones. You're one of the ones who care."

All right. I'd agree with her on that, but I wasn't exactly sure where this was going. Not all people were history buffs. They just weren't. No crime there, I suppose. Most of the time, though, when people were history buffs they would go out of their way to learn everything they could about a particular place or time.

"Yes," I said. "I care very much about where my people came from."

"I've waited eighty-three years to repay this debt. I didn't do it before now, because I was afraid," she said.

"Momma?" a voice said from behind me. It startled me a little, and I wondered why I had been so on edge since I'd come here.

I turned around to see a man in his late sixties with slicked back hair and shiny black shoes. Needless to say, his brown leisure suit was nearly as old as I was. I was probably in first grade when he bought it.

"Momma," he said, with his arms opened wide.

"Edwin?" Clarissa asked. "Is that you?"

"Who else ya think it'd be?" he asked. He walked over to her bed and kissed her on the forehead. He then produced, out of thin air, I might add, a Hershey's candy bar. "For you. Shh, don't tell nobody."

"I'll come back in the morning, Clarissa," I said and let myself out of the room.

On the way to my room, I saw a few other people that I did not have names for. A crack of thunder shook the boarding house and I squealed. Grown woman, here. Just thunder.

As I entered my room, I found my grandmother sitting on the edge of her bed, unpacking her suitcase. Her cane was leaned up against the oak nightstand, which matched all of the other antique furniture in the room. This room even had one of those old dressing tables with the scalloped mirrors. The only lights in the room were two lamps that were covered with old, maroon shades.

"Edwin just arrived," I said as I stepped into the room.

"Edwin was always a slick fart," she said. "Never trusted him."

"So what do you think of all of this?" I asked.

"All of what?"

"Nothing," I said with a sigh. "Did you really play with the Hart children?"

"I played with Lafayette a little. I was nine or so when he was . . . By the time the younger two, Edwin and Maribelle, came along . . . We played some. I was babysitting age."

"So you babysat them?" I asked, trying to make sense of her sentences. It was amazing. Sometimes she could talk for a whole ten minutes with no problems, and then other times her phrases came out unfinished and disjointed.

"Yeah, I was nine when—"

"No, did you babysit them, Gert? Edwin and Maribelle?" I asked, trying to keep her on track.

"Yup. I've seen all of their plumbing."

"Gee, that's great, Gert. Just what I wanted to know."

I sat down on the edge of one of the beds and took off my shoes. I was tired. I was going to go to bed and sleep as deep and long as I could. While I had that thought in my head, another crack of thunder exploded, reminding me that I might not sleep as well as I'd hoped to.

"I thought we'd go see your Aunt Millicent," Gert said. "Tomorrow or the next."

"Sounds good," I said. Aunt Milly—or Millicent—was one of my mother's sisters and the only sibling who stayed in West Virginia, the others all having moved to Missouri when their mother, Gert, moved back in the fifties.

Without really knowing how it happened, I was in my bed and

sound asleep within minutes. Not even my grandmother's snoring kept me awake. But, alas, an over-full bladder will do the trick every time. I awoke around two in the morning and had to use the bathroom. Which meant I had to get out of bed and walk down the hall.

I lay there a few more seconds, pondering if it was worth getting out of bed for. Rain crashed against the window in wild surges. I got up and went to the window and looked out. It was pretty cool how the lightning lit up the sky and all of the mountains surrounding this valley were silhouetted against the purple-blue sky. Then the lightning would die down and all would be pitch black again.

Once in the bathroom, I did my business and hurried back into my room, stubbing my toe on the overly thick floor runner. It must have been two inches thick. The hallway was pretty creepy, all dark and squeaky, and I really didn't want to stay out there any longer than I had to.

As I got in bed, I did give some thought as to how Clarissa could get her wheelchair up and over the floor runner. Her electric wheelchair must have a really good engine, I decided.

Just as my head hit the pillow, I heard this hair-raising scream that sounded like a woman being attacked. Goosebumps danced along my spine, and I sat straight up in bed. Well, as straight up as I could with a forty-five inch waist.

"What the heck was that?" I asked aloud. My voice sounded spooked and twelve years old.

"Panther," Gert said in between snores.

"What do you mean, panther?" I asked. "Don't panthers meow or something like that?"

"No. Panthers scream. Like a woman," she said, still without moving. How could she be this calm?

Then I heard it again. I sat in the bed unable to move, except for my eyes, which kept darting around the room expecting to see some rain-soaked crazy woman. The more I listened to it, the more

I knew the sound was coming from outside. The scream seemed to get louder or quieter as if it were moving closer to the boarding house and then farther away. The fact that it was outside made me feel a little bit better.

"I'm telling you, it's a panther. Go back to sleep."

"Panthers live in the wild," I argued. "In the mountains, in the boonies."

"Yes, and you are in the boonies, in the mountains, and this is called Panther Run for a reason. Now go back to sleep before I brain you a good one."

Enough said. Feeling very much like a scolded child, I snuggled back into my big fluffy bed with the covers up around my chin, but I still could not close my eyes. Rain pellets hit so hard against the glass that I thought for certain the window panes would break.

I lay like that until the storm moved on and the earliest rays of light caused shadows in my room. I heard the panther two more times in the middle of the night, and let me just say that it was the creepiest thing I've ever heard in my life.

At about six in the morning I had to use the bathroom again. I'd had to go for the last hour, but I waited until it became light enough to see where I was walking. As I stepped out into the hallway, I heard a creak. I looked up and down the hallway but didn't see anybody. Between each room, bronze sconces with curved votive cups came out of the walls, and I wondered why they weren't on. I felt inside of one and surmised that all the sconces like this one had no lightbulbs in any of them. The plush maroon floor runner was centered down the hallway floor. About three quarters of the way down on the left, the stairs exited into the great room below. A few feet of balcony stretched beyond the stairway until the very end of the hall, where Clarissa's elevator was. Which was the opposite end of the hall where her room was. All of the doors in the hall were shut, except the one I'd just come out of.

I went to the bathroom and then walked back down the hall

toward my room. Just as I was about to go into my room, I looked up and saw that the door to Clarissa's room was open about six inches. I stood there a minute waiting for somebody to come out, but nobody did. I glanced up and down the hallway and saw nobody, so I decided to go down and at least check on her.

"Clarissa?" I asked as quietly as I could without it being a whisper.

No answer. I should have turned around and gone back to my room, but I couldn't. I pushed on the already partially open door, and in the dim light of morning I could see Clarissa Hart lying on her throne of pillows, with one of the pillows covering her face.

It took a second for it to register that the old woman who had to use oxygen was lying with a pillow on her face. In all likelihood she would suffocate if I didn't do something.

I rushed into the room and lifted the pillow. "Clarissa?" I said.

A noise at the window made me turn and look at it. Some sort of white bird flapped its wings and seemed to look into the room through the window right at me. It then made a chirping sound and flew away.

When I turned back around, Norville Gross was standing at the doorway looking at me with an astonished expression. He looked at the pillow in my hand and then at Clarissa, who didn't seem to be breathing. Then ever so slowly he looked back to me.

This could be very bad.